The World: According to Graham

Layne Harper

The World: According to Graham is a work of fiction. Names, characters, places and incidents either are the product of the author's imagination or are used fictitiously. Any resemblance to actual persons, living or dead, events or locales is entirely coincidental.

The World: According to Graham

ISBN 978-0-9960854-3-4 (ebook)

Cover Design: Michelle Preast
Editor: Lauren McKellar
Polishing Editor: Kristi Zeller
Formatting: Polgarus Studio

Other Works By Layne Harper

Infinity Universe:
Falling Into Infinity
From Now Until Infinity
Finding Infinity
Infinity.
The World: According to Rachael
The World: According to Graham

Infinity Series Short Story:
Aiden's Broken Heart

Dedication

To my children. . . If everything in life comes easily to you then you never gain the thrill of working hard, pushing through mental blocks, and overcoming obstacles, to finally achieve something that you are so immensely proud of that you want to share it with the world. I love you enough to wish you struggles and failures because ultimately you will learn from them and become better people.

Contents

Dear Reader,

First of all, thank you for purchasing this book. As an indie author, your support means everything to my family and me.

Second of all, let me give you a brief explanation of how this book came to be if you haven't read the *Infinity* Series. Rachael is a secondary character that makes appearances in all four books. However, you do not need to have read the *Infinity* books to enjoy *The World: According to Rachael*. However, you really need to read the *The World: According to Rachael* before you start this book or you're going to be completely lost.

Rachael developed a bit of a fan following, and I was asked if I would ever write her story. Honestly, I never thought that I would. She's certainly not your typical romance leading lady, but that's what I love about her. Anyway, I had a three a.m. epiphany which lead to Rachael's book and now the conclusion to their story in Graham's book.

Finally, your support is what keeps us Indie writers going. Love or hate this book? It's okay. Please leave a review. Also, follow me on Facebook. I'm Layne-Harper-Author. I'm also on Twitter @Layne_Harper. My email is Layne@LayneHarper.com.

And before I leave you to settle into your favorite reading chair, I want to thank all the bloggers who have made my career. You ladies rock my world. I so appreciate everything that you do to give us Indie authors a voice. Without you, these are just words that live in my computer. And a super big shout out to the ladies who have joined my fan page on Facebook at Infinity Series –By Layne Harper. You're always good for a laugh or a pick-me-up. I've learned so much from you. And Christi, there are no words other than thank you for all that you do from the bottom of my heart, and I can't wait to have a glass of wine with you one day.

Okay, you can now begin reading . . .

Sincerely,
Layne Harper

"Some stories don't have a clear beginning, middle, and end. Life is about not knowing, having to change, taking the moment and making the best of it, without knowing what's going to happen next. Delicious ambiguity." – Gilda Radner

Prologue

"Yes."

It's three simple letters, and translates in every spoken language. Y-E-S. In Spanish it's *sí*. In French it's pronounced *oui*. In German it's *ja*, and in Portuguese it is *sim*. I speak all of these languages fluently. But answering Graham's question . . . *Would we have a future together if you weren't pregnant? And not the kind of future where we have to hide behind closed doors. I mean a future that is out in the open where I hold your hand in public and I proudly tell everyone who my girl is* . . . is the most difficult *yes* that I've ever said.

Why is this particular *yes* so grueling? Because Graham now knows what he means to me. My *yes* is what he has been trying to convince me to admit. It's the ammunition that we need to work through the trenches of despair that I, and we, have created by our stubborn, unbending personalities. I just don't know how much more pain our hearts can endure.

Here we stand at a rest stop on the side of a highway in Virginia. We left the out-of-the-way Cracker Barrel restaurant that I asked him to meet me at about thirty minutes ago. I knew that he wasn't going to handle the news of the baby well. Not because he's a bad guy or doesn't want to be a father, but because it was such a shock. It was a shock to me and I'm the one who is growing a human.

In the car, he began asking me all of these questions. I must have given

1

him an answer that he didn't like because like a mad man, he whipped across two lanes of traffic to park the car in this place that has seen better days. The blue restroom sign painted on the side of the brick wall is faded with neglect. There are four metal picnic tables that dot the yellow-ish brown grassy hill. There's no clear definition where the grass and weeds meet the shrub-lined entrance to the dense forest. It's a jagged battle for sunlight, and right now the tall weeds seem to be winning. *God, what a metaphor for my heart.*

Protectively, I place my right hand over my stomach, as if I'm shielding my baby from the tornado of emotions swirling through me.

My other hand strokes Graham's tightly strung bicep. He's bracing himself on the edge of a picnic table with his head hung. I'm tuned into this man's emotions like a radio with a broken dial. I would give anything to not feel like this—for him to not feel this way. Shouldn't love be easy? *Is it always this painful?*

His jaw is clenched in such a way that I worry about his poor molars that are taking a beating. The cords in his neck strain against his dark olive complexion. Mahogany brown hair is tousled by the wind, and his eyes are clenched so tightly that the lines etched in his face look like the trenches that are crisscrossing my heart.

I've done this to him. My inability to put my entire being into our relationship has created the angry, highly emotional man that is gripping the edge of a picnic table so hard that his knuckles are white.

My palm slides over my pubic bones, comforting the life inside of me. *He's done this to me.*

Every night for the past three months, I've prayed for amnesia. There had to be some way to remove Graham's imprint from my soul. For three months, I've felt completely void of a life force—the only time I felt my heart beat again was when he had his hands on me either possessively taking me in my office during the White House Christmas party, or desperately making love to me while we sought some sort of solace in each other's bodies. Every time, when we had to go our separate ways I fell into a deep depression, working myself to the point that I was ill and waking up in the middle of the night sobbing for his touch.

I love him.

I don't really know him.

I've given up everything that I've worked my entire life for for the man who is so angry that he can't look at me right now, and the baby that we made while he was trying desperately to convince me to embrace us with the same intensity that I give my career.

Little did I know, but that night, he made the greatest argument yet. We created a life that can't wait ten more months for President Jones to leave office.

I give my lower abdomen a squeeze, and then wrap my arms around Graham's bicep, hugging his arm desperately, hoping that I'm telling him with my body how much he means to me. *I've reached the place where I can give us a chance. Is it too late for you, Graham?*

But I'm so conflicted. We are a mess. We had two perfect weeks of falling in love, which has led to four months of torture that we've put ourselves through. I know so little about him. I don't know if he's ever been in love before. Hell, I don't even know his favorite color. Walking away from him and never telling him about this child would have been so much easier.

Easier on who? Me. I don't know if I have the strength to leave my dream career behind while I prepare to be a new mom at thirty-eight and try to repair this very damaged relationship with a man that I don't really know. Without Graham's knowledge of the life we created, I could have slipped away from D.C. in the middle of the night without having to battle through the hurt feelings that surround our time together.

If he could be a lesser man then I could nurse my broken heart in private while I prepared to raise this child alone. I knew that he would never agree to walk away from his baby.

I'm so tired of feeling this miserable. I crave my life before Graham. Yes, it was filled with work and mostly meaningless sexual relationships, but at least I didn't feel constantly sick to my stomach with an unrelenting tightness in my chest, feeling drawn to someone who I didn't know if I could have a future with. My life was so much easier before the President's invitation only fight night at the White House back in November.

Graham shakes me off, leaving me an empty vessel. I need his comfort and strength. I need him to tell me that I'm going to be okay. He still hasn't opened his eyes. Or moved. Or maybe even taken a breath.

A gust of wind whips around me, sending a wave of shivers through my body. I wrap my arms around myself, trying to block out the chill. I'm not sure if it's the cool March weather making me shake or the ice-cold shoulder that I'm being shown. But whatever the cause, my teeth begin to chatter.

Say something Graham. I want him to acknowledge that I admitted that even if I wasn't carrying his baby that we would have a future. Frankly, it's not even a question anymore. After months of begging God to help me forget Graham Jackson and move on, I received the news that I was going to be a mom.

Terminating the pregnancy would have been the easy choice, but I honestly never considered it. The idea of being a single mom is daunting, but I'm Rachael Early. I eat Senators for breakfast and bust balls for lunch. How hard can it be raising a child? I've essentially been in charge of a daycare for the past seven years.

After I recovered from the initial shock that I wasn't going into early menopause, I was indeed pregnant, I spent about an hour having an epic pity party, complete with a mental breakdown. Then I remembered what some famous person once said—that sometimes God whispers in your ear, and sometimes he knocks you upside the head. Not that I'm a particularly religious person, but after all those nights of wishing that something would happen to make me love Graham Jackson less, I get the news that we created a life together. Sometimes you just have to sit back and toast the universe. I mean, I thought I had my life figured out and in one-third of a year, I've experienced a complete one-eighty, and I don't know what my future looks like three minutes from now, let alone three weeks. I've never been in this position before, and frankly I'm scared beyond belief.

I'm a planner—an executer. I make a decision and ride it to the bitter end. I'm strategic. I play hard ball in a man's world. Why, dear God, why has Graham thrown me so off-kilter?

"Graham, please talk to me," I beg, over the cars racing by not more than fifty feet from us, trying my damnedest to keep the fear out of my voice while I mentally chastise myself for stooping so low.

He doesn't move a muscle. "Go wait in the car. I'll be there in a moment." He says this in a very controlled voice, but I detect the anger that he's working to suppress.

Blame it on my pregnancy hormones, lack of sleep, or straight-up despair, but I can't do what he asks. I throw myself against his back, wrapping my arms desperately around his waist. My cheek presses against his shoulder blade and I hold on to him as if he's my life preserver in the raging sea of my turbulent emotions. Every muscle in his body is tense, and warmth seeps from his shirt causing him to be fiery to the touch. I'm giving everything up for him and our child. I need him to reassure me that it's going to be okay.

I hate this version of me right now. I'm allowing Graham Jackson to reduce me to a stupid, needy, clingy teenage girl, but at the moment, I just don't give a damn.

He doesn't acknowledge me, but I don't give up. I cling to him fiercely—desperately. The cars on the freeway whiz past us, oblivious to fact that right next to them my future hangs in the balance.

I can survive without him. I'll have our child and love him or her enough for two parents. There are plenty of universities that will hire me to teach political science classes. We'll live in some quaint college town where I will bike to class and write political theory papers about how to fix Washington from my utopian perch.

But in my dreams, in the place that I dare to visit when I'm feeling like a dumb girl in a romantic comedy, Graham and I find a way to overcome all of the pain that we've created and become partners.

He rises to his full height, which is much taller than me. He has to feel my determination to make him see that we're better together than functioning in this shitty existence apart.

Still with his back turned and me cocooning him with every ounce of strength that I have, his body shifts. My head raises, anticipating his next move. Then, he reaches up and rubs his thumb over his eyes. Is he crying? God, that makes my eyes burn and my mouth flood with too much liquid. This big, strong, tough man has been reduced to tears.

Sometimes I really hate being me. This is all my fault. I wish I could know the words to say to make this better, but I'm at a loss. So I just speak from my heart. "Forgive me, please," I plead into his back. "I need you, Graham. Tell me what to do to make this right. Tell me what I have to do to make you forgive me."

He breaks free of my grasp and flips me around so I'm now the one in his embrace. His arms tuck me possessively against his chest, my face fitting perfectly against his hard pecs. He leans down and whispers in my ear in a scratchy voice, "I need time, Rachael. Time and some space to process all of this."

If it's even possible, my lungs tighten so painfully that I have to gasp for a breath of air. The juxtaposition of his body cocooning mine and his words are somewhat laughable. Space? There isn't a molecule of air between our bodies.

I want to ask what "time and space" means. I like timeframes, deadlines. Does the proper amount of time and space equal one day, one week, one month, one year, ten years? I hate his response. It's not definitive. It leaves my heart flapping in the wind waiting, once again, for one of us to step up to the plate.

The lack of planning in his response makes me feel as if I'm walking on quicksand. I can give him time. I can also give him space. But in the moment, I become resolved to continue on with my plans of being a single mom. I have three more weeks as the White House Chief of Staff. I've already given notice on my town home. My final day is the last Wednesday of the month. Colin and Caroline have agreed that I can live in one of their guest houses until I've come up with my next plan—finding a job, a place to live, and some town that I can blend in to. This is so not how I saw my days at the White House coming to a close.

Now it's time to focus on what's important, and it's this baby who didn't ask to be conceived. This can no longer be about Graham and me torturing each other, him unwilling to embrace my private relationship demands, and me not able to publicly support his brand of humor and politics. This is now about a baby that is owed a better upbringing than I was given.

One day, if Graham comes around after he's taken his time and used his space, I'll welcome him back into my life. I owe him that. I'll be his whenever and wherever. I just hope that it won't be too late.

Chapter One

Rachael

"Jab. Cross. Left hook. Uppercut. Right hook. Jab. Cross," my trainer, Malik, instructs as he blocks my punches. With each throw, my back, then my shoulder, followed by my arm muscles burn with intensity. Sweat trickles in a steady stream off of my forehead, blurring my vision. This is my last boxing session with Malik.

This gym has been my five-o'clock-in-the-morning, Monday-Wednesday-Friday ritual for the past eight years. Here is where I work out my aggression, battle my demons, and find a reprieve from my over-active mind. This place feels like my home much more than my townhouse ever has.

"Focus, Rachael. Give me everything that you got. One minute left." Malik holds the red pads in front of his chest, and I throw all of my intensity into the final minute of my last workout with him for at least the foreseeable future. My jabs are quick and hit with force as I aerobically push myself to a place of exhaustion. It's sixty seconds. I can do anything for sixty seconds.

Jab.

Cross.

Uppercut.

The timer dings, indicating that we're finished. My arms fall listlessly to my sides and I stumble for a brief moment, working to gain my equilibrium. Then, I feel it. My sweat-drenched body heats uncomfortably and abnormally hot. My stomach roils. I stagger to the barf bucket that I've never had to use.

Malik drops his pads and looks at me, satisfaction painted on his sculpted features. "Ha! Last day. I knew I could make you puke."

Smug son-of-a-bitch doesn't know that I'm pregnant.

At least he has the decency to grab my thermos of water and hand it to me when I'm done. I swish the water around my mouth and spit it into the garbage can.

This morning sickness business is a new addition to my pregnancy. The only evidence that I've got a baby on board is a slight bump just above my pubic bone. However, I seem to get nauseated at the drop of a hat. My doctor says that this is a good symptom. It means that this is a healthy pregnancy, but it sure would be nice to have a steaming-hot cup of coffee again without feeling violently ill.

"You alright?" he asks as I collapse onto the rusted metal chair in the corner of the gym. Sweat is running down his cheeks, and his dreadlocks, pulled away from his face, show perspiration beaded along his hairline.

"I guess you finally got me." I toast him as I take a drink of water, praying that it stays in my stomach.

He pulls up a chair near me and touches my knee. "I'm going to miss the hell outta ya."

Malik and I have a very professional relationship. However, you can't spend three mornings a week with someone and not consider them somewhat a friend.

"Me too." I smile.

"You'll stop by when you're in town?" He removes his hand from my knee and grabs his own water bottle.

I smile and lean back against the chair, finally feeling my stomach settle. "I will. But it'll be a while. I'm dropping off the D.C. radar. I need to figure out what's next for me, and I can't do that here," I reply, glancing around his simplistic gym.

"Understandable," he says, placing his water bottle on the ground. He opens his gym bag and rummages for something. Then he produces a small piece of paper and a pen. He takes the top off and scribbles something on the paper.

I take another sip of water, as the thudding in my wrists slowly begins to return to normal.

He stands up and walks to where I'm sitting. He hands me a business card. The white cardstock has the gym logo on it, and his name and phone number written in a block font. I look up at him, very confused. "I have your number, Malik. I've texted you before."

He smiles. "Turn it over."

I flip the card over in my hand and see his email and mailing address on the back. "Your home address?" I think I sound as perplexed as I am.

"I expect an invite to the wedding and pictures of the baby," he says, with a smirk.

I leap to my feet, blood pounding in my ears. *How does he know?* No one knows about the baby except for Graham, President Jones, Shelby, Caroline and Colin.

He chuckles. "No one told me," he reassures me, while shaking his hands. "I just assumed. Graham was clearly a man in love when you brought him in here."

Graham was a man in love the first and only time he met Malik. Unfortunately, shortly after that, I discovered Graham's secret. He's one of the Sons of Liberty, a political radio show with shock-jock humor thrown in for good measure. His night job makes my day job very difficult. As the White House Chief of Staff, it's my duty to protect the President and his policies from those who disagree. The Sons of Liberty have been reasonably fair to the administration so far, but the public perception of me, one of the President's top advisors, being in a relationship with someone who is so politically polarizing would reflect poorly on the White House. Plus, they discuss topics like strippers' breasts, how to avoid giving oral pleasure, and my favorite topic, my love life.

We played a four-month game of Russian Roulette with our emotions before I told him a few weeks ago that I was stepping down from my White

House position because I was carrying his child. As of right now, our relationship can be described as complicated.

My hand instinctively covers my abdomen. "How do you know that . . . I'm . . . I'm pregnant?"

"I have three kids, Rachael. You were green when you entered my gym."

I put my hands on my hips, and glare at him. "Why did you push me so hard, then?" I want to add *asshole*, but I refrain because I really adore Malik.

"Because you wouldn't have wanted to have been treated any other way." He chuckles.

I grab my black gym bag, water bottle, and towel. I tuck the card into the side pocket of my bag before I toss it over my shoulder. "Look. This needs to stay between us. Graham and I aren't exactly together at the moment, and I need to figure a lot of stuff out."

He pulls me tightly against him, giving me a sweaty hug. When he releases me, he says, "It's all good. I'm like a therapist. You wouldn't believe some of the stories that I hear."

"Thanks for everything," I call over my shoulder as I walk out the gym's glass doors for the last time.

"Later," he replies. Then, he adds, "Good luck."

He doesn't know how much I'll need it.

Lou opens the car door for me, and I slide into the back of the town car. Letting out a sigh, I mumble, "Time for the next goodbye."

***

My favorite winter white suit with the gold knot buttons is hanging in my closet, ready for one last wear. There will be no need for business suits in the middle-of-nowhere Texas, hiding out in Colin and Caroline's compound.

I stand in front of my full-length mirror in the second bedroom that I use for a closet, looking for any telltale signs of my secret. My breasts still fit comfortably in my padded bra. The control-top pantyhose have taken care of any bump, flattening my stomach. I slide the skirt over my hips, zipping it in the back. I button the jacket over my bra, and slip my black heels on my feet. I examine my appearance from every angle, as I know that I will be photographed incessantly today. Once I'm confident that my secret is safe, I exit the closet and enter my bathroom to complete my last-day look. My hair needs to be secured back in one of my signature knots.

Usually, I keep the hair pins in the drawer next to the sink. Today, they rest on the counter next to my overnight cosmetic bag. Everything is packed except for what I need just for this morning.

As I begin running the brush through my hair, my phone dings. My heartbeat picks up, hoping that it's a message from Graham. Today is one of the hardest days of my life. I could use a bit of encouragement right about now. Granted, he didn't plan on knocking me up, and I have complicated his life, but "a thinking of you" text would be nice.

Graham: *Movers will be there in fifteen minutes. I'm booked on the 5:00 flight. Meet you at my place.*

I exhale. That's it. I mean, I know that we're not in a good place, but a "have a nice day" message would have gone a long way to making me feel better about my decision. Hell, I would even accept a "don't suck on your last day of employment."

Sighing, I turn back to my task at hand—making myself presentable for my final day spent holding the title of White House Chief of Staff.

For the hundredth or maybe the thousandth time, I wish that I didn't love him. Today I walk away from my career. My life that I built for myself—every bit of normalcy that I have—to begin a new life as a mother, a person responsible for another human being. With Graham still taking his time and space, I don't know if my new life and responsibilities will be shared by him. I have no idea why he wants to meet me at his home this evening. All I received was a few-word text a few days back asking me to spend the night at his place after I completed my last day at the White House. Not an ounce of further details. I replied asking a few questions but so far, they've been ignored but like the drone that I've become, I agreed.

Just as the last pin secures the tight chignon at the nape of my neck, there's a knock on my front door. Quickly, I toss my remaining bathroom toiletries into the bag and bring it downstairs, dropping it on my over-used

12

chair by the front window that will be donated to charity.

Exhaling, I open the door and greet Lou along with Rita, the move coordinator. We walk to the middle of my living room. I have previously discussed with Rita what should be donated, what should be shipped to Texas, and what should just be destined for the dumpster.

I've known that this day was coming. The majority of my belongings don't hold an ounce of sentimental value. However, the few things that I do have are very important to me. My closet being one of them. Not that I have particularly expensive taste, but my business suits and high-heeled shoes mark time for me. I can tell you what jacket and pencil skirt I was wearing when important events happened. My navy heels with the pointed toe are the shoes I wore when I had to make a trip to Capitol Hill to convince a Congressman to come around to the White House's way of thinking. My clothing is a trip down memory lane—my career scrapbook.

Rita opens her notebook and takes notes as I point out important reminders. When I mention my closet, her eyes shift to the carpet, then she looks up at me rather timidly. "Have you spoken to Mr. Jackson yet?"

"What does Mr. Jackson have to do with this?" I ask in a high-pitched voice. Graham has not shown the least bit of interest in my move, other than to make the initial contact with the moving company. One of his friends from college owns the business. Graham called on my behalf, hoping that the moving company would take extra care with my things if they knew that I was friends with the owner.

Rita clears her throat, and says, "Mr. Jackson phoned on Monday and requested that everything that was to be shipped to Texas should instead move to his residence, including your closet." I'm spending one night with Graham. Why would I need my entire closet for this? I have a feeling that his online text invite to his house after work tonight holds more significance than I had originally thought.

Lou looks away and scurries out the front door. Smart man, that Lou is. Lou and I have never discussed my relationship with Graham, but you can't spend as much time together as we do without a working knowledge of each other's lives. "Rita, if you'll excuse me for a moment. I'm going to go upstairs and make a call."

Rita, who is about my age, with unnaturally red hair and whiskey brown eyes, gives me an uncomfortable smile and walks into my kitchen to begin inventorying my cabinets, or at least I think that's what she's doing by all the banging sounds.

I'm fuming mad. If I was the Tinker Bell cartoon character that the Sons of Liberty call me, my face would be apple red and steam would be billowing out of my ears. I stomp up the stairs, snatching my phone off the bathroom counter and hit send when I locate his number.

"Hello," Graham says with a hint of apprehension in his voice.

"Hi," I spit into the phone. I don't want pleasantries. I want to rip his head off.

"Are you okay? The baby?"

"Baby is fine. I'm not even close to being okay though. What's up with you changing the shipping address for my things?" I pause for a second and hear what sounds like sheets rumpling in the background. "Were you asleep? How can you have texted me fifteen minutes ago and be asleep?"

He laughs. The bastard actually laughs at me. "Oh. I didn't text you. Veronica did."

Is he intentionally trying to ruin my day? "Who is Veronica?" I demand as I take note that I'm standing in my bathroom with the door shut like a teenage girl hiding her phone conversation from her parents. Why do I care if Rita hears me arguing with Graham?

I don't have time to contemplate my motivations because Graham interrupts my thoughts.

"She's my assistant." At least he has the decency to sound a bit apologetic when he delivers that gem of information.

"So Veronica is your assistant who has access to your hotel room where I am assuming your phone is while you are sleeping."

Graham and I are not back together by a long shot, but I am having his child. I assumed that he wasn't seeing anyone else at the moment, as he is taking his time and some space to process all of this. In my humble opinion, it's difficult to do that if your space is inserted inside of Veronica.

"You make it sound so dirty." He chuckles.

I walk over and sit down on the closed toilet seat lid. *Geez, I'm fighting with my Baby Daddy while I sit on the toilet. How did my life become this?* I decide to drop the subject of Veronica and focus on what's important which right now which is my closet. Graham and I are spending tonight and tomorrow in D.C. before he leaves for his next tour stop and I head for Texas. We'll have plenty of time to discuss her then.

"Why is Rita under the impression that the contents of my closet and personal belongings should no longer be shipped to Texas and instead moved to your place?" I almost laugh at myself. I sound so professional. It's a strange question to ask the man who I know that I still love.

The line is silent for a couple of heartbeats. Then he responds neutrally. "That's where I told her they should go."

"I figured that much, genius. But riddle me this. How am I supposed to access my underwear if they're in D.C. and I'm in Texas?" I stomp my foot while I'm perched on a toilet seat lid. I actually stomp my high-heeled shoe as if I'm twelve again. The sound echoes off the vacant bathroom walls and tiled floor reminding me of a spook house. And then, just to further my pre-teen temper tantrum, I tap said foot until he responds.

It takes him a few breaths, but when he does, all I get is "There's been a change of plans."

I've really been trying to quit saying cuss words. I'm going to be a mom, and moms shouldn't drop the "F" bomb like it's going out of style. However, Graham Jackson has me so mad that *fuck* is really the best and only way to respond to him. "You've got to be fucking kidding me. You don't get to change the plans. You don't have the right to change where my belongings are being shipped to." I stand up and begin to pace in my no-longer-mine tiny bathroom. My heels click, click, click against the tile while my hand is planted firmly on my hip. "You aren't even speaking to me, except to check on the baby while you take your time and space. So fuck you, Graham Jackson. You aren't changing anything. You haven't earned that right."

This conversation is much bigger than just where my panties will reside.

This is about me telling him I'm pregnant and him essentially ignoring me. This is about me finally giving him everything that he's wanted and then him turning a cold shoulder.

I check my watch, noting that I should have left five minutes ago. It's my last day. Hopefully no one will be too upset that I'm late.

"Look, Rach. I may not have handled things well lately . . ."

"Ya think?" I interrupt taking a good look at myself in the mirror. I look like me—same platinum-blond hair, the same too-large-for-my-face green eyes, but I'm not sure where the tough-as-nails version of me has gone. Six months ago, I wouldn't have even given someone a chance to explain, let alone put up with Graham's time and space. Why I'm doing it now baffles me.

He ignores my snide comment and continues, "But please just trust me. Have your stuff go to my place. Veronica overnighted Rita the key. We'll talk about it tonight." He says this in his bedroom dominate voice. "Please," he adds, in a kind tone.

I sigh and lean against the bathroom counter top, wondering who the hell I've turned into. The Rachael Early that eats Senators for breakfast would never acquiesce so easily. However, I'm late on the last day of my White House employment and frankly have lost my will to fight when it comes to him.

"Fine." I can ship my things just as easily from his house as mine. It will cost more, but right now, there's no fire left in me.

There's a very pregnant pause.

Then, quietly, he says, "Have a great last day of work," and adds, "I'm so proud of you."

Damn pregnancy hormones make my eyes well up. I tilt my chin to the ceiling and fan my face, attempting to keep the tears at bay so they don't ruin my mascara. "Thanks. I needed to hear that this morning."

"Knock 'em dead, kid. I'll see you in a little while."

I smile, in spite of my hormonal, messed-up state. "Have a safe trip."

"Love you, Rachael."

Then the phone goes dead. Staring at the device for a few heartbeats, I wonder if we'll ever reach a point where we can just have a normal phone conversation without my heart rate going to stroke-inducing levels?

I say to no one in particular, "I love you too, but I don't like you very much at all."

***

Fortunately, Evan Atkins has my back and tipped me off that I was going to have to ceremoniously leave my office and walk the halls of the West Wing one last time while everyone lines the walls and clapped.

"They're ready for you, Rachael," Evan says with glee. He is smiling so big that I'm surprised his face hasn't split in two.

I stand up and walk around my desk. "Who came up with this asinine idea anyway? Can't I just grab my purse and stroll out of here like I do every night?"

He smirks. "You did. It was your idea three weeks ago. You said it would look great for the presidential historical video." *Damn pregnancy brain.*

Evan is dressed in a navy suit with a navy and green striped tie. His dirty blond hair is tousled, as if he had a nooner instead of lunch. "I believe the reasoning was that you are the first ever female White House Chief of Staff, and seeing how beloved you are by the staff will do wonders for smashing the glass ceiling."

I stare up into his soft blue eyes. I really love him. He's the brother that I don't have. I ball up my fist and punch him in the arm.

He yelps and grabs his tricep, as if I actually hurt him. "What was that for?"

I smile sweetly. "For not telling me that my idea was horrible."

He pulls me to him and gives me a tight hug. When we step back, he places his hands on my shoulders and has such a serious look on his face that I bite the inside of my lip to keep the tears away. *Don't ruin my makeup.*

Evan looks into my eyes and in a very solemn tone, says, "You know, I tried to talk the President into letting you mud wrestle the female Senator from Florida. Thought we could drink beer and place bets. Maybe eat a little pizza. Smoke a few cigars. He thought it would be a shitty match up. Said you'd take her in about three seconds."

God, I'm going to miss you. I punch him again. "You're such an asshole."

Laughing, I rub my knuckles. I forget that Evan has arm muscles. He's one of the things that I'm going to miss the most about my job. Even when days were really awful, Evan was good for a quick banter. We've made jokes about some horrible things—jokes that I would never repeat—but humor is our way of coping. One day, he told me, "Kid, you either laugh or cry." That about sums up the seven years and two months that I've served the President as his White House Chief of Staff, and, more importantly, as his friend. Fortunately, I've chosen to laugh more than I've cried. I consider that a huge success.

No one has been in the trenches with me like Evan has. We share a history that can never be explained.

Who am I going to talk to when I'm alone in Texas or living in a cottage in some pretentious college town, debating the merits of a monarchy system of rule?

I put my hands on my hips and give him my sassiest look. "I'm not telling you goodbye. I'm going to be on your ass every day after I watch the daily press briefing. Let's be clear—the yahoo might be taking over my office, but I'm still the White House Chief of Staff. Rachael Early is irreplaceable."

He leans down as if he is going to share a big, juicy secret with me. "I know, Rach. Trust me. We all do." Evan grasps my shoulders and gets in my face as if I'm a prize fighter, and he's giving me a pep talk. His eyes shine with mirth when he says, "All you have to do is put one foot in front of the other, smile pretty for the multiple cameras that will be capturing your every move, and look like this is the best decision you've ever made instead of your funeral."

I quip, "I know how to put the fun in funeral."

Maggie, my assistant for more years than I care to think about, cracks my office door open and says, "The President is on his way down."

I exhale and run my hands over the sides of my hair to make sure that my knot is still smooth at the nape of my neck. Maggie smiles as her eyes fill with tears.

Evan slips wordlessly past us and out the door giving Maggie and I are moment to say goodbye.

"Maggie, I'd cry too if I had to work for Michael." She laughs at my joke about her new boss. Everyone hates Michael. I bet even his own mother thinks that he's a douche, but he's been the assistant White House Chief of Staff under me for the past seven years, so it only makes sense that this office becomes his.

Maggie places one hand on her hip and says, "You know he's never once commented on how cute my kitties are." Framed pictures of her cats decorate her desk, and every day she shares one "funny" store about them. She's a little odd, but she's loyal, hardworking, talks a mile a minute, and makes inappropriate comments when it's just her, Evan and me. Oh! And her coffee is so good that it could make a grown man weep. *God, after I have this baby maybe I could convince her to brew me a pot.*

I walk to her and give her a kiss on the cheek and a big hug. "You're the best, Mags. I'll stop by next time I'm in D.C."

She whispers in my ear, "Send me pics of the baby."

I look at her with my mouth hanging open and my eyes wide.

"Don't worry. I won't tell anyone. I heard you sick in your office, and you've quit drinking my coffee. I hope the father is the guy who sent those horrible red, white, and blue flowers."

Okay. That makes me smile. Graham's patriotic floral display was just the right amount of gaudy, hideous and perfection rolled into one gigantic demonstration of American pride.

Is my pregnancy the worst-kept secret in Washington? I'm beginning to think so.

Chapter Two

Graham

"This is bullshit, Graham," Max says as he pushes his chair back from the dining room table in his hotel suite. It tumbles over with a surprisingly loud thud. It's early in the morning—like so early that in our college days this would still be considered nighttime. The window curtains are open behind him, highlighting the pre-dawn sky.

Max's bright red hair has gotten more over-the-top since we began our Sons of Liberty tour. Our manager forced us to meet with a stylist who created "looks" for each of us. It's very boy band circa 1997. Jake is the California surfer meets thrift shop T-shirts. Here's a guy who grew up on the Upper East Side of Manhattan and went to the most expensive boarding schools on the continent who is dressed like a Venice Beach bum. I'm the all-American schoolboy with perfectly gelled hair, turned up collars, and loafers. If you ask me, I think I look like the preppy asshole in all teenager angst movies.

As for Max? The poor stylist. I'm sure that she's still suffering from nightmares. She helped Max embrace his Maxness. His hair is bigger and brighter. His shirts look as if they could hang in a modern art museum, and Max is reveling in our newfound fame.

"It's bullshit because I need to get my fucked up personal life figured out? Really, Max?" My voice is calm—cool. The white of my knuckles gripping the edge of the table are the only indication that I'm anything but.

Max runs his hand through his curls, making them stand straight up. With the pre-dawn grey light seeping through the windows, he almost appears angelic, as if God has Bozo the clown angels. He presses his back against the hotel window. "No, it's bullshit because you started the Sons of Liberty. This is your baby, and you're pissing away the biggest opportunity of our lives for a girl you dated for two weeks. YOU. DON'T. KNOW. HER." He steps forward, leaning on the table, and pronounces each word as if I don't speak English or am hard of hearing. My grip tightens, preventing me from beating the shit out of him.

He continues, "I get that she has some sort of vice grip on your dick, but let's be honest, man. You don't even know if you're the father. You were not together when she mysteriously wound up knocked up. And be real. She's not nineteen. She's like almost forty and supposedly got pregnant when she told you she was on birth control. She knows where babies come from. Sounds a bit suspicious to me."

Max is right. I release the table and fall back against the hard wood chair. It's this argument that keeps me up at night, that makes my chest tight and that has made a bottle of bourbon my best friend. The timing of her news could not have been any worse. I had quit/been asked to resign my coaching and teaching position at the private college prep school that I was working at when we revealed our identities. Even though I knew it was coming, it was damn hard to say goodbye to the students and sport that I loved. However, the media attention was too great of a distraction. As our agent says, we're on fire. Every media outlet wants a piece of us. The Sons of Liberty have done what the original Sons of Liberty did two hundred and fifty years ago. We've incited real change in this country.

We've brought politics to the people who didn't give a damn who was in office before they began listening to our radio show. We've shown our age demographic that you don't have to be old, rich, with grey hair to make a difference. It's the most thrilling experience of my life.

Unfortunately, my brainchild also stopped the most promising and real relationship I've had in its tracks. Rachael does not approve, and refuses to be associated with me because of the tactics that the Sons of Liberty use to reach males under the age of thirty-five. We use shock-jock humor. I'll admit some of our topics are crude, disgusting, and degrading to women. She can't see the greater good approach to what we're doing.

We broke up two weeks after we began dating. Fourteen days is a ridiculously short time to know someone. I slept with her three times after we ended things. She's pregnant. We weren't even texting each other, and she managed to get pregnant. She's told me that the baby is mine. Although, I didn't need to hear those words exit her mouth. The baby was mine as soon as she said, "I'm pregnant." But I get why Max and Jake are so pissed. They don't understand the connection that Rachael and I have. Max has been with Marissa since early college and doesn't remember what it's like to fall in love, and Jake probably doesn't fuck the same girl twice. They don't get the attraction—the connection that we share.

I turn to Jake and try to plead my case. "I'm not going to miss a single tour date. I'm just going to skip out on the public appearances and sponsor dinners during the week. I'll leave on Sunday after the show and be back on Thursday, but I'll be there for every radio show. We'll just record from different time zones."

As Jake shakes his head, his floppy blond hair falls in his eyes, reminding me of a shaggy dog from old cartoons. His voice is soft, regretful. "Sorry, man. I agree with Max. This is bullshit. She doesn't have a job any longer. You want to make this work with her, she can join us instead of you running to her." He pauses for a second, looking away from both Max and me. "Don't forget that this tour isn't making money yet. If anything, it's hemorrhaging. We've only done three live shows. We're still working out all the tour kinks. Now isn't the time to go play house with your baby mama."

My best friends, my fraternity brothers, my business partners think that this is the biggest mistake of my life. Why am I still considering doing this?

And I know. The answer has been clear to me since the day that we sat in a Cracker Barrel restaurant and she gave me the news. She said "yes." She confirmed that whatever feelings I have for her, she feels the same about me. How can I not do whatever it takes to make this work?

"Hopefully, it will only be for a couple of weeks," I quip. "I mean look what happened the last time we were together for fourteen days."

No one laughs. Max rights his chair and sits back down at the table. Neither guy will make eye contact with me, and for some reason that hurts more than their lack of support.

I sigh and drop my head. My heart is being pulled in two directions. My career needs me more than ever. We're still trying to find our on stage mojo, and we're losing money with every show, but that's why we've hired a manager. Hopefully, he can do a better job of managing the crew than I've been doing. The Sons of Liberty are on the brink of greatness. And the woman that I love is growing our child. I don't want to miss out on a single moment of it—of any of it.

"It's just for a couple of weeks." I don't recognize my own voice. I've never sounded so defeated. The stakes are high. I'm betting everything that I can keep the Sons of Liberty going and convince Rachael to join me on tour.

"You're not getting my blessing," Max states as if he's declaring war on Russia. "I will not lie for you or make apologies." Then he pulls the dagger out of his pocket and shoves it into my heart. "Just remember that I actually have a wife and kid also. Their future, my family's future, trumps your piece of pussy."

"Don't call her that," I growl as I fly to my feet, ready to beat the shit out of Max. I become feverishly hot and blood pounds so loudly in my ears that I can't hear anything other than my own rage.

Max jumps to his feet also, not even coming close to matching my height. The wooden four-inch thick by three-foot wide tabletop is keeping the two of us separated, but it won't for much longer if he talks about her again. "Fuck you, Jackson. I hope she's worth it," he says gesturing wildly around the room.

Jake stands up and walks out of the hotel suite without acknowledging either one of us. The door slams loudly behind him. Tension crackles the air. Max isn't backing down and neither am I. This might be a huge mistake, but I'll be damned if I let Max talk about the mother of my child that way.

He glares at me. His green eyes blaze with fury. I don't need his blessing to leave the tour, but I sure as shit would like his support. Fist fighting with Max is not something that I want to do, but I have to prove to him just what she means to me.

My phone buzzes in my pocket, giving me the perfect opportunity to look away and break the tense situation. As I fish for my cell, Max walks briskly away from the table and into the bedroom in the suite, slamming the door behind him.

At this early hour, I wouldn't be surprised if security doesn't show up with all the slammed doors and the knocked over chair.

The phone buzzes again. I know it's her. It's about the time she should be calling, madder than a swarm of hornets. I take a deep breath and exhale before I answer, preparing myself for the wrath of Hurricane Rachael, mentally reviewing the notes that I've made for this call. Rachael's reputation is not lost on me. For hand-to-hand combat with her, I have to be prepared.

1. Don't let her steamroll you.
2. Keep focused. This conversation means the difference between you seeing your child frequently or your nightmare coming true.
3. Do not under any circumstances tell her that you love her.

"Hello," I answer, trying to sound as if I haven't been expecting this phone call.

"Hi," Rachael says with enough venom that I almost laugh. Did she just overhear my conversation with the guys? I look around suspiciously as I exit Max's suite, without slamming a door, I might add, and head back to my hotel room.

"Are you okay? The baby?" I pretend to not know why she's calling. I'm not making this easy on her.

"Baby is fine. I'm not even close to being okay though. What's up with you changing the shipping address for my things?"

I slide my keycard into the lock on the door and enter my dreary, generic room. It's a nice enough space, with a large bed, swirl-patterned maroon carpet, and modern artwork hanging on the walls. I slip under the sheets and pull the duvet up as if it can shield me from her fury.

"Were you asleep? How can you have texted me and be asleep?"

I laugh, knowing that I'm adding fuel to her fire. I think I derive some sort of sick pleasure out of poking her with a stick. "Oh. I didn't text you. Veronica did."

"Who's Veronica?" she demands.

"She's my assistant." I glance at the hotel room clock that is exactly one hour and ten minutes incorrect. I never bothered correcting it. Realizing my clothes aren't going to pack themselves, I walk to the closet, pulling my pants from the hangers and tossing them into my suitcase.

"So Veronica is your assistant who has access to your hotel room where I am assuming your phone is while you're sleeping."

"You make it sound so dirty." I don't mention that Veronica had joined us for our very early meeting this morning and used my phone to text Rachael the reminder. Maybe she'll focus on Veronica and forget that I hijacked her things, but I know there's not a prayer of that happening.

"Why is Rita, my moving coordinator, under the impression that the contents of my closet and personal belongings should no longer be shipped to Texas and instead moved to your place?"

I muster the cockiest voice I can and reply, "That's where I told her they should go."

"I figured that much, genius. But, riddle me this. How am I supposed to access my underwear if they're in D.C. and I'm in Texas?" She's caustic in how she delivers that line. I imagine her forehead pulled into a deep *V* and her hand resting on her slight hip.

"There's been a change of plans," I state evenly, my voice not betraying the rush of blood through my body.

"You've got to be fucking kidding me. You don't get to change the plans. You don't have the right to change where my belongings are being shipped to. You aren't even speaking to me, except to check on the baby while you take your time and space. So fuck you, Graham Jackson. You aren't changing anything."

Yes. She's furious, but I detect something in her voice. Hope? A small degree of happiness? Does Rachael like that I'm taking control just like she wants me to do in the bedroom?

Change of tactics . . . "Look, Rach. I may not have handled things well lately, but please just trust me. Have your stuff go to my place. Veronica overnighted Rita the key. We'll talk about it tonight." I'm off-script, but I think this is good. "Please," I add.

She sighs loudly, and I imagine her rolling her eyes. "Fine."

That's it? She gave in that easily. This is what she wanted. Rachael has been wanting me to prove to her how much this relationship means to me. Okay. *I've got this.*

"Have a great last day of work. I'm so proud of you." She's agreed to part of my plan. I mentally high-five myself. Take the victory and move on.

Then, she breaks my heart. My tough-as-nails ball-breaker gets choked up. "Thanks. I needed to hear that this morning."

My jaw relaxes and my shoulders fall back to their natural position. And I smile. I don't know the last time that I've legitimately smiled. "Knock 'em dead, kid. I'll see you in a little while."

"Have a safe trip," she wishes me, barely above a whisper.

Then I break all my rules and tell her "Love you, Rachael" and hit end on the call. My heart can't take any form of rejection right now, so I don't wait for a response.

I spend the next thirty minutes analyzing every word spoken. If I don't stop this cycle, I'll go crazy so I throw on my workout clothes and hit the gym in the hotel. In the middle of my run, it dawns on me that I'm feeling something I haven't felt for a long time. In fact, it's been four months since I experienced this emotion. It's happiness. A smile spreads across my lips, and I increase the speed on the treadmill. *Maybe my plan does have a snowball's chance in hell.*

Since the last time Rachael and I had sex and then she rejected me, I've been so angry. I was the happy-go-lucky, easygoing guy before I met her. I had casual relationships—I certainly didn't fall in love. She was and is my game-changer. Now, we're bringing a new game-changer into this world. That doesn't seem so daunting right now.

Everyone is mad at me. The guys think I'm making an epic mistake, but I know that I've got to give us a chance. Two weeks . . . I just need two weeks to make her see our future my way.

Chapter Three

Rachael

My ceremonial walk down the staff-lined hall was hideous. I felt like a float during the Macy's Thanksgiving Day Parade. Everyone clapped and smiled, which was the opposite of my emotions. The world thought I was leaving for a glorious new job opportunity in the private sector. Not a total lie. I am leaving the White House to take on an exciting new career—one of dirty diapers, sore breasts, stretch marks, and sleepless nights. Geez . . . this is so hard.

Burying myself deeper into my favorite chair in the President's private office, I'm so glad that I did my walk for history's sake and then changed into cashmere lounging pants and a hoodie. My baby bump is quite thankful that the control-top pantyhose are now a thing of the past.

"One more minute, Rach . . ." the President says.

"Take your time," I reply as I pull out my smart phone. I've mastered *Angry Birds* and have moved on to *Candy Crush*.

As I slide my phone to on, I notice that I missed a text from Graham, or Veronica, or whomever else has access to his phone at the moment. "Flight delayed. I'll text when I know more."

I reply back, "No problem. I'll be here a bit longer."

I don't expect a response, so I close my messaging app and open my email. Just as my mail is loading, his text fills my screen.

Graham: *Reason #1112 that MMA is better than boxing: Matches are frequent enough that fans get to know the fighters.*

That's it. That's all there is. I actually open the text up to see if maybe the rest of his message was cut off my screen. Graham and I have barely spoken since I told him about the baby. After me essentially admitting that I would have wanted a future with him even if I wasn't pregnant, he shut down. Instead of us going back to his home to discuss our next steps, he dropped me off at my townhome repeating his excuse of "I just need time and space to think."

I thought this morning we were back in a good place. He told me he loved me before he hung up. *Those words lit up my heart.* Unfortunately, they also were like a lit match in a pitch-black room. I've spent the time since I told Graham about the baby preparing myself to raise this child alone. Hearing that he still loves me has given me hope that he might come around to the idea of us trying to co-parent this baby.

I read his words again and try to decipher what exactly he's trying to relay to me. Finally, giving up, I send something back that is equally cryptic so I don't lose our little game.

Rachael: *Reason #1120 that boxing is better than MMA: The strikes are precise and a boxer hones his punches over years of practice.*

Lame. But it was the best that I could come up with. In fact, there's a good chance that I've used it before. Unfortunately, my creativity is shot after my very emotional day. I'm looking forward to seeing Graham, whom I hope is in a good, non-brooding mood. I also hope he assures me Veronica is like ninety with skin that looks like a saddlebag and boobs that hang past her waist. Then, he'll tell me that he loves me, will quit talking about locker-room topics on his radio show, and we'll find a way to beat the odds and make this work. After I agree, we'll make love until the sun rises, because pregnancy has made me horny as hell.

"Ready, Rachael," the President says as he takes a seat across from me on the blue couch chosen by Shelby.

Once the President is no longer in office, the Smithsonian will choose some pieces from the White House to be displayed. Also, the curator of his Presidential Library will select some meaningful items from his terms in office. I make a mental note to remind whomever is chosen for that job to take the peacock-blue velvet sofa. That sofa is where the most important decisions of his administration have been made.

My phone drops into my open bag that is resting on an ornate oriental rug. I tug my feet under me and prepare for the last evening debriefing as the White House Chief of Staff.

"How are you feeling?" he asks as he takes a sip of his scotch. Carefully, I watch the ice in the high-ball glass for any signs of a tremble. His hand is steady. I hate his Parkinson's diagnosis, and that I will not be here to protect his secret.

My mouth waters for just a tiny, intsy, weentsy sip of his scotch. I swallow. "Fine. Except for the nausea every now and again, I can't tell that I'm pregnant."

"Good. Good." He nods and smiles. "Are you ready to share with me who the lucky dad is?"

When I told President Jones and Shelby my happy news, I opted to not share Graham's identity. For one thing, they were still reeling from the fact that one of the Sons of Liberty was their son's lacrosse coach and had been in their private residence. Also, until I'm absolutely positive of Graham's role in my baby's life, I don't want to share his identity. Graham didn't ask to be a dad. I want him to have every opportunity to walk away if that's what he wants.

"Sperm donor," I quip with a chuckle.

The President doesn't miss a beat, "Aren't we all?" A huge smile cracks his hardened face. "I'm going to miss the hell out of you."

"Feeling is mutual."

"So what's next?" he asks, as he takes another swig of his scotch.

"I'm going to hide out in Texas until after I have the baby, then who knows? I've been offered a book contract to write about breaking the political glass ceiling, or I might take you up on your offer to help me land a professor position." I adjust myself in the chair and stare at the fire. I don't think my accomplishments have been all that remarkable. I've worked hard and gotten lucky. I'm not sure what anyone can learn from that.

He chuckles. "I'll be more than happy to help you, but you don't need me to make a phone call. You're a pioneer, Rachael. Don't forget that. You have a lot to share with the world."

But do I? Do I really have a voice? I attribute most of my success to luck and hard work, but luck has played such a big part. I happened to graduate from grad school at the right time. I happened to be hired by Senator Jones's office. Now, I did work hard, proving to him that I was much more than the copy girl, but was that really enough for a book or to educate students?

"You're too talented to hide for long, Rachael," President Jones continues in a tight voice. "I get why you feel like you need to disappear until the baby is born. I might not agree, but I understand. However, I'm going to be very disappointed in you if you don't stay in the mix of Washington politics. The country needs you working behind the scenes. We're better off for it."

Damn, stupid pregnancy hormones for like the hundredth time today. My eyes fill with tears as I continue watching the red-orange flames dance around the crackling logs. I swallow hard and fight to regain my composure. Clearing my throat, I say, "Thank you, Mr. President. That means the world to me."

"So let's discuss your favorite person Roan Perez. What do you think of him as a possible Vice Presidential candidate?" Roan is a sore subject. I despise him personally, but admire and am even a bit jealous of his charisma. We attended many events together and photographed enough that the press thought we were dating. Ewww. . . I went home alone at the end of the night while he helped himself to the plethora of women flinging their panties his way.

"He is a despicable human, but the media loves him. He's probably a good candidate. I'll talk to the campaign manager and make sure that he's properly vetted." I reach in my bag and extract my notebook and pen and open to the section where I keep my to-do list. I make a note so I don't forget.

By the time we wrap up our meeting, it's after nine o'clock. I hug Shelby goodbye and promise to keep in touch. The President pulls me into a tight embrace and tells me to be careful. I feel like a kid being dropped off at college. Lou is waiting to take me on our last drive leaving the White House.

As we pull away through the enormous iron gates, I place my hand over my pubic bone and shed a few tears as I rest my head against the cool leather seat. Exhaling, I whisper, "Here's to new beginnings."

***

Graham's house looks exactly as it did in November, except his landscaping is beginning to show signs that spring is in the air. It's a ranch-style home that sits on a quiet neighborhood street. Now I know that it was the launching ground for the Sons of Liberty. The last time I walked to the front door, up this cement path, I was dressed in a trench-coat dress with ruby red lipstick painted on my lips. I wanted to hurt Graham for making me feel used—for tricking me into falling in love with him.

Oh, the difference time makes. My heart races knowing that in a few short steps, I'll see him again. *He told me he still loved me when we hung up this morning.* His words ping-pong around in my head. I've spent the time since I found out I was pregnant preparing for my last days in office and building a plan that revolved around me being a single mom. It's my preservation. Prepare for the worst and hope for the best.

"Do I need to escort you to the door?" Lou asks, in his very professional voice.

"No. I think you're finally rid of me." Laughing, I slide forward and grasp his arm. "I couldn't have asked for a better shadow."

Lou turns and I catch his eyes in the rearview mirror. "It's been an honor." He swallows hard and stoically looks forward. "I hope my daughter turns out just like you."

My eyes burn. Is there a greater compliment than a dad wishing his daughter is as successful as you've been? But I know that my success is only with my career. My personal life is a train wreck. I swallow the huge lump in my throat and whisper through a choked voice, "With a Dad like you, how could she not?"

I scamper out of the back of the car as if my hair is on fire. I can't take another damn goodbye today. It's just too painful.

I all but run to Graham's door and knock with so much force that I'm sure he thinks there's an emergency. Well, there is. There is a pregnant woman who needs to decompress—a two-hour horror flick and making fun of the girls who hide in the garage next to the chainsaws is just what I need.

My body shifts from side to side as I bounce on my toes, waiting for the door to open. I imagine him greeting me in nothing but a pair of soft, worn jeans resting on his hips. His chest is bare and lickably lush. Heavy blue eyes will drink in the sight of me waiting for him to pull me inside and devour me against the wall. I can feel his tongue caressing my ear and tracing my collarbone, and I lick my lips in anticipation. It was only a short text invite to come over tonight, but at the moment, I'm sure glad he sent it.

I become so lost in my fantasy that I almost scream when to my complete shock, a tall, raven-haired stunner with light green eyes opens the father to my child's front door instead of him. She's dressed in black jeans, a tight black sweater and dark boots. Her breasts are like perfect mounds, stretching the fabric to its limits. "Oh good, you're here." She sighs and grabs my arm, pulling me inside the house. "She'll be here shortly. We have a lot to do before Mr. Jackson arrives."

My mouth must be hanging open in shock because she turns her head and makes a strange face, saying very slowly, as if English isn't my first language, "You tackle organizing her closet while I unpack her personal things."

I don't move from my spot. This is not how this evening was supposed to go. "You are?" I manage to spit out, but I know exactly who this is in Graham's home. It would be Veronica, who texted me from Graham's phone during the early hours of the morning.

"Oh sorry," she says dismissively. "I'm Veronica, Mr. Jackson's personal assistant. I thought that the agency didn't have any help available, but I'm so glad you were," she relays, as she shuts the door behind me. We're standing in Graham's small foyer. It's just inside the door with a wall that blocks the rest of the house from view.

She's maybe twenty-three if I'm being generous, and she is gorgeous. She's an exotic beauty that looks like she is the perfect complement to Graham. In fact, they look eerily similar. Unfortunately, any hope that I might have that his assistant is hideous flies out of the window.

"Drop your bag," she instructs, as she points to a spot on the floor. I obey because I am curious to see where this is leading. "Mr. Jackson needs everything perfect before she arrives." She rolls her eyes and gives me a conspiratorial wink, as if I'm her partner-in-crime. "She's like ten years older than him. Total cougar."

In my catty thoughts, I conclude that Veronica was not hired for her politically-minded ways and more for her personal skills. I hope to God that she isn't the reason for his need for time and space.

"I'm restocking Graham's kitchen and finding some place for her things marked important. I just need help organizing her clothes. Mr. Jackson prefers that a professional handle this. He wants her to be like, you know, organized and stuff."

Nodding, I ignore her use of the words "and stuff." Veronica has no clue who I am. Probably if I was still dressed in a power suit she would have been tipped off. It's fine. Unless you watch the evening news or read political websites, I'm not particularly recognizable. I haven't been on the late-night talk shows, or the cover of a gossip magazine. However, I would have thought with her job as an assistant to one of the Sons of Liberty that she would have at the very least Googled me or, at the most, turned on a cable news channel so she was politically informed. Whatever. This further proves my point that she was hired for her boobs.

I walk past Veronica and into Graham's living room. It looks exactly like it did when I last saw it. Everything is in order and photography ready for the next issue of the Pottery Barn catalog except there is a wine glass with bright red lipstick prints on the rim resting on the coffee table. I bristle. There's something about seeing her lip imprints on his glass that makes my chest constrict. I have been struggling with the effects of early pregnancy while being the President's right-hand woman, and Graham has been drinking wine with his too-young-for-alcohol assistant. I'm sure that he just needed time and space to think. Yeah, right! With the help of the black-haired, green-eyed beauty in the kitchen. Inwardly, I roll my eyes, as I remind myself of her early morning text.

Then I spot George, Graham's gigantic black Labrador, in the backyard. He looks so sad with his droopy eyes, and his face is pressed against the glass. It's as if he's pleading with me to let him in. I walk over to the sliding glass door and flip the lock.

"What are you doing?" Veronica shrieks. She had walked into the kitchen and was unpacking a brown sack of groceries. A loaf of French bread slips out of her hand and tumbles to the kitchen counter. I make note of the bread for tomorrow morning when I'm reminded once again that there's a human growing inside of me.

"I'm letting George in," I state calmly as I slide the door back. The big beast greets me with such affection that I drop to my knees and cuddle his head. I'm not a dog fan, but George is beyond cool.

"Get him out!" Veronica screams as she rushes past me to grab his collar and attempts to drag him out.

I hug George tighter to my chest and reply firmly, "Leave him alone." I'm sure that the scene is quite comical. The poor dog is caught in the middle of a game of tug-of-war between two adult females.

Veronica places her hands on her hips and says very snidely, "I'm going to call the agency and have you fired. The dog stays outside."

George looks up at me with the saddest chocolate orbs in the history of puppy-dog eyes. I rise to my full height of a barely there five feet and reply, "George stays in."

"He's a filthy dog that sheds everywhere. Mr. Jackson wants his house perfect for the cougar. If you don't care about your job, fine. But I want to keep mine." She pulls her phone out of the back pocket of her jeans and begins to scroll through contacts. I stand there watching her, - daring her to make the call. Then the lightbulb inside her pretty little head turns on. She throws her hand over her mouth and backs away from me as if I'm a poisonous viper.

Yes. There have been a few congressmen that have had the same reaction.

I stand there stroking George's back, quite pleased that she's realized her mistake.

"You're the cougar. I mean Rachael," she corrects herself. The look on her face is priceless. Her mouth is gaping open displaying her lovely artificially white teeth, and her eyes are round as if she's seen a ghost.

Nodding, I lean down and give George a kiss on the top of his nose. Graham's sweet boy sighs in appreciation and licks my hand. "I think that it's time for you to leave."

I know that I have no right to throw her out. This isn't my house, and Graham and I aren't even a couple. However, Veronica was in his hotel room and had access to his phone this morning. She's at least going to know that I'm competition. He did say that he still loves me after all.

She scurries to her phone and at least she has the good sense to look apologetic as she grabs her purse. "I'm . . . I . . . I'm . . . sorry," she stutters as she rushes out. "I thought you were from the personal organization agency that's supposed to take care of Miss Early's clothes. I . . . I didn't know."

When she gets to the front door, Veronica reaches for the door knob but turns around and gives me an apprehensive smile. "If it's any consolation, you don't look almost forty."

I don't respond, because as I've learned navigating the underbelly of Washington politics, nothing good comes out of responding to a backhanded compliment.

After the front door closes, I turn and shut the sliding glass door, dropping to the floor beside George. Just his proximity is calming to my frayed nerves. Stroking his back, I look around Graham's home.

It really is a very comfortable place to live. I laugh as I remember how I asked in my snottiest voice which Betsy Ross, the Sons of Liberty's name for their female sources, had decorated his place. Graham had smirked and responded that his sister had. Ha! I guess the joke had been on me.

As if he understands me, I say to George, "I've missed you, big guy. Want to help me find my belongings?"

Standing, I walk to where I dropped my purse and pull my phone out of the side pocket. No missed calls from Graham or texts for that matter. I wish that before I'd kicked Veronica out I had asked what his flights status was. Hmmm . . . and if they were in the same city together, how was she here when he's not? More questions to ask him when he arrives.

First order of business though is to wash the wine glass. It's sitting there as a reminder of the girl that I'm probably biologically old enough to be the mother of. That thought inspires me to make finding a personal trainer priority number one when I get settled.

I use a Brillo pad to scrub the tramp red lip prints off the glass and note that the last drop of wine must have been sitting in it for a while. A hint of rose has stained the bottom. Oh well. I put in the drying rack. Graham can figure out what to do next with it. At least any trace of lipstick has been removed.

Next, I make my way down the hall, past the door that hid Graham's secret from the rest of the world. I've seen that room and the nasty things written on the "other white board." There's no need to dredge up those memories again. A shudder runs through me as I pass by.

Standing in front of the door at the end of the hall that I assume is the master bedroom, I pause a moment before I turn the knob. I feel a bit like a voyeur spying on Graham's life. I've only been in his home once. I didn't stay long enough to see where he sleeps.

As the door swings open, my breath catches in my chest. I was expecting another Pottery Barn regurgitated room complete with the wooden headboard, matching bedside tables and designer chest-of-drawers. Instead, I walk into a room that is a hodgepodge of the things that Graham must love.

Flipping on the light, I stare at the wall of canvas prints of different sizes hung in a collage. Local Washington D.C. landmarks are captured through the lens of a talented photographer, but I skip over those. What intrigues me the most are the black-and-white images of a young Graham and his teammates playing lacrosse. He must have gotten his fraternity letters tattooed on his calf soon after he left for college, because they are quite visible in this picture. There are pictures of the Sons of Liberty when they were young fraternity brothers. I love how they all look like kids—fresh, as if life hadn't inflicted hardships on them yet. Max had crazy hair even back then. In one shot, he has his red curls knotted in a bun on top of his head. I smile and touch the image, running my finger over Graham's chest.

My favorite one is of Graham, Max, and Jake dressed in tuxes with their arms wrapped around each other's shoulders. They could be going to a social or maybe it's Max's wedding day, but they look so carefree, young and uninhibited. Jake has a silver flask in his hand and there's a cigar pinched between Graham's lips. Whoever snapped the picture captured their spirits perfectly—or what little I know of them. I've only met them once.

Next, I study a canvas of Graham with his niece, sister, Mom and Dad. It looks more recent. Kelly, Graham's sister, and I went to high school together. He told me that she had survived breast cancer, and much to my happiness she looks to be thriving. A beautiful pre-teen girl is holding Graham's hand. She's looking up adoringly at her uncle. Graham's head is thrown back in laughter. Kelly looks very mischievous. I decide that she must have told a joke or said something that was inappropriate because Graham's mom doesn't look thrilled about whatever is causing Graham to laugh. Her hand is firmly gripping her hip and her lips are pinched. Graham's dad? Well, his face is blank. They all look so much alike—dark hair, light eyes and tall builds.

Instinctively, I run my hand over my stomach and wonder if Graham's genes are as strong as his parents' and sister's. Will my baby have almost black hair with light eyes or will he or she look more like me—petite with light blond hair? My cheeks warm as I smile and look down at my bulge, and I feel something that I haven't experienced in a long time. It's excitement. For the first time since I found out that I'm expecting, I allow myself to be excited about becoming a parent.

"I'm going to be a mom," I say to Graham's family canvas.

Then my eyes catch a black-and-white canvas of Graham and me. It's when we attended the fundraiser together. My hair is down and my short dress shows off the top of my legs, which I rarely display. Graham looks devastatingly handsome in his perfectly tailored tux, with his wavy long black hair and piercing blue eyes. His dimple is on display and he looks down at me with hungry eyes. I'm staring up into his as if I'm lost in the moment. Hours later we would make love for the first time, confirming our feelings for each other.

I'm honored that he would choose to add that image to his special picture wall. Actions speak louder than words. *Maybe Graham and I do have a chance of making this work.*

George brushes past me as he flops down on the red plaid cushion that rests at the foot of Graham's bed. George is a gentle giant. I like his chilled demeanor and non-demanding personality. Plus, I think it's impossible to not pet him. It's like my hand finds his head automatically.

"Hey boy," I coo as I walk past him towards Graham's fluffy comforter. Before my head even hits the pillow, his scent bathes me in warmth. It's masculine and rugged with a hint of cologne. I grasp his pillow, bringing it to my nose, and inhale like a stalker. I look over my shoulder just to make sure it's only George and me in the room. Odors and my pregnancy haven't gotten along well, but his scent? Wow. It makes me ache for its owner.

Tossing the pillow back on the bed before my fingers get a mind of their own, I open the bi-fold doors of Graham's closet, hoping to see my clothing in some semblance of an order. The only things before me are a row of neatly hung male jeans and slacks on the bottom, and T-shirts, sweaters, and shirts hung above. *Who hangs sweaters?* It's as if these doors trapped the essence of him inside. If I had hoped to avoid his scent, I seriously should have stayed out of his closet.

My mind floods with memories of our time together. His dominance that I love. Tender kisses left in trails over my ribs. His talented tongue and magic fingers. How I ever thought that I could forget and move on from him is really beyond me. I was such a fool. Even when he isn't here, just the smell of him makes me long for his attention.

I shake my head, clearing the thoughts as I exit Graham's room and head back to the foyer to grab my bag. Presuming that my clothes are still in wardrobe boxes, I don't think they have arrived.

This baby is the best thing that could have happened to me in more ways than one, I've come to decide. My recent dream of becoming a mother will be realized, but it also made me see just how much I love Graham. I would like to think that I would have eventually gotten out of my own way and forgiven him—Sons of Liberty politics and all. But I don't know if that's true. I could have let pride rule my emotions and been miserable the rest of my life. The thought saddens me. I hope that I would have been braver than that.

My phone still indicates no missed calls. I do have one text from a number that I don't recognize. I swipe my finger over the screen and read, "I'm very sorry for how I acted. Your things are in the SOL room."

Veronica.

I'm actually rather proud of her. Possessing the ability to apologize at such a young age is a gift. After Graham and I discuss assistants not being welcome in hotel rooms, maybe she won't be so bad after all.

Walking back to Graham's bedroom, I drop my bag just inside the door. Then I turn around and walk to the door that surprisingly no longer has a combination lock installed on it. It has been replaced with just a normal non-descript knob.

The close proximity to the space makes my stomach clench. When I stood in this spot months ago, I was angry and hurt, but most of all I felt betrayed. I'm still raw. Anxiety curls itself like a vine around my heart. My grip on the doorknob tightens, but I force myself to enter anyway.

Once again, I'm shocked by what I see, but in a very good way. I was expecting to find wardrobe boxes lining the wall; instead the oversized telephone booth is still there, but all the sound equipment, the round conference table, and the filthily-worded white boards are gone. They've been replaced with my business suits and clothing from the second bedroom in my town home hung in beautifully crafted white, open cabinets. There's a built-in vanity in between my evening gowns and shoe racks. My full-length mirror has been installed on the front of a cabinet door. I open it and discover that it's a cedar closet to protect my wool items.

Graham did all of this for me.

It's too much and mesmerizing at the same time. My clothes that were destined for a spare room in Caroline's guest house are now being displayed like works of art in this beautifully crafted closet—for me. "For me," I repeat as I spin around, trying to grasp that this was crafted with me in mind. He saw my spare bedroom and realized what my clothes meant to me so he created this in a room that used to be associated with vile feelings.

The walls are painted a gorgeous shade of green that makes me think of the stems of wildflowers growing in a meadow. *I told him that my favorite color is green.* A crystal chandelier now hangs in the middle of the room. Its prisms cut the light, creating a rainbow effect on the ceiling. It's a room crafted for a princess. Not even in my wildest dreams could I imagine something so wonderful.

It's not like I ever fantasized about having a real closet one day; the thought actually never entered my mind. However, this . . . this is something that I didn't think existed, except for Kim Kardashian and the First Lady. So much attention to detail has been shown. Graham gets it. Gets me.

In the corner of the room, where complicated panels of knobs and slides used to reside, is now a beautiful mahogany desk with intricate wood detail that has been placed near the only window in the room.

I run my fingers over the ornate detail as if I'm blind and memorizing every detail. Perfection. But then I gasp as I realize that the desk is very similar to the one that I just vacated at the White House. The chair is even similar, or maybe the same.

Graham copied my office desk and chair.

But how did he know what they looked like? He's only been to my office once and neither one of us were in a talking mood. He'd been possessive—angry that I had danced with Roan Perez at the White House Christmas party.

I hadn't attended the event with either one of them. I'd been too upset about my breakup with Graham to bring anyone. When I'd seen him there with another woman, my stomach had twisted into a knot resembling something that even a Boy Scout couldn't unravel. The other woman had been young, pretty. I didn't know her. After I'd done a bit of snooping— finding Lou and asking him to pull the guest list—I'd discovered that she was a lobbyist at one of the bigger firms. Graham had definitely been her plus one.

Was she a Betsy Ross? I'd tried to focus on the conversations that I'd kept getting trapped in, but inadvertently, my eyes had wandered around the great expanse of the room and locked with Graham's. It had been as if he and I were the only ones in attendance at the Christmas party. He'd been dressed in a tux that was perfectly tailored for his tall form—probably the same one he wore the first night that we made love. Casually, his date had touched his arm or placed her hand on his back. It had made me crazy. That was my jacket. My man.

I'd attempted to forget him with two glasses of wine—my limit at White House functions. That hadn't worked. I'd danced with a couple of male friends. All that did was remind me of our dance that we'd shared together when he sang "You Look Wonderful Tonight" while we twirled across the floor.

It has been as if we were playing a one-up game. He'd flirted with his date. I'd danced with a staffer. He'd let her feed him a bite of salmon croquettes. I'd sat by Roan at dinner. His forehead had creased and his eyes had become the shade of dark blue that I had grown to read as upset, so I'd asked Roan to dance.

Before I'd been able to register what was happening, Graham had grabbed my hand and led me to an alcove just outside the entrance to the ballroom. His eyes had been wild and his hair flopped over his eyebrows as he'd stared down at me.

"You only danced with him to piss me off," he'd stated, glaring with such a look that I should have known what would happen next.

"You flirted with her shamelessly and let her feed you, for God's sake.

Are you a child? Can you not feed yourself food?" I'd replied, gesturing wildly behind me, as if she were standing right there.

"She's a friend and you know how I feel about Roan. I'd call him slime but that would be an insult to the snail that left it behind."

"He's a colleague." Geez, I'd been defending the guy who—I agree with Graham—is slime.

Graham had looked up to the ceiling and said more calmly, "You know how I feel about you and you did that to . . ." he'd paused and then dropped his eyes to mine. He'd taken my face between his palms, "to hurt me—make me jealous."

He'd run his fingers tenderly over my forehead as if he'd been brushing imaginary hair out of my eyes. "I'm right here, Rachael. I'm yours. No need to make me want you more. That isn't possible. All you have to do is acknowledge me."

My body had tingled everywhere he'd touched. My cells had recognized his as their counterpart. Graham was mine. I'd wanted him to erase Roan's too soft, sweaty palms from my back. I'd wanted to replace his date's touch with my own.

I'd stood on my tiptoes and grabbed him around the neck, bringing his lips to mine. At first our kiss had been tentative. Both of us had known that we shouldn't have been doing this and definitely not so publicly. At any moment, one of the guests could have walked by and spotted the White House Chief of Staff making out with, well, a high school history teacher and coach. Not very professional at all. But as his tongue had become more forceful, demanding, the less I had cared about a code of ethics.

"My office," I'd groaned into his mouth.

He'd pulled away and grabbed my hand. I'd straightened my dress. "Do I look presentable?" I'd asked, attempting to make myself appear sophisticated and classy instead of horny as hell.

"Your lips are swollen and your cheeks are flushed. You're the most goddamn beautiful thing that I've ever seen," he'd growled.

I'd smiled and showed him the way to my office where he'd pushed my dress up around my waist and had taken me from behind, bent over the arm of my sofa. It was the roughest sex that I've ever had. He'd used my body and I'd let him. He'd spanked my ass, leaving palm prints on it that had lasted for a week and I'd loved every minute of it. What I'd learned that night was that I like to run every facet of my life except for in the bedroom. I'd loved that Graham dominated my body.

Afterwards, we'd taken turns cleaning up in my small bathroom just off my office. He'd asked me to come home with him. I'd stupidly declined, letting my insecurities trump my heart. He'd looked miserable and I'd cried all the way home.

Reliving that night makes me nauseous. *How I hurt you, Graham, and yet you still did all of this for me.* I drop into the chair, too overwhelmed to process it.

A new laptop rests on top of the desk and trophies of sorts lines the walls. Graham took highlights of my career and turned them into black-and-white canvases, like the ones in his bedroom. Tears prick my eyes when I see the now famous picture of my delivering the news to Senator Langford Jones that his new title was President-elect Jones. I'm dressed in a campaign T-shirt and yoga pants because I had spilled coffee all over my beautiful suit earlier in the day. Graham had this picture and article in the notebook that he'd kept on my career. I spin around in the chair, looking for all of those colorful notebooks. They've been replaced with cabinets that hold my jeans, hats and sweaters.

Before I open the desk drawers, I know what I will find. It's Graham. He thinks of everything. They are stocked with pencils, pens, notebooks and other office essentials.

This wasn't the plan though, I think, as I spin around in my desk chair. I have to leave Washington. I can't have a watermelon under my shirt and go out in public here. Everyone knows who I am. My pregnancy will be exposed, which is not good for President Jones or Graham for that matter.

Even though I tried to avoid the newsstand on my corner, I still caught glimpses of the cover of gossip magazines flaunting Graham's single status. Of course, they call him Revere, which makes me crazy. Graham is his name, and he loves me. Revere and some supermodel at a party. Revere and a pop singer dancing at a night club. His target demographic for the Sons of Liberty tour is men between the ages of eighteen and thirty-five. Those magazine covers are good for his image.

Just to torture myself a little more, I lean forward and peek out of the closed blinds just to see what my view would be. "Oh God," I sigh as I sit back in my chair. It's not the White House lawn, but Graham's home backs up to a ravine with a stream that runs through it. It's so tranquil and just what I enjoy staring at when my mind needs to wander.

Closing the door on my beautiful room makes me sad. I know Graham's motivations for building it for me. He's showing me that he wants me in his life. He may have needed time and space, not been able to properly tell me where his head was at, so he decided to show me. The message has been received loud and clear. I'm just not sure if I can stay in D.C. or even want to. He's on the road touring for the next eighteen months. That's no place for a family. I've had a taste of that life when President Jones traveled by bus all over the country campaigning. It was hell, and it took a real toll on Shelby and the boys.

One night, Shelby broke down in tears. It was over something simple, but I knew that it was the overwhelming frustration of not having a place to call home—of losing her privacy and her boys missing their friends and schoolmates. Through her sobs, she told me that she felt all alone. That night, we ditched the campaign and found a movie theater. We watched a chick flick, ate popcorn mixed with M&M's, and then finished the evening off with mint chocolate-chip ice cream. The night made both of us feel human again.

I smile at the memory, but also know that if I join Graham on tour I will become Shelby. I'll be friendless, lonely and lose my privacy, all while experiencing changes to my body that I can't even fathom. A tour bus is no place for an infant. And there's no point in me staying in Washington. I might as well go to Texas. At least I will not be alone.

My head falls back against the desk chair. It gives a weak squeak of protest. It's not quite exactly like the one in my office. This one is new and needs to be broken in.

How did my life become so complicated? Before Graham I could play my life like a board game. Everything was predictable. I knew with the roll of a dice where my next move was. Now, I'm a flag flapping the in the wind. The room—it's just too much.

One of the bonuses of my pregnancy is that the more exhausted I become, the more nauseous I get. I'm beginning to feel queasy. It could be the hormones or it could be the personal space that he created and my turmoil over what to do. I decide to let it rest tonight and I'll discuss it with Graham tomorrow. I note the time on my watch. His flight must have been very delayed.

My overnight bag is where I dropped it. I carry it into Graham's room and unzip it. My pajamas are on top, but I can't bring myself to wear them. I want Graham to hold me—for him to surround me—so I walk back to his closet. It's so pathetic and I wish that I could fight off these girly impulses but tonight is not the night. I succumb to being a lovesick sappy girl.

One of the last shirts towards the back of his closet is a blue button-up that looks as if it has seen better days as a thin layer of dust that rests on the shoulders. I pull it off the hanger giving it a brush and bring it to my nose. Inhaling deeply, I sigh. It's the scent of him that I crave so much. As I button it over my bump, I imagine his arms pulling me against his chest and him whispering in my ear how much I mean to him. Sighing at how pitiful I've become, I grab my toiletries bag and phone and head to the bathroom that I assume Graham's guests use. After a face scrub and tooth brushing, I make my way back to his bedroom. The bed looks so inviting. I fold his comforter back and slide in between his incredibly soft sheets. I choose to sleep on the left side of his bed because the couple of times that we've spent the night together, he always chose the right.

As I drift off to sleep, I allow myself to believe that this could be our future, and the smile on my face is so foreign that my cheeks ache from lack of use.

Chapter Four

Graham

The airport is a cluster fuck. Veronica, who was on an earlier flight, had no issue getting out of town. I had to record our radio program, which was tense, but we got through it without killing each other, and we still have all of our teeth. Sometimes you just have to label days like this as survival. It would have been easier to call in sick, but I showed up—showed the guys that I'm still committed to the Sons of Liberty. It has to count for something. *Man, I sure hope so.*

"You have to get me on a plane," I plead to the harassed lady behind the counter who doesn't care that I have to get back to D.C. to Rachael . . . to my baby.

She bangs on the keyboard for a bit making little "hmm" noises. "Okay. It looks like I can get you on the next flight. It leaves in an hour. ID?"

I almost kiss her. She hands me back my driver's license. I settle into the executive lounge and order a bourbon. I don't have a lot of time, but it's enough that I can start working on notes for tomorrow's show.

Unfortunately, I check email first. I scan my inbox for anything that requires my immediate attention. Sure enough, I spot an email from David Riker, the Sons of Liberty's agent.

The subject line is "Graham: READ IMMEDIATELY." I roll my eyes as I click on the email. David is a bit high-strung. Like if it were still the 1980s I would swear that he has a coke problem. He's one of my least favorite people that I've had the pleasure of working with. However, Max fought for us to hire him because he's a shark in the entertainment ocean. And as much of a jerk as I think he is, he did negotiate us one hell of a sweet package deal with the concert promotions company.

> *Revere,*
>
> *I just hung up with Solomon. I'm assuming that he misunderstood you when you told him that you were leaving for D.C. IT'S WEDNESDAY! May I direct you to the attachment that lists the SOL calendar. You have a show on Saturday, with a radio show to record and appearances every hour of the morning and night. A quick trip home is NOT on the itinerary. Now, get your ass back on a plane, and we'll visit in person tomorrow about this stunt.*
>
> *D.R.*

I delete the email without responding. What's done is done. *He works for me.*

I down my drink without tasting it and settle back against the plush seat. My guilty subconscious reminds me that I signed a contract. Not the Sons of Liberty, but Graham Jackson used a Mont Blanc pen to scratch my name on the 'sign here' line. I agreed to make our tour my number-one priority.

That was before her.

My head falls into my hands, and I stare at the green and grey abstract squares decorating the carpet. David is going to lose his mind when he realizes that I'm leaving after every live show to spend the next four days with Rachael before I have to be in the next city. I decide that it's best to not mention that little detail yet.

My phone dings with a text.

Veronica: *All is good here. Desk is set up. Clothes need organizing, but everything survived the move. Anything you want from the store?*

Me: *The usual stuff and grab a few things that you think a girl would like.*

Veronica: *Eye-eye Captain*

I smirk at my phone and whisper to myself. It's "A-y-e, Veronica." David certainly didn't hire her for her knowledge of the English language, but she is efficient.

My flight is called, so I pack up my little-used laptop and head for the gate. I just have to keep all the balls in the air for a few weeks. Hopefully, that's all it will take to convince Rachael to see things my way.

***

"Hey, man." I get the cab driver's attention by tapping him on the shoulder. "Can we make a detour?" Our plane had to make an emergency stop in Denver because some asshole decided to have heart palpitations. Rachael has probably been asleep for hours. No use in rushing home at this point.

"It's your dime." His voice is deep and rich. He sounds as if he should be playing the sax at a smoky jazz club in New Orleans instead of driving a dingy yellow cab in D.C.

About ten minutes later, we pull up in front of the high school where I used to work. I never really had a chance to say goodbye. The day before we revealed that we were the Sons of Liberty, I met with my principal. I gave him the news and told him that I would be resigning at the end of the month.

It didn't go well. He was very upset and accused me of jeopardizing the school's reputation and putting the students in danger. I still don't know how hosting a radio show endangers the youth of America, but I wasn't in a decent position to argue. I thought that I would get to say goodbye to my students and work with the new lacrosse coach, helping him transition to coaching such a talented group of guys. Instead, the principal slapped me with a letter informing me that if I stepped foot on the grounds of the school, they would seek a restraining order.

I climb out of the back of the cab and walk across the yellowish brown grass of the lacrosse field and take a seat on the home team's bench. It's a chilly evening, so I pull my wool coat tightly around my chest, flipping the collar up to keep the cold wind from my neck.

After the plane touched down in D.C., I made the mistake of checking emails again. You would have thought that I had learned my lesson the last time. There were six more from David making sure that his displeasure at my absence was noted. I deleted his voicemails without listening to them and did the same with his text messages. That's not why my chest feels like an elephant is performing a pirouette on it. Max and Jake have been radio silent. Normally, we text throughout the day. Some of it's about the Sons of Liberty, but mostly it's just good-natured ribbing each other. These guys are my brothers and right now our family doesn't seem to be speaking to each other—or just me.

I ask the night sky, "Why the fuck can't I just be a history teacher and lacrosse coach?"

Of course, I know the answer. The Sons of Liberty were my passion, my baby. Rachael inspired me so many years ago to make a change—to see a problem and fix it. I put my heart and soul into building our radio show into what it is today. Proud is an understatement. It's my life. Now, I have a complicated relationship with Rachael and a baby on the way because I was much more than a history teacher and lacrosse coach.

I block that thought from my mind and instead focus on telling my beloved sport goodbye. I hope that my students and players know that I was not perfect, but I worked hard to be the perfect teacher and coach for them. Maybe one day, they'll follow their own dreams and realize that anything worth having means blood, sweat and tears, and sacrifices that you never planned on making. I hope that Rachael is not one of my success casualties.

Lacrosse matches play in my head, while I relive some of my favorite moments. Those make me smile. I even catch myself laughing out loud when I remember the look on one of the player's faces when I told him that he was going to start. He was a hard-working kid, but he didn't have a lot of talent. It was his senior year. I announced his name in the locker room before the game. His face lit up like the Fourth of July. Then in the next second he turned green, saying, "Oh God. That means I'm actually going to have to play."

But as always, the good memories went hand in hand with the bad. The time one of my players failed a drug test and I had to suspend him, or when I had to tell one of my favorite players that his mom didn't make it out of surgery. Those memories are so vivid and overshadow the disappointments that come along with the game, like losing a championship.

I say goodbye to the sport that helped shape my life to this point. Without lacrosse, I would have never made it to Virginia and met Max and Jake. There would have been no Sons of Liberty, or Rachael for that matter. Lacrosse will always be my first love.

Climbing down from the bleachers, I walk to the center of the field. Bending down, I pick a tuft of grass, bringing it to my nose. I'm sure it's just my imagination, but I can smell the sweat and determination of my guys in the dirt. The plug slides easily into my pocket. One last memento of the game that made me.

"Play hard, boys," I yell to the universe. Then, I turn and make my way back to the yellow cab.

As I duck through the door, the driver asks, "Where to now, man?"

"Home," I reply, as I settle against the seat.

I haven't seen my house in almost a month. The place still looks the same. There are four outside walls, a driveway, and trees in the front yard. It was purchased with the Sons of Liberty in mind. After looking at hundreds of homes with my realtor, I finally found one that had a room that could work as a studio. Now, it houses Rachael's extensive shoe collection, her business suits, and office. It was a small gesture on my part, but one I hope she sees for what it truly is. An olive branch. My way of showing her that I want her as a part of my life.

From the outside, my home looks similar to all the others. Each house is a shade of red brick, one-story, with four windows across the front. But what makes my pulse beat in my ears is knowing that she's inside its four walls, waiting for me.

The key slips easily into the lock, and I open the front door with care not to disturb the sleeping souls inside. Despite my best efforts, George comes bounding down the hallway to greet me right inside the front door.

Poor guy has been in boarding all of this time.

"Hi my big, silly boy," I greet him.

Sinking to the floor, I take his enormous head in my hands and give his ears a good scratching. He whines in appreciation and keeps nudging my hands with his nose if I try to stop. "I've missed you so much. No more awful kennel for you. We're going on a road trip. We just have to convince Rachael to join us," I tell him.

Finally, George lets me stand and make my way into the house. I throw my coat over one of the arm chairs and make myself a drink in the kitchen. After the day I've had, I deserve something strong. The burn of the whiskey makes my mouth pucker, and I wince from the heat.

It's so damn strange to be back in my house.

I take the bit of earth from the lacrosse field out of my jeans pocket and place it in a zip-lock bag. It looks out of place resting on my kitchen counter, so I open my junk drawer and drop it in. That feels awkward also, but at least it's in safekeeping.

The place that I've called home feels foreign to me. Yes. This is where I live, but it seems colder, vacant. I'm not sure why, but I don't like it. The air smells musty, not like it did when I lived here.

There's a pile of mail on the counter, and I am thankful that Veronica sorted through all the junk and just left me the things that I need to look at. Most are bills. I guess I need to forward them. To where? A tour bus? A hotel room? The thought is depressing. There's a graduation invitation from one of my former students. I check the date and know automatically that I will not be able to attend. Not sure what city I'll be in, but it's a Saturday night.

The thought heaps on to my already foul mood. I haven't missed a graduation ceremony since I began teaching. *You're not a teacher anymore.*

Finishing my whiskey, I leave the glass on the counter. I look for signs that Rachael is in my home, but everything looks pristine, untouched. I'm not sure what I was hoping to see, but there is something about the starkness of my living room that makes me a bit sad. It looks as generic as the hotel rooms I've been living in.

I wish she had left her shoes laying haphazardly in the middle of the room and her purse on the hook by the door. The navy blue blanket should be crumbled on the couch and a dog-eared magazine lying nearby—not one perfectly draped over the arm of the couch and the other in a fan on the coffee table.

Standing up straight hits me like a burden as the whiskey begins to soak my brain. I shuffle down the hallway to my bedroom door. The closer I get, the more excited I become to sleep in my own bed again. I didn't realize how much I'd missed it until I saw George disappear around the corner. The door is open, and I come this close to flipping on the light switch. But I stop dead in my tracks. The blue light from my alarm clock illuminates the bed, and on the side of the mattress where I sleep is her tiny frame snuggled into my pillow. Blond hair is piled around her angelic face looking like spun silk, and her knees are drawn tightly to her chest. She looks childlike against the vastness of the mattress. In this moment, there is nothing that I want more than to slide under the sheets and wake her with soft kisses against her lips that are slightly parted. Then, as she wakes, I'll make my way to her soaked panties—wet because of me—and devour her sweet pussy as if it's my last meal on this earth.

Images of her naked body flood my mind. I haven't gotten to enjoy her visually since we ended things. The ability to stare at her now is like candy for my brain.

This sleeping beauty can't deny us happiness because of my job, or tell me that we can only work after President Jones leaves office. No. When Rachael is asleep, I can pretend that she is all mine.

I unbutton the top button on my jeans and pull the zipper down. As I go to hook my thumbs through the belt loop of my jeans, my brain reminds my dick what a bad idea this is. If Rachael and I put sex back into play between us, we'll never take the step back that we both need and learn to become friends—to trust each other. The two weeks that we spent together changed our lives. It's time we handled this relationship like we should have from the beginning. We need to quit thinking like the horny teenagers in my class and approach this relationship like adults. Especially because these adults are about to be parents. Rachael and I need to build a solid foundation of forgiveness first and then begin developing a relationship based on values that last—not just orgasms.

The hardest thing I've done is turn around and walk back down the hallway to the room that I had prepared for Rachael. I fling open the door with too much force. The doorknob hits the wall, probably leaving a dent, and bounces back, banging into my shoulder. I don't care. I'm pissed at myself. Why shouldn't I walk back into my bedroom and own her body?

Because you want to own her mind also.

I take off my clothes and leave them in a pile on the floor, and pull the quilt back, climbing into the bed that once was used by Jake when he came into town every weekend to work on the Sons of Liberty. Instead of it smelling like my college roommate—which would be disgusting—I'm flooded with the sweet scent of Rachael. I had her bedding from her townhome moved into this room. Her pillow smells of her shampoo. It's a floral, lavender scent that makes my dick even more livid that we're in here and she's out there. I toss and turn for a little while before I finally switch pillows. I'm going back in that room if I have to smell her all night. It's like the sweetest form of torture.

Damn! I sit up straight in bed, remembering that I didn't take out my contacts or brush my teeth. For about two seconds I contemplate skipping my nighttime hygiene, but I swear it's like I have some sort of neural link with my mother and I hear her reminding me that I'll get an eye infection and cavities. In my thirties, I still shuffle to the bathroom to perform my nighttime duties just to quiet my mom's nagging voice in my head.

Crawling back in bed, I remind myself that I should not lecture my kid so much about hygiene. It's okay to sleep in your contacts sometimes, isn't it? *You did when you slept with Rachael.*

That just takes me back to my dick asking again why we are in the guest room.

At some point, I must finally drift off to sleep. Then the dreams come as they have every night since she told me that one plus one was about to equal three.

Ba . . . boom . . . ba . . . boom . . . My heart thuds against my chest.

Rachael! Rachael has taken the baby.

Images of a man who isn't me holding a black-haired, blue-eyed little boy's hand race through my dreams just like they did last night and the night before. Every night the dream is different, but the characters haven't changed. A nameless, faceless man is raising my son, teaching him to play lacrosse, and the dream ends with my little boy not recognizing me when I show up for one of his games.

Just like all the nights before, I wake up drenched with sweat. The quilt, her scent, seems to be suffocating me. I untangle my legs from the material and lie naked on top of the sheets, letting the cool night air dry my damp skin. I'm panting like a dog after a long run. It's pathetic really. These dreams must stop.

It's like the fog is cleared away or the veil lifted or some other contrived saying that means I'm kicking my own ass. My reasons for concocting this crazy plan become clear to me. I'm not taking some time off from the Sons of Liberty to try to make things right with Rachael for her sake or even our baby's sake. I'm doing it to save myself. I'm not just betting my career on this move—I've gone all in with my soul. Gasping at the realization of just how fucked I am, I ball my hand into a fist and push it into my breastbone. Right now, that horrible dream is my reality if we can't get our shit straight.

I roll over and pretend to sleep for a while. I might actually doze a bit, but it's no use. My mind is racing. Anytime I find sleep, the dream begins again as if it's looped. I wake myself up and stare at the ceiling again. I'm terrified that she's going to follow through with her plan to run away to Texas and hide. *Maybe the closet was enough to get her to stay.*

I know better. It's Rachael Early, the most stubborn woman on the planet. It's going to take more than clothes organization to get her to see life my way.

It might be easier committing a felony—kidnapping and imprisonment.

***

The opening and shutting of my kitchen cabinets wakes me from my shallow sleep. I stare at the wall next to the bed for a couple of heartbeats, trying to collect myself. I have to remind my brain that I'm in the guest room in my house, and the person clanking around my kitchen is the mother of my child. Before I bolt out of bed and see my Tinker Bell—I call her that only in my head—I take a deep breath and work to restore my heartbeat to something other than a stroke level. This feels like a job interview. If I don't get "hired" I might as well be fired from my life.

I slip on some of Jake's pajama bottoms that I find in the bottom drawer of the dresser, and my glasses. It crosses my mind that I should put on a shirt but I decide that I need to use my advantages where I can. She likes/liked to run her hand over my pecs and stomach. Maybe a reminder of better times?

Entering the living room, my eyes track to her immediately. She's sitting on a chair at the kitchen table with a box of crackers in front of her. She has a flour square in her right hand, nibbling on it like she's a mouse, while her other hand supports her forehead. Rachael's white blond hair is draped over one shoulder creating a screen of sorts, blocking what's on the other side. My first thought is she got plastered last night.

Obviously, I quickly correct myself. There's one thing that I don't have to worry about and that's Rachael taking good care of the baby.

"You okay?" I ask as I walk past her to the coffee pot. I have to stop my lips from finding her forehead and giving her a good morning kiss.

Trying to be nonchalant, as if we do this every morning, and this isn't the first morning we've spent together since her impromptu invite to the hotel back in November, I turn my back to her and start the coffee.

"Fine . . . just have to get through this reminder that I'm pregnant." She takes another bite of the cracker.

"Coffee?" I know the answer. The woman loves her coffee. Without hearing her response, I automatically make double what I would normally brew.

"Oh God, no!" She moans, and the plastic sleeve from the box makes a crackling noise.

My forehead crinkles in concern as I turn around and walk towards her. There is no doubt in my mind that I still love her. I might have told myself that I'm doing all of this for the baby and myself, but that's only the partial truth. As much as I wish that my heart didn't ache at seeing her sick, it does. And I want to make it better.

"Hey," I soothe, as I pull one of the other kitchen chairs near her. "It'll be okay. Can I get you something? Water? Milk? Orange juice."

"A glass of water would be nice," she says, as she nibbles on the corner of another saltine.

"No problem." I leap to my feet, thankful that she has given me something to do.

"What's with the glasses?"

Her question takes me aback. I've worn contacts since I completed law school. Has she never seen me in glasses? As I fill the red tumbler with water, I think back to the mornings that I've shared with Rachael. Yeah. It's true. I always slept in my contacts.

"Wear them every morning until I put my contacts in." I set the glass down in front of her and walk to the double doors to let George in. "Thanks for putting George out."

"He wasn't taking no for an answer. Whoever has been caring for him has spoiled him rotten." She sounds better. Her voice is stronger and there's a hint of humor, maybe even fondness, when she talks about George. That's good, because he's not going back to the kennel that he's lived at while I have been gone.

George almost knocks me over when he comes barreling into the house. I kneel in front of him, rubbing his ears and stroking his back. I was worried that he would have forgotten who I was, but after his reaction last night and this morning, there's no doubt that George and I are still buddies.

"You two are very cute together. He was happy to see me last night. I had to inform your assistant"—there's the Rachael that I know and love. Venom laces the word "assistant." Apparently, she wasn't pleased that it was my assistant who texted her from my phone yesterday morning. Good. I like a little bit of jealousy. Makes me happy that she gives a damn—"that George is an inside dog and does not appreciate being kept outside at night."

"Thank goodness Rachael was here to save you, big boy," I coo.

"Veronica didn't realize who I was and called me your cougar."

I can't tell from her tone or body language if the fact that she's seven years older than me bothers her. I've joked about it, and she teased back. It's not a big deal to me. I can't imagine why she would care. However, I bet that she wasn't too pleased to be called a cougar by my young assistant.

I will have a talk with Veronica though. She's twenty-five, and was hired by the Sons of Liberty manager for her ASSets and not her PA skills. I'm sure she was supposed to be a distraction from Rachael, because Jake's assistant is post-menopausal age and acts like his mother. Max's assistant is male because Marissa did the hiring.

Standing up, I walk to the kitchen to get my coffee and breakfast for George. The conversation that the two of us need to have is sitting like a rock in my stomach. The cavemen really had the right idea. I'm bigger than she is. Why shouldn't I just be able to throw her over my shoulder and make her see that this is the only chance that we have?

George's food makes a loud pinging noise as the hard chunks hit the stainless steel. After I set the bowl down in front of him and give him his command to eat, I pick my mug up and take a gulp. *I can do this.*

Ready . . . .

One . . .

Two . . .

Three . . .

Her phone rings from somewhere in the house. She jumps to her feet and races out of the kitchen as if this is the most important call ever. As she exits the living room, I catch a glimpse of what she's wearing and a groan escapes my throat. I stare at the ceiling, as if hoping for divine inspiration to keep my hands to myself. She has on just about the sexiest thing that a woman can sleep in besides nothing at all. It's my cornflower blue dress shirt from law school.

I haven't worn it in years. In fact, I didn't realize that I still had it. It must have been shoved towards the back of my closet. I guess she was looking for something to sleep in and pulled a shirt that she didn't think I cared about. I didn't give a damn about that shirt until I just saw her in it, but now it's my favorite. It hits her just above the knees, with the slits on the side revealing her muscular thighs. My dick remembers what it felt like to have those legs wrapped around my waist, and I groan again.

Her hair swishes along her middle back as she turns the corner and I have to stop myself from following her. If having mind-blowing orgasms built a relationship, then Rachael and I would be destined to be some romantic movie success story.

I'm still standing in the same spot, lost in my vivid thoughts of this woman that has taken my brain hostage, when she dances into the living room with the phone pressed against her shoulder while she's attempting to slide on yoga pants.

"I'm still in D.C. I can be there in fifteen minutes," she says to whomever is on the other end of the phone.

"Change of plans . . . It doesn't matter . . . Sure. I'm leaving . . ."

She's leaving. Did she just say that she's leaving me? We've only shared the same oxygen for about ten minutes. She's not going anywhere.

Before I can stop myself, I've snatched the phone out of her hand and ended her call. "Now . . ." She finishes as if she had to say that last word in the sentence.

I hold the phone high over my head and give it a jiggle, anticipating the wildfire that I just ignited.

"What do you think that you're doing?" she demands, standing in front of me in my shirt with her yoga pant leg only pulled up to the knee on one leg. Her face is flushed with anger and her eyes are slits. A little *V* forms between them.

Somewhere on the edge of my consciousness, I get a nudge that this maybe wasn't the best idea that I've ever had. Quickly, I dismiss it. I started this war so I might as well win it.

I smirk. "Saving me the time and energy of explaining that you're not going to work. Yesterday was your last day. Today you are unemployed."

"Don't remind me." She taps her foot against the tile, not bothering to reach for her phone.

She begins her speech with "she may not be paid by the White House any longer, but she will always take the White House phone calls" and ends it with something about national security and me being an asshole.

All I hear is the teacher from the Charlie Brown cartoons.

In the middle of her tirade, I turn around and walk back into the kitchen to pour myself a cup of coffee. Apparently, this was not the best move either because she follows behind me, continuing her speech, only now it's about how I don't listen to her.

Whatever.

I continue to ignore her while I casually fill my mug. She's drawing closer to my back. I know this because she's getting louder, lecturing me on how I don't have the right to dictate something or another, when I've finally had enough.

I spin around quickly and grab her under her arms, lifting her off the ground. She screeches like a hyena, demanding that I put her down. Her face is pink and hair flying as she balls up her fists, attempting to hit me. I dodge her punches and raise her up, placing her on top of my refrigerator. I note that during some part of her fit, she'd removed the yoga pants and is back only in my shirt. Works for me.

"What in the fuck do you think you're doing, Graham Jackson? Get me down from here," she demands. She's looks just like Tinker Bell when she's mad: rosy red cheeks, brows drawn together, lips thin as slits, arms crossed over her chest. Even when she's furious she's gorgeous. Her alabaster-toned legs cross at the ankle and contrast beautifully against my black refrigerator. Stepping back, I admire just how fuckably luscious she is when she's making bodily threats against me.

Turning around, I walk to my coffee mug, attempting to camouflage the smile that is cracking my cheeks. A thought crosses my mind that makes me have to bite the inside of my lip to keep from laughing out loud. *How much money could I make by selling tickets to see the great Rachael Early helpless on top of a refrigerator? Millions. I could make millions.*

Leaning against the counter, I take my first sip of coffee and face the wrath of my pissed-off Tinker Bell.

"Quit smiling," she seethes. "None of this is funny. The White House needs me and I'm stuck up"—she gestures wildly at her perch—"up here."

"So you are," I reply as I take another sip, smirking at how damn cute she looks.

Her arms unfold and she lets out a *hmmmph.*

This is a Mexican standoff, except that I'm winning. She's pregnant, and if she's anything like my sister was, she'll eventually have to use the restroom, and she can't get down without my help.

Her phone is still in my hand. I place it dramatically on the counter, as if I'm presenting a precious jewel. A little part of my brain says that I should turn it into a puppet and make it do a hilarious dance, but then I think better of that plan. No need to poke the bear.

I take my time finishing my cup and rinse it in the sink before placing it on the drying rack. As I turn back around and walk towards the coffee pot to unplug it, I freeze. The wine glass is washed and resting on my drying rack. *What the fuck?*

"I told her that this was off-limits." The first time I met Veronica and we discussed her job duties, I showed her the wine glass on the coffee table. I made it perfectly clear that it was not to be touched. Now it's resting in my drying rack with all hints of the red lipstick removed. I'm going to fire her. There wasn't much I actually asked of her. The damn wine glass was important.

"I washed that," Rachael states. She must have caught me examining it. "It had been sitting there a while. I couldn't rinse the red wine stain from the bottom." She doesn't realize that during some lonely, shitty nights, that wine glass—her wine glass—was the physical proof that I needed to remind me that whatever we had was real.

"It has been sitting there a while," I reply tightly while I examine the glass, holding it up to the light, realizing that it can't be unwashed. It's clean. What's done is done. Maybe this is a metaphor for our relationship. I turn and meet her eyes. "Exactly four months."

Yes. This is my sign to let the past go and focus on our future together. I have to forgive Rachael for the hurt that she's caused, and she has to forgive me for demanding her to embrace our relationship publicly and for needing time and space. The washing of the wine glass from her one and only visit to my home is a baptismal of sorts—a cleansing of our sins.

I place the wine glass near the sink and make a note to pack it in the travel trailer.

"You might try baking soda. I've heard that it takes out stains like that."

I lean forward, gripping the edge of the counter, and my back and shoulders tense painfully. I don't know why I'm so angry. It's not her fault she washed the glass. I guess I just want her to acknowledge that the wine glass was important. I want her to get it—maybe to see that she hurt me deeply also.

"That was your wine glass."

"What?" she asks, raising her left cheek and giving me a look as if I've lost my marbles.

"That was your wine glass," I state more clearly.

"No it wasn't," she says, rolling her eyes while her feet kick back and forth against the refrigerator door. "It was Veronica's. After she called me a cougar, I decided that any trace of her annoyance had to be wiped out. Besides, Graham, you should really do a better job at cleaning. It was kind of gross. And while we're on the subject, she is an issue for . . ." She trails off.

I've never in my life wanted to simultaneously kill and fuck someone at the same time. I grit my teeth and stalk toward the refrigerator where she looks so damn sexy, helplessly trapped on her perch. "That was your goddamn wine glass that you drank out of when you came over here the only other time you've been to my house, you annoying woman."

"Then you really should have washed it sooner. My point is made. And by the way, keeping a wine glass with my lipstick on it is a bit creepy don't you think?" She huffs and tightens her arms across her chest.

Her comment makes me want to throttle her. "Do you know how many nights that I stared at that glass? Do you have a clue how many times that I ran my finger over those red lip prints, wishing that I had the real thing?

Damn, Rachael. Did you ever once consider how much I was hurting, or were you too selfish to think of me? Was this about you? Has this always been just about you?" I pause and turn away from her, not wanting to see the hurt look on her face. "Never mind. Don't answer that. I don't want to know."

I've never been a big fan of silence, so I decide to change the subject. "I didn't know that you had morning sickness."

"Well, if you had talked to me recently, I would have told you. Instead you needed your time and space." God, the mocking way she says "time and space" makes me want to spank her ass until its bright pink and then fuck her until she can't walk.

I grab a bar stool and sit down so I'm facing her, but far enough away that she realizes that I'm not letting her down until we chat. "I've texted or called every single day to ask how you are and you reply 'fine.' Were you lying to me?"

Her eyes squint. "No. I wasn't lying to you, asshole. I just didn't feel like discussing the intricacies of the changes happening to my body with the guy who needed 'space and time to think,'" she says, making the stupid quotation marks with her fingers which I absolutely hate.

"Intricacies," I repeat, as I think about what she said. I get it. The news that she was pregnant was shocking. I maybe didn't handle it as well as I should have. The reality is that I haven't handled anything having to do with our relationship well. Unfortunately, I can't change history, but I can move us forward.

Now is as good of a time as any. "I want to talk to you about something."

"Really, Graham? You want to talk to me now? Get me off the refrigerator and then we can chat."

"No."

"No. No. What do you mean no? You can't hold me against my will!" she points out like I'm an idiot.

"Oh, but I can." I smirk. "I'm bigger than you are."

Chapter Five

Rachael

I hate him so much right now that I could claw his eyes out. Bastard! How dare he? Who does he think he is? On top of a refrigerator? Really? Can this be any more sexist? It's like a bad *I Love Lucy* episode. I should have known that the guy who could found the Sons of Liberty and talk about such sexist trash on the radio would be the one to put a woman on top of a refrigerator. I hope he meets an untimely demise by getting stomped to death by women wearing spiked high-heeled shoes. And unfortunately for me, this Neanderthal is my baby's daddy.

"Uncross your arms, Rachael. Wipe the scowl off of your face. I want to share with you how the next two weeks are going to go." He has the nerve to punctuate the end of his statement with a gorgeous smile that makes that damn dimple under his eye appear. I hate the dimple, and I hate what he does to me. *Will our baby have that same dimple?*

I do uncross my arms, but the scowl is permanent until I'm on solid ground. "I know exactly how the next two weeks and months are going to go. I'm leaving tomorrow for Texas. I'm staying with Caroline and Colin until I determine where I want to live." He's so smug that I wish I could throw something at him, hitting him right between the eyes. Yes. That would make me feel better.

Just as he opens his mouth to respond, I add, "And I'm going to write a book on how I broke the glass ceiling in D.C. politics, and why women should just say no to player pretty boys with dimples and seemingly normal jobs because they turn out to be assholes." Where did that come from? I haven't seriously considered writing my biography.

He smirks. "Like my dimple, do you?"

Have I called him a bastard in the last five minutes? Doesn't matter. If the term fits . . .

The smile fades and his face becomes stoic. His shoulders tense and the muscles in his sculpted arms bulge unnaturally against his skin. Damn him for not putting on a T-shirt this morning. My pregnancy hormones make it hard for me to remember why I'm so angry with him right now.

Oh yeah! Refrigerator. Focus on where you are and not looking at his abs.

But they're so pretty.

"Seriously, we need to talk about us," he begins. His tortoiseshell glasses enhance his serious demeanor, and I contemplate why he doesn't wear them more often. He looks like freaking Clark Kent and images of him taking me from behind in a phone booth penetrate my brain.

"Are you listening to me, Rachael?" he asks, while I try to remember where I've seen a phone booth recently.

"I'm at too high of an altitude to listen," I reply with a shrug.

He sighs. "This is serious."

"I'm sure it is. Serious enough that my feet can't touch the ground because I might bolt."

"Fuck," he yells, as his hands slap the counter. I jump, startled by his behavior. Okay. That got my attention. I sit up straight and pay attention. "Will you just let me speak?"

It's at the tip of my tongue—a sarcastic response—but I keep it to myself, and instead just nod.

"Good," he says, shooting me a dirty look. He stands up and walks around the bar and sits on the kitchen counter across from me. "First I want to apologize to you for how I reacted when you gave me the news about the baby. I have to say, Rach, when you asked me to meet you at a restaurant in the middle of nowhere, a baby never crossed my mind."

"Yay. Imagine my surprise when I—"

He cuts me off. "I'm talking. You're listening," gesturing back and forth between us.

I roll my eyes, but shut up.

"I'm not saying for a second that I don't want our baby. So hear that. What I am trying to tell you is that I just . . ."

"I know. Needed some time and space to think," I helpfully offer with a wink.

Now it's his turn to roll his eyes. "Yes, I needed to process the news. You're right. I wish this baby was coming under different circumstances. I wish that I wasn't committed to an eighteen-month tour, but well, I am. I've been doing some thinking . . ."

His phone rings somewhere in the house, and I wait to see if he'll get me down before he answers it. He ignores it and keeps going. "Here. I'm just going to say it." He pauses too dramatically for my taste, and then states, "You're not going to stay with Caroline and Colin. You're—"

"The hell I'm not. My things are being shipped to Texas as we speak. I have an overnight bag and plane ticket that says otherwise."

"No, you don't. I canceled your plane ticket and well, you know that your closet and other stuff moved to my house."

It all becomes perfectly clear now why I've been manhandled and stored on top of this refrigerator like the sugary cereal that a mom wants to keep away from her snotty-nose five-year-old. He knew if I could reach him that I would kill him. He's also trying to bribe me with the fantasy closet and lovely desk. It wasn't a peace offering; it's manipulation.

I've explained to him why I can't stay in D.C. The former White House Chief of Staff can't be pregnant and unmarried strolling through the halls of the West Wing. President Jones ran on a family values platform. I look down at my stomach. Family it is. Values would be greatly debated by the religious leaders that have the President's ear.

"Just listen," he pleads. My face becomes unnaturally warm, and I debate how I can safely get back to the ground. After all of my theories end with me flat on my face, I become resigned to hear him out.

Normally, I would be immune to the desperate tone of his voice, but there is something about his body language that makes me believe I should at least not ignore him. I don't see the confident, in control, man who I met and fell in love with. Instead, I see someone who appears to be at his wit's end. What I've learned from my time in navigating Washington politics is that sometimes it's best to shut up, listen, observe and then judge.

I do exactly what he asks and not say a word. His phone rings again and he continues to pretend that it doesn't exist.

"Rach, I'm not asking for sympathy or for you to even give a damn. I know you despise the Sons of Liberty, but I am the father of this baby, and that at least gives me the right to be a part of this pregnancy. It will not be easy. I signed a contract that says that I will be in a different city each week, but I've managed to shuffle some priorities and I think that I can make it work."

He doesn't seem to be talking to me anymore. His eyes are focused somewhere else—a place where maybe I listen. He's talking to the universe or himself, I'm not sure.

". . . I mean it's not going to be ideal. But, we'll get to know each other, Rachael. I've screwed so many things up, and so have you. Let's try to do this right."

He pauses long enough for me to realize that it's my turn to speak. "I really have no clue what you're saying. You know why I can't stay in D.C. I need to go to Texas until the President's term is over at least." Mentally, I'm calculating what it's going to cost to purchase a last-minute one-way ticket. Then I'm curious how he could have canceled my ticket. I hope to God that he's bluffing. As for my clothes and other things, well, they will just have to move again.

"That's just it. I've come up with the perfect way for us to be together and for you to keep the pregnancy out of the media."

"Really? Call me skeptical." My eyebrow cocks uncomfortably high.

A horn blares from somewhere in the distance. It's a loud horn. Much deeper than a regular car horn.

Graham's eyes grow wide and he looks towards the front of the house as if he has X-ray vision and can see what's making the noise. *I think in the cartoon Clark Kent had to remove his glasses to use his x-ray vision.* Then he glances back up at me. "Want to see your new home?"

One side of my lip curls up. "I can't from on top of a refrigerator."

He stalks towards me and looks up at me with pleading eyes. His voice is soft with a twinge of desperation. "Please give this a chance, Rachael. Please." Then he drops the worst, most guilt-ridden line in the history of lines. "Don't do this for us. Do it for our baby." Even he can't deliver that cheese without a little smirk.

My heart skips a beat when he reaches for me and I scoot into his outstretched arms. My body connects with his and I slide down his chiseled chest, not wanting my feet to reach the ground. As hard as it is to admit to myself, in his embrace is where I'm the happiest and most content.

"You are so beautiful." He compliments me as he brushes the hair out of my eyes.

I lean in, craving more contact. Nestling into his pecs, I turn my head so I can feel his soft chest hair against my cheek. His long arms pin me against him. For a brief second I ponder how I can be so damn angry at him one second and desperate for him the next. *This must be love.*

He steps out of my embrace and places his hands on my shoulders. His eyes are heavy with lust and his pulse is beating double time against his smooth, olive skin. His full, red lips part and his tongue darts, swiping around his mouth before his teeth bite the corner of his bottom lip.

I look into those clear blue eyes and melt for the father of my baby. Me being manhandled like a child is forgotten. I lick my lips and watch his complexion flush with desire. The pull between us is magnetic. I've never wanted more for him to be inside of me without an agenda. Not him-reminding-me-of-how-good-we-are-together sex, or jealousy sex. I just want to make love to him with passion and intensity, knowing that we no longer have any secrets between us.

Rising on my tiptoes, I wrap my arms around his neck bringing him down for a kiss. He lets me lead him toward my needy lips. As our mouths are just about to touch, he pulls away, breaking our moment.

I'm left feeling lost. Why did he do that? Why would he deny me? Am I still being punished for my crime of wanting to keep our relationship a secret?

He turns away and walks towards the ringing of the phone that hasn't stopped. Even though the sound is high-pitched and annoying, Graham's silence is deafening.

Finally, I can't take it any longer. "What have I done?" I throw my arms up in frustration. It sounds much more like a plea than I wish it did.

He shakes his head, as he turns the corner. He's not gone long, but when he returns, he ignores my frozen body in the middle of his kitchen and drops to the chair I had vacated at the kitchen table. Once he's seated, he turns his phone off and replies stoically, "I'm just not ready yet."

I explode. "Not ready? How can that be? Is it because Veronica is helping to give you the time and space you need?" I stalk towards him and lean down so we're eye to eye. "I couldn't stand the thought of another man near me. Yet, you? You sleep with your adolescent assistant, whom I'm sure earned the job for her excellent typing skills. Well fuck you, Graham, you take all the time and space that you need. In the meantime, I'll be growing our child and focusing on making a home for him or her."

I'm on a roll now and couldn't stop if I tried. I take a step back from him and put my hand on my hip, looking to the floor, before I meet his eyes again. "You know, when you told me that you loved me yesterday, I believed you. However, I think you just said it to calm me down and get me to agree to have my things moved here. Is this some sick revenge you have planned? Make me want you, then fuck me over? Have your baby mama in D.C. and your fling on the road? Because, if it is . . ."

Before I can calculate what's happening, my back hits the side of the refrigerator, and he growls "shut up" before his lips slam against mine. My mouth willingly lets his tongue slide against my teeth. It's such a demanding kiss. Graham is not asking for permission, he's taking what belongs to him, and I gladly allow him full access to my body.

"Does this feel like I'm fucking you over?" he growls.

"No," I breathlessly reply as my tongue meets his.

Graham parts my legs with his flannel-clad thigh as he raises the dress shirt which is draped over my body so that it bunches under my breasts. His hands tangle in my hair. I wrap my arms around his hips, cupping his firm ass, and pull him closer to me. His erection is hard against my abdomen and I gasp as I feel it twitch.

Like the hormonal, crazed woman I am, my pelvis begins to grind against his thick thigh. God, the friction feels so good. It's not lost on me that I'm dry humping his leg, but in this moment I don't care. I just want the intense pressure building in my lower stomach to be expelled. I want Graham to hold me while I come, even if it's just on his leg.

"That's it, Rach," he coaxes though frantic kisses. "I can feel your wetness and how much you need this."

My hips rock back and forth until I find the perfect angle and ultimately my release. My head drops back, separating our lips, as I bang it against the refrigerator. A throbbing pain shoots through my skull but soon the pain is lost on me. The orgasm is so intense that it reminds me just how much better it is when you experience it with someone you love.

"That's it," Graham whispers softly in my ear as he supports my weight. "That's what my girl needed."

When I open my eyes, I look at his beautiful face. His features are soft and relaxed, and his lips are puffy from our bruising kiss.

"Hi there, gorgeous," he says as he kisses my forehead. "See? Isn't that better than you yelling at me?"

I nod like a stupid bobble-head doll. "Now, it's my turn," I state as I reach between us, grasping his throbbing cock in my hands.

He captures my wrist, halting my movement. He brings it up to his mouth and kisses my palm. "Not right now," he says.

I'm so perplexed. His body is definitely ready for my touch. Emotionally he was just as much into our make-out session as I was. There were no walls between us. What happened between then and now?

"Is it because of the baby?" I ask out of desperation. It's the only thing that I can think of that might be an issue for him. I remember when my best friend Caroline was first pregnant with her daughter Ainsley. She worried that her husband, Colin, would not want to have sex with her out of fear of hurting her. Fortunately for Caroline, that wasn't the case. Maybe that's what is going on with Graham.

"It's perfectly healthy for us to have sex. The baby is so well insulated that . . ."

He shakes his head, silently stopping the conversation. I wait for him to share with me why exactly it's okay for me to ride his leg to orgasm, but I can't touch his cock.

He pulls me to him, pressing our bodies together. I want to lash out at him. I want to demand that he tells me what's going through his head, but I don't. Instead, I open my heart just a bit and let him take what he needs from me.

Then he does something so unexpected that it causes me to gasp. He steps away from me and places his hand over my barely there protruding abdomen. No one but me has touched the sensitive skin protecting my child. My immediate instinct is to move out of his reach until I look up into his sparkling eyes. A soft smile curls his lips, and a look of wonderment dances across his relaxed features. "You have a bump."

My heart melts. The hurt that I've felt since his "I need time and space" comment and his rejection leaves me in a rush, and it's replaced with a determination to see this look on his gorgeous face every single day for the rest of my life.

"I do." I giggle. I'm not a giggler. If you took a poll of the people who I've spent the last seven years working with and asked them if Rachael Early giggled, you wouldn't find a single one who would answer yes. Graham makes me giggle.

"I love it," he says with awe.

"I'm sure that I'll like it better now, since I don't have to hide it with tight pantyhose." Why can't I just gush with him? This is a personality flaw that I've got to work on.

His phone rings again, and once again he ignores it. "Ready to see my plan?" he asks hopefully.

I nod, and he grabs my hand leading me to his way of thinking.

Chapter Six

Graham

"What is that?" She gasps as her face contorts into a very unpleasant expression. She looks as if I just forced a Sour Apple Warhead into her mouth. There are a lot of things that I would like to slide between those beautiful full lips—making her look like this is not my objective. She grasps my hand so tightly it tingles from lack of blood flow, but I don't dare pull away.

Her touch and trust after my rejection in the kitchen is nothing short of a gigantic step for her. I want this to work so desperately that she can do whatever she wants to me as long as she just agrees. God it was hot watching her come on my thigh. That's an image that I will not soon forget.

"That's our home," I exclaim, as I turn and give the side of the travel trailer a tap. I got this idea a little more than a week ago. It was a three-in-the-morning inspiration. We have nothing else to do as we drive this across the country to meet up with the tour but talk. Hours and hours of no distractions, just us working through our shit. Plus, George doesn't have to be kenneled, and if she gets really, really pissed at me, what's she going to do? We'll be in the middle of nowhere.

"What . . . how?" She stammers as she drops my hand and begins to fidget with her hair.

Turning, I admire my stroke of genius before flashing her my best smile.

"Well, I found a guy not far from here that retrofits these."

"What?" Her forehead crinkles in confusion.

"Retrofits," I repeat. "I had the Sons of Liberty equipment moved into the second bedroom and had it turned into a recording studio. I'll still be able to tape the show while we're on the road."

"On the road?" She pauses and then walks towards the entrance to our new home away from home. "We sound like parrots," she remarks.

She opens the door and proceeds up the steps and into the living room, kitchen and dining room. They've all been condensed into a tiny space. The kitchen starts next to the door and extends along the wall until it hits the door to the bathroom. It's really got everything that we need: a small refrigerator, two-burner stove, microwave, and sink. The living room and dining room are on the opposite wall. A table that can be converted to a bed is screwed to the floor and bench seating surrounds it on three sides. There's a flat-screen TV that is mounted to the wall on the other side of the entrance door, and just behind it is the master bedroom.

I follow her up the stairs, watching her examine the small space. Déjà vu almost brings me to my knees as I remember feeling this way once before when she was checking out the Sons of Liberty's studio. Her face is expressionless. Years of training, I presume, have taught her to shield her emotions.

"What's back there?" She points towards the back of the travel trailer.

"That's the second bedroom that's been turned into my studio."

"And there?" She motions to the closed door next to the kitchen refrigerator.

"That's the bathroom. It has a standup shower, sink, and toilet. Want to take a look?"

She shakes her head, turns around and points to the closed door behind her. "And that's?"

"That is the master bedroom. I had the guy that I bought it from switch out the mattress to the nicest one they make." I don't know why I told her that, and I feel like an idiot. I guess I just wanted her to know that I was thinking about her when I was planning this.

She walks over and sits down on one of the bench seats. "So what's your plan, Graham? This obviously wasn't cheap, and you've thought it through. I'm a planner. A strategist. I need to know your end game here."

I join her at the table but sit on the opposite side. Her mood is somber and serious. She's got her game face on—the one that has been photographed incessantly. This feels more like a board meeting than a conversation with the mother of my child. "End game is that we find a way to make this work, and you and I are lovers, friends, partners and parents together."

"And why do we need this," she says, gesturing around the trailer, "to make that happen?"

I sigh and drop my head back against the wall. Closing my eyes, I rehearse the words that I've spoken so many times inside of my head. She gives me the time I need and when I open them again, I take a deep breath and share my plan with her. "Rach, we were so busy ripping each other's clothes off that we forgot to build any sort of base for a life together." I pause to gauge her reaction. Nothing. So I continue. "There is no denying the sexual chemistry that we have between us."

Her eyes cut to the floor for a split second, and I know that after my rejection of her in the kitchen she's doubting my words. Quickly, I rush to reassure her. "You make me crazy. Your sexy little body was made for me. I could make love to you non-stop for the rest of my life and it still wouldn't be enough."

A small smile plays across her lips which causes me to relax just a bit. "But, when we conceived this child I had laid it all on the line for you. It was my last attempt to make you see that you needed to give us a chance and you rejected me." I swallow hard, "again."

"I know that you said that even without a baby that you wanted a relationship with me, but I'm just not sure that I believe you."

Her jaw clenches and her back goes so straight that it looks unnatural. "I told you, Graham. I said 'yes.' What else do you want for me to do? Should I—"

I cut her off. "You should agree to take this journey with me. Let's work on a friendship. Rachael, you didn't even know that I wear contacts and glasses. It's a small example of how much there is for us to discover about each other. Don't go to Caroline's. Join me and the Sons of Liberty."

Her eyes dart back and forth. "I'm going to start showing soon. I can't join you at one of the most heavily attended media events happening in this country and not expect to keep this baby off the radar. CNN has as correspondent at all of your shows for goodness sake."

"We have this." It's now my turn to gesture around the trailer. "You can live in it with George. I can sneak you into my hotels through back entrances." I can't help myself. "You should be used to doing that with your politicians."

She smirks just a bit, but it's good enough for me. "Look. I hope that you realize that your pregnancy shouldn't have to be a secret. I hope that soon you'll allow me to scream it from the rooftops that I'm in love with Rachael Early, and she's carrying our child."

Her smirk is replaced with the clenched jaw and panicked eyes so I reassure her. "I'm not asking for that immediately. I just want you to agree to take this journey with me."

"What does this journey entail?"

At least she's open to listening. "I want us to travel together across the country to catch up to my tour. We'll spend the night in this and spend the days getting to know each other like we should have done in the first place."

"And once we catch up to the tour?"

"We'll play it by ear. We can drive to the next location. You can stay on the travel trailer or in the hotel. You can work on the book that you just mentioned writing. We'll figure it out as long as we're together."

Her face betrays nothing, but her thumb rubs over her forefinger on her right hand. I think this is an anxious tell. I dive in, hoping to bring her out of her own head. "Say yes to being a part of my world."

I study her body language. Rachael is getting more anxious. Her lip slips between her teeth, and she looks as if she was just handed a death sentence. *That's not good.* "It's now your turn to give me some time and space." She jumps to her feet and swiftly exits the trailer.

Standing up, my first instinct is to follow her out, but I pause at the doorway, watching her walk away from me. She stomps up the driveway. I don't know how it's possible for someone who weighs nothing to make so much noise when they walk. It's as if she can control gravity, along with the rest of the political universe.

Closing my eyes for just a moment, I pinch the bridge of my nose, hoping to fight off the stress headache that is threatening. When I open them again, she's paused halfway up the driveway. Her hands are firmly planted on her hips, her shoulders back and her chin up. "I'm not sure if you intentionally chose this model because of the name 'Cougar' written all over the exterior, but bad, bad choice Mr. Jackson."

What is she talking about? I walk down the stairs and back up enough from the trailer so that I can take in the entire exterior. Sure enough, I read the logo that is painted quite prominently on the side. She's right. It does say "Cougar." Laughter begins to bubble up from my toes and erupts out of my mouth in hysterics. Somehow, I managed to purchase a travel trailer that is the Cougar model. The irony is not lost on me. I laugh so hard that tears are rolling down my face, and I use the back of my hand to wipe my cheeks.

Can't I catch a break?

I could walk up the driveway into the house and fight with her. We could have an all-out battle complete with name calling, slammed doors and hurtful accusations. We've been there and done that already. I'm tired of arguing. The drama has to end. Therefore, she's doing this my way, even if I have to kidnap her.

When I walk in the house, I don't bother to look for her. She's not in the living room or kitchen, so I reason that she's most likely in the space that I created for her. That's good. I'm happy that she sees it as a safe place.

After locating my travel bag, I dig out a pair of jeans and a royal blue long-sleeved T-shirt. I skip the shower, reasoning that I'm about to fill a trailer with everything we'll need for the next couple of weeks. No point in getting too clean to just get dirty again.

Next, I start loading. I grab George's dog food and other supplies, and haul them out to "our home." Next, I carry out cleaning supplies from under my sink and grab pantry food staples.

As I make the trips in and out of the house hauling clothes and other things that we need, I keep hoping that she'll come to me on her own— that I'll find her in the kitchen helping to pack. Realistically, I know that's not going to happen. I fell in love with someone who doesn't back down or give in. She didn't become the White House Chief of Staff by being a pansy.

She might give me a hard time for saying that I need time and space after the pregnancy bombshell, but there's no doubt in my mind that she needs it also. Rachael is holed up in my house weighing her options and considering what she should do. When she's rational, she'll see that this is a good choice for us. *Or she'll take your child and move to some small remote part of the world and never let me be a part of their lives while some other guy tucks your son into bed at night.*

"Fuck!" I yell to the emptiness in my house and my heart. I set off looking for her. This is a battle for us—for the three of us.

I'd like for us to get at least five hours out of D.C. today. That's not going to happen if we don't get on the road.

My house isn't big so it's not hard to find her. I was right. She's in her space sitting at her desk with her back to me. Her feet are propped up on a moving box, and she's leaning back in her chair looking out of the window.

She's so gorgeous that I forget to breathe. Her hair is flowing down the back of the chair and her profile is relaxed—serene. She looks just like the fairy that she hates being compared to.

I'm not sure what to say. Do I apologize? I'm not sure what to apologize for though. For wanting a relationship with her? That seems ridiculous. Do I plead my case? It hasn't worked in the past. So far, our relationship has been on Rachael's terms only. I'm ready for a fifty/fifty split. Hell, I would even take sixty/forty if she would just not fight me on this.

"I can hear you breathing," she says, as her hand immediately covers her stomach. This gesture makes my heart clinch. I get the impression that she does this as if she's protecting our child from me. I may not have been the most supportive new father, but I would never, ever hurt her or the baby.

"I can hear your brain churning up all the reasons that you aren't going with me," I reply as I walk towards her. When I draw close enough, I take the back of the chair and spin it so she's facing me. Then, I drop to my knees so we're eye level. "I don't want to hear those reasons. I'm going to tell you why you are."

I grasp the hand that is shielding her stomach and bring it to my lips, planting kisses along the underside of her wrist until I locate her pulse. A soft moan breaks the stillness of the room. A plum vein pushes against her alabaster skin—God, the things that she does to me . . .

Gently, I rest her hand on the arm of the chair and lean down, kissing her stomach through the well-worn dress shirt fabric. Being so close to our child causes my breath to catch in my throat, and I know in this instant that I'm doing the right thing. When I find the courage to look in her eyes, I see that my gesture has warmed them. She no longer looks as if she wants to break my neck or stomp on my favorite appendage. This gives me the courage to say the words that I haven't been able to.

I swallow hard. "You love me, Rachael. You may not agree with the topics discussed on my radio show. You may not approve of my political views all the time. But, you love the way I make you feel in here." I lean forward, kissing her chest right above her heart. "A month ago that wasn't enough to make you fight for us. But things have changed." I place my palm over her stomach, hoping that she gets my message that it's my job now to protect the life we made. "We really only spent two weeks getting to know each other, and four months fighting this pull that we have between us. Give us the chance to see if we can turn this into a real relationship. One where we love and respect each other enough to call ourselves a family."

Her eyes shoot to the ceiling, sparkling with unshed tears. I may have actually persuaded the great Rachael Early to see the world through my eyes. This accomplishment has to win some sort of medal. When she finally looks my way, I wait with breath trapped in my chest, hanging on the precipice of what she's going to say. This is it. I just laid my best lines on her. If they don't do the trick, then I'm going to have to go with Plan B, which is a felony.

She smiles and takes the hand that is resting on her stomach in both of hers. I think I have her. I wait like a lovesick puppy for the strokes to my head. Then she delivers this. "Those were a lot of words. As a girl, they are exactly the words that I want to hear. Unfortunately, my time in Washington has hardened me against words. I like actions. That's why I'm going to agree to this crazy idea of yours. I've thought about it. The fact that you're skipping out of whatever contractual public appearances that I assume you've agreed to, which I'm sure is pissing off everyone around you, plus you've gone to all of the trouble to outfit that hunk of metal into a recording studio and place for us to sleep? Well, those actions show me that I should at least give this a chance."

My face falls. Yes. I'm happy that she's agreed to join me, to give us a chance on making us work while I'm on tour, but I don't particularly care for the verbal lashing. She continues, "However, remember this. I am going on this trek across America because I'm choosing to go. I'm choosing you, Graham. I'm risking all that I've worked for. My reputation, for you. Backlash on the President . . . for you. You didn't coerce me. If at any point I don't think that it's the best for me or the baby, then we're on the next plane to Texas. And I mean it, Graham. If at any point I feel like I'm a pawn in a political game that you're playing, or if I think there's anything going on with your assistant, I'm out of there so fast that your head will spin. Got it?"

"I can live with that," I reply, stroking the back of her hand.

Yay! No felony charges today. The rest of the trip? I'm not sure. I guess we'll take it one day at a time, but she's agreed to join me, and she's not running away to Texas.

Chapter Seven

Rachael

"Hi, this is Rachael Early. May I please speak to Candace Wilson?" I tap the desk with my long fingernails. Pregnancy has been a real treat for them. They've never looked better. I don't think that I've remembered to thank Graham yet for my desk, closet—well, this whole set- up. It's pretty amazing—even though he did it to anchor me to him. I remind myself to thank him when he gets back from buying? Renting? Procuring whatever it takes to haul my new home away from home.

"Rachael." The masculine voice booms on the other end of the line. If you didn't know that Candace was female, you'd think you were speaking to a man. She had a stroke when she was in her twenties that paralyzed her vocal cords. The sound that comes out is raspy and deep as if she's smoked a couple of packs of cigarettes a day her entire life.

"Candace. I hope I caught you at a good time."

"I'll always make time to talk to my favorite new author." I've known her for years. She's a publishing agent for many politicians and former presidents. We're kindred spirits in that we both play well in male-dominated worlds.

Her words make me smile, even though she can't see me. "Not yet. I've been unemployed for exactly one whole day. But I've never been known to let grass grow under my feet. Would you mind forwarding me the book contract that we discussed? It might make for some interesting pool-side reading."

Her deep laugh matches her voice. "Absolutely. Why the change of heart?"

I'm not sure what to say. *Candace, I'm taking the biggest gamble of my life by agreeing to travel cross country with a man who talks about disgusting things for a living so I thought that the book would be a great insurance policy. Or I'm about to be single mom and my kid will need diapers, food, and clothes.* Instead of those gems, I reply, "You know. Always have to keep my options open."

"That's my girl." I can hear the smile in her voice. "Headed to the Caribbean for a little R and R?"

More like the Poconos. "Something like that." I fake-laugh.

"You deserve it. Have a Mai Thai for me, and I'll touch base with you next week."

"Perfect," I reply as I end the call.

Being an author is not something that I've really ever considered. However, I've had a job since I was sixteen. Before then, I taught swim lessons to the neighborhood kids for spending money. I didn't walk away from my career because I was burned out or needed "time and space." I require something to occupy my mind, especially if I'm cruising America's heartland.

Yes. I'll just mentally brainstorm book ideas, reflect on my time at the White House, and try to be as agreeable as possible so Graham and I can work through our issues. The idea makes me feel useful.

Graham should be back soon so I throw my clothes for the road in a duffle bag. I've done this road-trip thing before. President Jones, Shelby, the boys, me, Evan, and some staffers lived on a bus for weeks on end during both presidential campaigns. Instead of packing a combination of yoga pants and business suits, this time I aim for many more pairs of yoga pants and stretchy tops, jeans, and two nice dresses. My shoes are limited to track shoes, one pair of boots, two pairs of flats, and neutral heels.

I look at my bag and feel nothing but despair. Calling Caroline and telling her my change of plans sucked. I had been looking forward to spending time with her and her family, although she was ridiculously proud of me for taking this step and she encouraged me to pursue the book idea. I don't think I could have made the phone call to Candace without her support. The decision to write this book was knee-jerk at best. I just blurted it out. There had been no forethought or planning. I've never written anything more than research papers in college and reports when I was more junior in my career. I don't know the first thing about being an author.

Before I can stop myself, I let the brick wall that I've erected around my feelings towards this idea crumble just a bit. Fear is the first feeling that escapes. It tightens my chest, making my heart race. Then self-doubt rears its ugly head. I'm not a writer. I didn't even write my own bio for the media. Evan carefully crafted it. How long should a book be? Do I start with chapter one, or do I write what flows? What happens if the words don't come?

Unfortunately, the river of self-loathing takes out the wall around my insecurities when it comes to Graham. Before I can get my act together, the moving wall of water inside my head comes gushing out in torrents of gasping sobs. I drop to the floor and pull my knees to my chin, burying my head in my hands. I've never in my life been so scared. I don't know how to be this new version of me. I don't know how to be somebody's partner, and I certainly don't know how to hold my tongue and be pleasant all the time. I don't know how to be a mother, or unemployed, or forty. I don't know how to support Graham and his career.

This isn't the life that I asked for. No. All I wanted from Graham was good sex. Why did I have to fall in love?

Slowly the tears turn to just a trickle, and I'm able to see the forest through the trees. *Get a grip, Rachael.* I'm scared. No. That's not right. I'm so terrified that I can't trust myself to make a good decision for me or my baby. I'm the stupid girl in the horror movie that Graham and I enjoy making fun of who hides in the closet when the man with the chainsaw is after her instead of jumping out of the window. I'm the . . . And the word sears my brain so hard that I actually stop crying and begin to panic.

"I'm . . . I'm helpless."

I fly to my feet and bolt for the bathroom across the hall. I'm not sure if

I'm going to be sick or what's going to happen. I just know that I need cold water on my face STAT.

The chill is a grounding agent, reminding my body that I don't have the luxury to lose my shit. Graham is going to be home soon. He expects to find the happy-go-lucky version of Rachael that has decided to embrace this crazy journey. He can't find the insane, self-loathing girl that has a purple face and swollen eyes.

George wanders into the bathroom to keep me company while I turn the shower to cold and strip off my clothes submersing myself under the numbing stream.

"Helpless," I repeat over and over again as I catch the cold water in my mouth and spit it out. "I'm helpless." My bank account is at a place where I can survive for a little while. I'm certainly not destitute, but I don't have enough in savings that I could support two people for long. What are my skills? Yes. I ran the White House. Okay. Those are somewhat impressive skills, but do they translate to a life outside of Washington? I don't know. Will the Republicans accept me back if I even try to play in Washington politics again? Family values are a huge pillar of the party. Does a single mom have a place? I don't know that either.

I've allowed myself a good fifteen-minute pity party. *Suck it up, Rachael. One foot in front of the other. Trust in Graham that you can make this work.*

I now do what I do best. Walls are repaired around my self-loathing, and I take control of my life. The soft towel blankets me with a false sense of comfort as I walk across the hall to my new office. After logging into my email, I find the contract from Candace. Before I even get dressed, I sit down and give it a quick read-through. The terms look good and the projected advance pay is enough that I could buy a small house for the baby and me. That's what matters. Survival. I print it on the new printer provided by Graham and sign my name to the dotted line. Then, I scan it in and email it back to Candace with a little note. "Can't wait to get started."

What a lie. I'm a joke. Yes. This gives me options that aren't dependent on an existence with Graham. Yes. Knowing I'm no longer trapped in a relationship if we can't make it work does relieve a bit of my anxiety.

This book is my Plan B. It's my ticket to independence and will give my career validity, even if I never play in the political world again. The thought makes me sad, but also gives me the opportunity to take a deep cleansing breath, which I haven't been able to do since I missed a period and peed on a stick.

The feeling of helplessness has been pushed to the recesses of my mind for the time being. Now, I just need to make sure that it stays there.

My happy face is plastered on and I'm ready to tackle this new life that I'm calling Rachael 2.0.

Chapter Eight

Graham

Forty-nine missed calls and it's barely noon. "Fuck," I mutter as I turn my phone back to silent. I didn't bother to read the one-hundred-and-two texts or eighty-five new email messages. We have a manager. The guy takes his percentage of our paychecks, but I'm not sure exactly what he does. Can he or my over-paid assistant really not handle any of this?

I send Hank a text. "My phone is blowing up. Everything okay?"

The dots appear, letting me know that he's immediately replying. "Sponsors are pissed. Wanted three SOL, not two. I'm trying to deal."

I wait, assuming that there's more. We don't have that many sponsors to be pissed. When I get nothing back, I send another message. "Reassure them that it's only for a couple of weeks. How's everything else?"

The phone rings. It's him. "Hank," I answer. "I've got just a few minutes."

"What? To busy hittin' it to talk about your fuckin' career?" he replies.

I roll my eyes, but I don't respond. Hank doesn't know about the baby, and I'm in no mood to explain myself or my actions again. I remind myself once again that I'm paying him and not the other way around. "What's going on?"

"Well, let's see." He pauses, as if he's mentally calculating. "I had to fire the pyro guys because I caught them smokin' pot under the stage. Tryin' to find replacements, but who knows. The band that's opening for ya is not agreein' to the lighting cues. Someone placed the gun control people next to the gun owner's rights folks. I've called in extra security. What else you want to know?"

Yup. I'm pretty sure this is why we have a tour manager, so I don't have to deal with these problems. "Call the union. They can send some temp pyro experts. That was part of the contract that we negotiated. Inform the guys of ToGetHer that we understand that they're an extremely popular band, and we're so honored that they're playing for free at our show. Work with lighting to accommodate them, even it means sacrificing a bit of our lighting. We can change our stage cues. It's harder for them." I pause and swallow. "Remember you catch more flies with honey than vinegar. And yes. Extra security sounds necessary."

"We're already crazy over budget, Revere. Where is this money supposed to come from?" Hank asks.

"Give me a few days to figure it out." I end the call and lean back against the hood of the truck that I just bought to haul The Cougar travel trailer. My stomach feels as if I swallowed a gallon of bleach. So far, the tour is way over budget. The guys and I don't start earning a paycheck until we've paid back the advance from the promoter to get the concert off the ground. The Sons of Liberty are responsible for everyone's paychecks— venue rental and the forty-three people that we employee to make the show happen every Saturday night. This is a stress like I've never experienced before. I went from a teacher and coach to essentially the CEO of a company, and I don't have a bit of experience unless you count my law degree, which is worthless, but I can proudly say that I can interrupt legalese in a contract.

On the flip side, ticket sales are through the roof. We're sold out in every city so far. Plus our merchandise sales have been healthy. We're bringing in wheelbarrows full of cash, but it's quickly being deposited and going back out of the bank accounts.

We hired Hank to manage the tour and us. He came highly recommended from our agent and concert promotion company. The guy has managed several huge tours—The Rolling Stones, Cher, and U2.

But what we're doing is different. We aren't a concert. We're an all-day festival. The gates open at ten in the morning. Local bands start playing at noon. We welcome every local political action group to set up a booth to promote their cause. We don't charge for this. The only thing that we require is that a group that represents the other side of the issue also be present. This is where the gun control versus gun owner rights gets a little sticky, and we have to hire extra security.

Our number-one goal is to make our target demographic care about what's happening in our government. This gives them the opportunity to talk to both sides of a political cause and determine what their beliefs are. I want informed citizens, not drones.

So far, at every tour stop we've had a popular band who believes in what we're doing taking the stage to get the crowd pumped. It's very surreal that these bands aren't asking for dollars. They're just volunteering their talents to our cause. That's not entirely true. We do let them sell their merchandise, so they do make something off of the gig.

Once they're finished, we take the stage at around ten o'clock. Like our radio show, our live show is not scripted. We have talking points and play off of each other's cues. We try to discuss local issues and explain them in ways that our audience will understand—taking macro problems and giving them a micro spin. Our part of the evening lasts two hours, with two ten minute breaks. That's when the local talented girls, aka exotic dancers, perform their Betsy Ross pole dances. The crowd loves it—even the girls in attendance.

Hank is well qualified, I just don't think that he's ever managed anything as complicated as what we've put together, and especially in this short amount of time.

We taped enough yesterday to cover the radio shows for today and tomorrow. Thank God. I feel like the five foot, hundred pounds of nothing back at my house has kicked my ass all over the square or octagon fighting ring. Should loving another human being be this damn difficult?

"Sir, here are your keys," the elderly gentleman who sold me the truck says, as he places the keys in my hand. He reminds me of Colonel Sanders from the Kentucky Fried Chicken restaurants. "By the way, Revere, can I get your autograph? You're my favorite one."

"Sure," I mutter, as I sign a blank sheet of paper with some sort of nicety. It takes all the restraint in my body not to sign it with something flippant like "Eat more chicken." This newfound fame is bizarre. A couple of months ago, my name couldn't get me a cup of hot coffee. Now, it opens doors that I had never dreamt possible. People want my signature— well my stage name. Why? It's just a scribble. It's not even really who I am. Revere is a piece of me, of course. But what I don't think anyone but Rachael and the guys understand is that this is an act—a nightly performance. I still have to write checks at the end of the evening.

I climb into the new extended cab truck and adjust the seat and mirrors. It's not a new vehicle, but it's new to me. It's grey, although the sales guy said that it's silver. It has grey leather seats with black carpet. It has all sorts of features that Colonel Sanders was eager to demonstrate. I couldn't have cared less, but I politely nodded and acted interested. What it does have is GPS, satellite radio, and a backseat for my best dog.

That's right, I think, as I buckle my seatbelt. *The open road, my dog and my girl.* If only life was that easy.

***

"Rachael! Rachael," I yell as soon as I walk into the house. Before I can open my mouth to yell "Rach" again, she rounds the corner and enters the living room, dragging a suitcase behind her.

I approach her with caution. Which Rachael Early am I facing? The viper or the pussycat?

"I didn't really know what to pack so I just grabbed a bit of different stuff. I assume that if I need something, we can stop and purchase it. Oh, and I am bringing my new computer. Thank you, by the way, for creating my own room for me. It's really something special. Are we ready to go?" She rambles, sounding like her former assistant, Maggie.

This is a new Rachael. I don't think that I've ever met amenable Rachael before. This one knocks me for a loop, and I'm not sure if I can trust her. I decide to proceed with caution just in case it's a trap. "We need to get your stuff in the trailer, then we're ready."

"Let's do it," she says with a touch too much enthusiasm, reminding me of the cheerleaders at my old school. They would have nasty scowls on their faces as they said hateful things about someone, but when they performed, their shiny white-toothed smiles would emerge. So fake.

"Fuck," I mumble under my breath. I need a Rachael manual.

Chapter Nine

Rachael

"Look, Evan, I don't see what the problem is. The White House has already released the emails. The news agency has them. Let their reporters do the leg work. We aren't doing their job for them." Gripping the phone, I note just how quickly the cement jungle of D.C. fades to the green rolling hills, tall lush trees, and clear blue sky.

About two hours ago, Graham locked up his house, walked George and got him settled in the backseat, and pointed the gigantic truck with the home-away-from-home attached to it, west. Traffic wasn't too awful leaving D.C. thank goodness. Now, I feel as if we're in the middle of nowhere.

"I'm afraid that we look guilty by not just stating the truth. Don't you see that?" Evan pleads his case.

"I stand by what I said." I state a little too forcefully as Graham makes a rather loud guttural noise. I look over and see the vein just above his right eye throbbing unnaturally. "Umm . . . Evan. I need to go."

I don't want a repeat of this morning when my phone was snatched out of my hand and turned off. Then I was incapacitated on top of the refrigerator. Looking around nervously, I don't see any place where he could store me. *The bed of the truck? Surely not.*

Ending the call, I bury the phone in my lap and decide the best course of action is to ignore Graham until he's finished brooding.

The silence becomes thick. Just the buzz of the road noise and George's gentle snores fill the car. I don't handle being ignored very well. I'd like to pull out my phone and check email or play a game of *Candy Crush*, but I'm afraid that Graham might have a stroke so instead I just stare ahead at the endless miles of asphalt.

God, this is boring. Thank goodness I have my book to concentrate on.

After what feels like days of quiet tension, I lean forward and start fiddling with the radio controls. Human voices fill the car, singing a jingle about milk. It's literally music to my ears.

Graham has orchestrated this car trip for us to get to know each other better, so I decide that now is as good of a time as any to ask "What's your favorite kind of music?"

"Pretty much everything," he mumbles, and doesn't take his eyes off of the road. *Well that clears that question right up.*

Okay. I'll keep trying. "I like classical when I'm working. But when I'm exercising, give me some good late eighties or early nineties heavy metal. Pantera, White Zombie, Marilyn Manson, Primus, Korn—those are just a few of the bands that I listen to. Oh, I love Sublime. I'm sure the Chairman of the Republican Party would get a kick out of that playlist. Working for President Jones for so long has made me appreciate good zydeco and jazz. You know, he's from Louisiana. But I guess at the end of the day, I'm just a pop princess at heart. It was so cool . . ." I ramble on and on, determined to make Graham speak to me.

He's brooding, for some obscure reason. Is he mad that I dared to answer my ringing phone? He doesn't want me to take phone calls. He made that clear this morning. Well, too damn bad. I'm here of my own free will—as I made crystal clear when I agreed to this journey.

Is this about him having to step away from his tour and deal with me being pregnant? If so, that's his own issue. I was perfectly content with going to Texas. I never asked him to partially abandon the Sons of Liberty. This trip was his choice.

He could possibly still be pissed that I wouldn't openly date him when I found out about his other job. Well, I guess he has the right to be a little angry about that, but that ship has long sailed, and I'm in a truck towing The Cougar across rural America.

Most likely it's a combination of the three. Fine. I'm trying this his way because he asked me to. He's got to give in a little bit and let me answer my phone when it rings and forgive me for the past few months. It's time to make peace and move on or just let me go back to Texas and prepare for my new future.

Determined to make him talk, I keep rambling. "So this one time, Caroline and I saw this band in college. They were still pretty new. No one had really heard of them, and then—"

His face softens. "How much longer can you talk?" He smirks, without looking in my direction.

"All of a sudden, a week later they were on the radio, and Caroline and I couldn't believe that we had just been to their show. We even shared a beer with the drummer." I smile, rather satisfied with myself. He also seems to not want to kill me or store me in the bed of the truck any longer. Mission accomplished.

I settle back against the passenger's seat, a bit smug. Being Agreeable Rachael is kind of fun.

"How about you and I make some road trip rules. Seem like a good idea?" he asks, clearly amused at my rambling. There's laughter in his voice and I know that I've broken him down.

"I have to warn you. My parents didn't believe in car trips when we could fly, so the only road trips I've done have been campaign tours. I'm used to a restroom on the bus and a chef."

That actually solicits a laugh from Mr. Grumpy. "No chef or bathrooms here, well at least while we're on the road. However, I do promise you some fantastic roadside dives and christening truck-stop toilets."

"Ewww." I shiver a bit. How the mighty have fallen. I had a private restroom in my office at the White House, and our cafeteria was pretty darn good. Now, I have to use public toilets and greasy spoons. My hand instinctively moves to my pelvis. *I can do this,* I reassure my baby bump.

"Rule number one," he says, holding up his index finger. "Phones can only be turned on in the morning while we're getting dressed, when we stop for lunch, and one hour after dinner. That means no texting, or calling, or answering, or playing games."

No phones? Seriously, am I his prisoner? Is this some sort of mind-fuck that he's planning? "That's not fair," I state aggressively. "The White House still needs me. How can they reach me? Come on, Graham. Be reasonable. I say we can take work calls, just not personal calls." I cross my arms. Sounds like a good deal to me.

"Grab my phone from the arm rest," he instructs.

"Why?"

"Just get my phone, Rachael." He sounds exasperated again, so I do as he asks.

After opening the center console, I see it plugged into a charger. "Got it."

"Now turn it on."

I hit the on button on the top of the phone and wait a couple of moments for it to power up and the passcode screen to appear. "Code, or you can type it in?"

He rolls his eyes. "Four-three-five-nine."

I punch in the numbers and then his phone blows up—not like an explosion. More like he must be the most popular guy in the world.

After all the dings and pings and chirps stop, he says, "That's why we have to have phone rules."

"Graham, who are all of these people?" I ask in shock.

"They're all people who want a piece of the Sons of Liberty. Politicians, media outlets, deep pocket money donors, small pocket money donors, people wanting us to sign something for charity, crazies who claim that we are their political puppets, financial managers who want to invest our income, women who think we're hot, little old ladies who want to share their opinion, and usually one or two stylists or designers who just know they can improve our image. Then there's the guy that we actually pay to deal with this, who is overwhelmed with the tour, and the guy who writes the checks and keeps asking when more money is coming in."

My mouth gapes open. I know that I've been a bit isolated in my White House world, lately even more than usual because I was preparing for my departure, as well as getting used to the whole idea of being a mom. However, this is beyond belief.

"Isn't this your manager and Veronica's job? I mean, why do you employ them if you still have to deal with this? Change your number." I gesture toward the phone as if it's done something wrong instead of just being the bearer of bad news.

"Do you know how long the world has known who we are?"

I do a quick calculation in my head, but I realize there is no need. It's exactly one week less than I've been pregnant. "Nine weeks."

"Nine weeks. I've had to get used to going from being a nobody to a household name. Nine weeks to go from only the people on my favorite's list calling me to thousands of people wanting a little piece of the Sons of Liberty." His voice cracks as he's gripping the steering wheel with such force that one of the veins that runs through his corded arm muscle is standing at attention.

I take off my seatbelt and push the center console up, wanting to comfort him. Despite the hurt that we've caused each other, by his side is still the place that I long to be. My body craves being near him—to soothe the wounds that the outside world has inflicted on his soul. I scoot closer and reach for his thigh, but he stops my hand. It's a subtle movement—a quick, gentle grasp of my wrist as he places my hand back in my lap. Before he lets me go, his fingers press against my pulse point a beat longer than necessary. With a sigh, his palm opens, releasing his grasp, and he grips the steering wheel again with the same force.

My heart plummets. Rebuffed by him twice in the same day. That makes it incredibly difficult to be Agreeable Rachael.

I move back to my side of the truck, feeling dejected and physically bruised. I fasten the seatbelt and stare out the passenger window at the vast nothingness.

"Let me get this off my chest, Rachael." His voice startles me out of the dark spiral that I'm falling down. "I can't do that with your hand touching me." His voice is laced with what I think is regret. I imagine his crinkled forehead and downturned pouty lips, but I don't dare look his way.

I don't respond, feeling too hurt to reply and mostly there is nothing to say. This is not the best time to point out what a walking contradiction he his. On one hand, he wants the baby and me in his life so much that he's left a portion of his tour and all the chaos in his wake. On the other hand, somehow being sexual or me even touching his leg is abhorrent to him. I understand and agree that we need to work on our relationship outside of the bedroom, but if he thinks for one minute that I will agree to have a platonic friendship with him, he's crazy. We're too attracted to each other for that to work.

"I'm going to need to stop and use the restroom." I don't really, but this truck is feeling claustrophobic.

"I'll pull over at the next gas station that we come to."

"Thank you." My voice sounds meek, and my fingernails bite into the small flesh of my palm in disgust at myself for being so weak. Why don't I put him in his place like I would with the rest of the world? He makes me—what's the word for it? Oh yeah. Reasonable.

"Anyway," he continues with the conversation that we should have had the day that I shared the pregnancy news, "I asked you to be a part of the announcement. I begged you that night to be my side. Do you remember that night, Rachael?"

He pauses, waiting for me to respond. I was hoping that it was a rhetorical question. I remember that night very well, I just don't care to discuss it. It's not something that I'm particularly fond of and definitely will not be a story we share with our child.

"You were waiting for me on my stoop when I arrived home from the White House. I was wearing a yellow suit. I'd chosen it because I woke up that morning and could barely get out of bed because I was so discontent with my life. I missed you. I was tired of feeling loss. I thought to myself that yellow would make me feel better. It didn't. I worked that day like a mad woman. Poor Maggie. She was my tornado sidekick."

My mind gets lost in that evening. The whole day I had a feeling that I was on the brink of a tipping point—something had to change. I was mourning a relationship that in the span of normal physical time didn't make sense that I should still feel such attachment. Two weeks. Just fourteen measly days. That shouldn't translate to the tremendous amount of absence I was feeling. However, this is what I've come to learn about love. It doesn't follow Einstein's rules of the universe. It doesn't march across a linear plane of time. No. Love is otherworldly. It doesn't make sense. It doesn't believe in rules and timelines and logical next steps. My brain kept reasoning with my heart that we couldn't feel this strongly about Graham Jackson, the guy who I only dated for two weeks, but what I've come to learn about my heart is that it just doesn't listen to reason.

Graham picks up our story where I left off. He's distant. I glance at him and see that he's looking at the road ahead, but his eyes are glossy, as if he's viewing the past—ten weeks ago on a brutally cold Wednesday night. "I was dressed in my lacrosse sweatshirt and track pants. Practice that day was for shit. It was like the entire team suffered from a brain-eating parasite that erased their stick-handling skills," he says this so wistfully that it contradicts the nature of the conversation. "After practice, I took George on a long run. My mind was all over the place. Chaotic. I couldn't concentrate on anything and everything at once. Make sense?" He pauses and waits for me to nod.

"My team was a mess, and I knew I was about to quit on them. My personal life was shit. I finished my run at a breakneck pace, came home and ran my finger over the rim of your wine glass, remembering what your sweet lips tasted like just to torture myself a bit more."

I keep my face neutral and pretend that his confession about our similar mental states doesn't faze me. It does. Until this moment, I didn't know what had prompted him to show up on my stoop that evening. Since we'd stopped seeing each other, I'd listened to every one of the Sons of Liberty shows, hoping for a sign that he was as miserable as I was. His voice was strong, locker-room humor intact, and I was still referred to as Tinker Bell frequently. Professionally, he never betrayed our connection to his listeners.

In a way, this made our breakup worse. I guess there is that girly part of me, which has watched too many romance movies, that was hoping that he would send me some sort of message only intended for me. I'd hear it, and we would declare our love for each other and find a way to make it work. I guess that we did in a way. . . It was just in the form of a new life.

"I was waiting for you when you got home," he finishes.

"You were sitting on my stoop, and I asked Lou to not do a house security sweep. He wasn't thrilled, but he obliged." I fill in the blank, pleased that this is a memory that we can share even if it's a hard trip down memory lane. I had felt guilty when Graham told me about my life-changing trip to campaign headquarters when he was working there between college and law school. He said that my speech inspired the Sons of Liberty. For me, it was just another day on my calendar, nothing special.

"The moment I saw you stepping out of the back of the black town car I knew that you were mine. Not in some metaphorical sense, but that you belonged with me, by my side."

Turning towards him, I try to read his body language. His eyes are fixed on the road and his jaw is set in a rigid line, which is a contradiction to his hunched shoulders making him look like an old man. I think he's as gutted by the rehashing of this night as I am. "We made love . . ." His voice trails off.

I pick up where he stopped. "It was so much more than just making love. At least that's what I felt."

"Really?" he asks, cocking his eyebrow and turning for the first time to look at me. "You felt it also?"

I nod. "You . . . ummm . . . you . . ."

"I what?" His smirk is cocky, and I swear the temperature in the car rises ten degrees. I lean forward to adjust the air vents.

Sticking my chin out, I reply, "You dominated me." And boy, did he.

Glancing at his lap, I see the denim is straining to contain his erection. I lick my lips, longing to reach over and unzip his pants, freeing what I so desire from its tight constraints. My mouth fills with too much saliva at the thought of tasting his beautiful cock. I want to suck him until he grabs my hair tugging it with desire, see his eyes rolling back in his head as I get a rare opportunity to top him. *But he will not let me touch him,* I remind myself. We're stuck in his self-imposed purgatory.

"Had you ever played with zip-ties before?" His eyes are hooded and his voice is raspy.

I swallow the extra liquid and reply, "No, Graham. Only you. You're the only lover that I've ever trusted to tie me up."

His eyes close briefly, and then he slaps the dash so hard that it startles me, and I jump. "I wanted to fuck some sense in to you. I wanted to show you what our life could be like if you would just publicly support me." He takes a hand off of the wheel and runs it through his dark hair. "I wanted you by my side."

My head falls with shame. If I could go back in time, I would have agreed to Graham's plan that he had formulated for us to have an open, public relationship. He outlined the fine details for me while my arms were fastened to my headboard and my feet spread.

"Why did you deny us again, Rachael? How could you, after everything that I told you? I bared my soul to you, and you still were able to say that nothing had changed."

I shake my head back and forth. His words cut me to the quick. I hate this. I hate myself for not being braver and bolder. I hate that it took getting pregnant to make me see how foolish I was being.

"Graham, I could spend the next twenty-four hours giving you reasons why I made that choice that night. I could throw out catch phrases like 'valuing my privacy.' But after many sleepless nights, what I've come to realize is that I'm terrified of this." I motion back and forth between us. "I've never felt this. And even though you've told me over and over again that you love me and feel the same way about me, I guess there's a part of me that doesn't feel worthy of it."

I pause for a moment and then decide to forge ahead with a dark confession about me that I had discovered through our difficult breakup. "Look. Only Caroline really knows the depth of this." Then I backtrack. "This is not a pity story or an excuse. I believe that at some point you have to take ownership of your character flaws and can't blame them on others.

But I do think that you need to understand something about me. My family is not like yours."

We whiz past a truck stop on the right-hand side of the road. "Don't forget I need to use the restroom." Now, I actually do.

"You're finally opening up to me. We aren't stopping." It's the dominant voice that he uses in the bedroom that my body instantly obeys. "Continue." He motions.

Shifting in my seat, my hands ball into fists and I push them against my thighs. I hate talking about my past. I've been out of my childhood home longer than I lived there. I've accomplished so much. Reliving it reminds me of just how cold they were, and it's not a pleasant trip down memory lane. "My parents are ophthalmologists. They pioneered a new surgical technique for correcting vision issues. This was back when I was little. They were never home. I mean, we had a nice house, and I never wanted for material things, but they were never available. It was my nanny who attended my school open houses and hosted my birthday parties. My nanny taught me how to drive, helped me buy my first bra, and pick out a prom dress."

I went to high school with Graham's sister. I remember how his mom volunteered in the school library and how envious I was of her family support. "Unfortunately, my parents didn't even keep the same nanny for long periods of time, so I never bothered to bond with any of them because they were gone too quickly.

"Let me put it this way. When I was hired as the White House Chief of Staff, I called Caroline and Colin, and then I told my parents eventually a week later. They still don't know that I'm pregnant. In the seven years that I worked in the White House, my parents didn't visit one time. There's not a doubt in my mind that they love me. They are just too consumed with their careers, with each other and their life, to be parents."

Graham's features soften, but when he takes his eyes off the road to look at me they aren't filled with pity. Fortunately for me, they are filled with understanding. My fists loosen in relief. "So you think that because I was going public as one of the Sons of Liberty that I wouldn't have time for you anymore?" He gestures behind us. "Does that prove to you that I will always be here for you and the baby? Does my phone being turned off and me giving you this time prove how much I want you?"

I bite my lip and nod, trying my damnedest to keep the tears at bay.

"So was all that about 'not wanting to associate with me publicly because it might reflect poorly on the White House' bullshit?" he asks in a hushed tone.

My heart clenches at his words, and I shake my head. "No. That's still a concern of mine." I swallow and continue. "Look. I have a lot of concerns. What it boils down to is that I'm terrified of this." It's like current of energy seem to flow between us. "I'm terrified that I don't have a purpose right—"

"Stop it." He cuts me off. I dart my eyes towards him, admiring his rigid body. He's serious, focused on this conversation, and my heart swells with love and admiration for this man. "Oh, you have a purpose. Never let me hear you say again that you don't have a purpose, because that just pisses me off. Your purpose right now is to grow our child. Your purpose is to let me worry about the effect of our relationship on the White House, and how to keep you safe. It's now my job to make sure that you feel loved and wanted, and let you know how much I want to be your future."

No one has ever said they would take care of me. Not my parents when I was a child. Not President Jones. No one. I learned at a very young age to be self-sufficient—to take care of myself. I depend on no one—a one-man island.

There's the girly side of me that longs for his words to be true. I would like to have my only concern be growing our baby, but I'm a skeptic. Don't tell me, show me through actions. Yes. This grand gesture with The Cougar and taking time from the tour is showing, but will this last? I'm frankly terrified of trusting anyone to take care of me, especially the man who needed time and space when I told him the news.

"I see a rest-stop sign up ahead. Please pull over." My voice quivers, and I look at my hands resting on my knees. They're shaking. Crossing my arms over my chest, it's clear I need distance from Graham. The cab of this truck is too tight. My body aches for him to punctuate his sentiments with action, to bend me over the couch like he did at the White House Christmas party, to pin me to the wall like he did in the hotel, or to tie me up again. Something. Anything to make these feelings go away.

"Ready to stop for the night?"

"Yes," I reply too loudly. I'll do anything right now to make these feelings go away. They make it hard to be Agreeable Rachael.

Chapter Ten

Graham

"How's it going?" Max asks when I finally turn my phone on after I have "The Cougar," the only thing that Rachael will call the travel trailer, set-up. It makes me grin every time she says it. She's in the kitchen microwaving something for dinner while I'm headed to the closest grocery store for some fresh fruit and vegetables.

"It's going." Max and I are ready to beat the shit out of each other one minute and best friends the next. I guess the shunning of me is over, because he took my call. Thank God our friendship works like this, because I need his advice. "I think that I may have scared the shit out of her."

"That's great. Should we expect you sooner?" His voice is biting in a teasing way. "How long will it take to fix this fuck-up?"

"Look, I need advice. If you can't help me, then put Marissa on the phone." I pull into a small grocery store in Blacksburg, Virginia. It's the closest large town to the campgrounds where we are staying the night.

"I'm listening. No need to involve Marissa in your crotch problems."

Marissa yells from somewhere in the distance, "Call me anytime."

My chest unclenches just a bit knowing that they still have my back. "So in less than twenty-four hours of us being together, I told her that I loved her and essentially asked her to marry me."

"What?" he screams so loudly that I pull the phone from my ear, giving my lobe a rub.

"I mean I didn't ask her. I just defined our new jobs. Hers is to take care of herself and my baby. Mine is to worry about everything else." I decide to hang out in the truck until this phone call has ended. No need to have the conversation recounted on TMZ by someone trying to make a quick buck.

Max makes a dramatic whooshing noise, as if he's held his breath for a couple of minutes. "Not near as bad as I thought. Now, go back to the tin can and fuck her brains out. Make her scream your name, big papa. Spank her ass and have her call you Daddy. Then get her on a plane, and we'll see you tomorrow in San Diego."

"Listen, Max. Focus for just a second, okay?" I love this guy, but I actually need real help here, and not just sex help. I've got that department covered—or not. God, this not sleeping with her is seeming more and more like a bad idea.

"Full attention, bro."

"What if I scared her off?" And then, as if I needed a further dose of reality, I stare out the truck's front window and watch a dad grab a little boy's hand, who is about three years old. The little boy looks up at his father with round, adoring eyes. The dad must say something funny, because the little guy laughs and swings their connected arms. What a reminder of how much I have to lose.

"Then you contact a family attorney and file for your paternal rights," he says it as if he's telling me to buy her flowers. This is not the first or even the twentieth time he's given me this advice. When I first told him about the baby, he instructed me to make the call and even did the research to find an attorney.

"Put Marissa on the phone," I grit out through a locked jaw.

"Sorry. Can't help myself. It's like I suffer from some sort of affliction. The words just pop into my head, and they exit my mouth before I can stop them." He pauses for a beat. "I'm working on it, but not too hard, because it's what makes me lovable."

With that, I slam the truck door and head into the grocery store to grab the supplies that we need.

Finally, Max gives me some decent advice. "She's scared shitless. No job. Pregnant. Hell, Mar was terrified, and we planned for the kid. Just keep showing her how much you want and need her. Chicks love that shit. Buy her something special at the store. Be thoughtful. Mar likes it when I bring her the latest issue of *People* magazine. Trust your gut, Graham. I mean, look where it's gotten you."

I don't bother to ask if "where it's gotten me" is a good place. "Thanks, man. Now catch me up on the SOL. I don't feel like listening to or reading all the messages."

***

An hour later, I have enough fruit to feed us for a week and a smattering of fresh veggies. I grabbed us snack food for the truck and bottled water to throw in our new red Igloo cooler. I bought seven types of crackers, not knowing which kind helps her morning sickness, and George has some new dog treats that they don't sell in D.C.

I pull up to the tin can that's nestled in a grove of trees. This RV Park is nice and clean, and it feels safe. I haven't asked Rachael yet if she plans on joining me in San Diego this weekend for our show. Fortunately, the lady who lives on the property and handles check-ins said that she would watch George for me if Rachael decides to go. We've tackled enough hard topics today. I'll save the tour for tomorrow.

"Hey, Lucy! I'm home," I call in my best Ricky Ricardo voice. My grandma made me watch *I Love Lucy* reruns in the summer. Can't say that I liked the show, but there's something very appropriate about the line tonight as I carry in bags of groceries.

"Just a sec," she calls, as the door to the bathroom opens. "I knew you had watched that show at some point in your life." She's dressed in one of my white cotton sweaters. On her, it brushes across her legs at mid-thigh. She's rolled the sleeves up to her wrist, and her long hair is damp from a shower. She looks even more fuckable than she did this morning. Mentally, I explain to myself why it would be a bad idea to pin her against the bathroom door and make The Cougar rock back and forth, creating quite the show for our neighbors.

"I think I found everything that you asked for." I rest the bags in the sink, because we are lacking in counter space, and begin unpacking. My back is towards her as I try to calm my racing pulse. "Not sure what kind of crackers you wanted so I bought different kinds."

I open the cabinet over the sink and pull down the bottle of Johnny Walker Black and prepare myself a drink. I sip it while I finish unpacking the grocery bags, struggling to find room. This kitchen is definitely fun-sized, like Rachael is.

"I made us sandwiches for supper. Seemed like the easiest. Points for me that I remembered your aversion to mayonnaise," she says as she brushes against my back while opening the refrigerator door. I'm not sure if the touch was intentional or not, but my skin is inflamed where we made contact, and a low groan escapes from my throat.

Quickly, a quarter of the drink slides down my throat to cool me off.

"Want chips with yours?" she asks as she stands on her tip toes reaching for the bag of Lay's on top of the freezer. My eyes travel down her legs and watch my sweater ride up, revealing her toned hip. There is just a hint of her pale pink lace that slips out. It's teasing—mocking me.

Dear God, please give me whiskey dick. I slam another quarter of the drink. What guy has ever prayed for that?

We sit across from each other at the table. I have no idea what kind of sandwich she made. I don't taste it. It's as if one minute there's a plate full of food in front of me, and the next minute it's gone.

She talks through dinner. I'm not paying attention. Maybe something about writing her book? I can't focus. I must respond appropriately, because she doesn't call me out. Her lips wrapped around the top of a water bottle make me fucking jealous of the bottle.

"I'm going into the studio to work. I'll see you in the morning." I fly into the second bedroom and slam the door behind me.

"What the hell am I doing?" I ask myself as I take a seat in front of the computer. My testosterone-addled brain can't focus on anything but her. She's like some sort of siren that calls to every cell of my body. I remind myself why I can't have her sexually yet. *Yet.* We're learning to communicate verbally instead of just physically. Our conversations in the car were tough but necessary. No. This is good. Although my dick would beg to differ.

It's clear to a blind man that I'm still crazy in love with her. She has me behaving like a teenage boy. The first time I touch her body again I might explode in my pants, like the time that I lost my porno virginity.

"She's just a girl, like every other girl," I tell the wood-paneled wall. But even I know that's not true. No. She's my muse—my *it* girl who I've been fawning over since I was a stupid college graduate interning for then Senator Jones's campaign.

I need a distraction, so I decide to focus on my job. I open clips of the daily political talk shows that we watch to make sure our topics are relevant. The videos begin and end, and I watch them with a small degree of focus. Work is always a good distraction from my pixie, but today not even the most insightful commentary can fully replace Rachael in my brain. The brainstormed list of topics for future shows that I send to the guys is thoughtful at best, and at least they can see that I'm contributing.

The Betsy Ross email folder on my computer is a great place to check when I'm looking for interesting tips for the show or a much needed laugh. We get some crazy leads. *Attention! Attention! The President is being mind controlled by Aliens* or *President Jones has a terminal illness and the First Lady is running the White House.* Those leads get moved into the comedy folder.

I've created a network of sources around D.C. —everyone from bartenders, to strippers, to high-end call girls, to Uber drivers, to secretaries, to waitresses, to housekeepers—politicians themselves even email us gossip, overheard snippets of conversation and complete stories. Some of our best insider knowledge came from the students at my school. It's amazing how little candor kids have.

Rachael hasn't asked who my inside source at the White House is. She'd die if she knew that her assistant, Maggie, is one of my Betsy Rosses. We met at the vet's office. George needed his yearly checkup, and she was in the waiting room with one of her cats. I make it a habit to visit with everyone. Being friendly has paid off more than once and yielded some nice tips. She mentioned that she worked for Rachael Early and my heart had caught in my throat. This was the assistant to the woman who had inspired the Sons of Liberty. We'd traded information as I'd pretended to be a journalist. A few email and text exchanges later and Maggie had been more than happy to share tidbits of interesting information—nothing that has compromised Rachael, but I still think I'll keep this bit of information to myself.

As I scroll through the leads, my mind drifts back to Rachael. I think what would happen to me if I had all of this taken away. She's walked away from her career—her safety net. I know that she's scared. She admitted as much. I know that she feels unlovable. I sensed that on our first date. It's my job to make sure that she knows how important she is to me. It's also my job to ensure that the Sons of Liberty continue profitably. Max's words of "don't forget I have a wife and child" resonate with me. SOL is our financial future.

Focus, I tell myself. I need to focus on the Sons of Liberty, for my sake as well as the guys'.

The Betsy Ross folder has a few notable tips, but nothing that we can build a full segment around. Next, I check my email inbox. It's flooded with more requests for my time. I ignore it and turn my attention to my phone. More problems. We still don't have a pyro team in place. The right-to-life people are complaining about their location versus the women's rights group. We have too many strippers hired for the pole-dancing routine when we break in between our first and second set, and some asshole has been printing fake tickets and selling them on Craigslist. Unfortunately, these problems ultimately become my issue.

I handle what I can and decide that San Diego might just be a shit show, which will, of course, do nothing to inspire the guys' confidence in my absence.

This is for you, Rachael . . . and for me. I push back from the computer and spin around in the chair, looking at the makeshift studio. It's small, but it has what I need to tape our show and still spend this time with her. Bill, the guy who installed all of this, told me that he could make it work. The fact that he built me a studio with one week's notice is nothing short of spectacular.

"I did this for us," I mumble under my breath.

Standing up, the rolling chair slides backwards and I exit the studio. *I can just hold her tonight, right?* No making love, just feeling her body pressed against mine. To show her that I can make her feel safe and wanted without an orgasm.

I open the studio door and walk through the main room towards the front bedroom, needing her more right now than I've ever needed another human being. I'm a man on a mission . . . I want to fall asleep protecting her baby bump. I need to prove to her that it's now my job and I can be trusted—that I'm the only man she needs.

As I approach the door, I hear a faint buzzing sound and gentle moans of pleasure coming from behind the wall. Instantly, my head registers what's happening before my heart will admit it. *She's doing my job because I'm not.*

The realization doubles me over, and I grasp the wall for support. It's one thing to have a lover pleasure herself when you can't be there or for your entrainment. I mean, that's really fucking hot. It's another thing to be fifteen feet away and she chooses a toy over the real thing. *She wanted you. You denied her.*

I slide down the wall, letting my legs splay out in front of me. Listening to her whimpers and quiet cries of pleasure simultaneously makes my heart ache and my dick hard. I deny myself the pleasure of zipping down my pants and finishing with her. My fist clenches and I repeatedly pound my thigh until I'm sure there will be a bruise. It's my punishment—my cross to bear for denying her and myself. I will not give in to my needs.

This is pathetic. I should storm into the room, smash the vibrator against the wall and make her come until her bones turn liquid. I should tell her that her pleasure is mine to worry about also. I'm in charge of that along with everything else. She has one job and one job only—to take care of our baby.

Her tortured cry of pleasure shatters what's left of my control. I leap to my feet, not bothering to adjust myself, so the zipper of my jeans bites painfully against my throbbing cock. I leash George in a sprint out of The Cougar.

The chilly night air stings my inflamed, sweat-drenched skin. I feel wild, as if I've become feral. When I'm far enough away from the camper, I scream out, "Rachael." The release is cathartic. I double over, resting my arms on my knees while I work to get my breathing under control. Finally, I give in to gravity and sit on a fallen tree near the path.

"What the fuck just happened in there?" I question George. He walks over to my resting spot and lies down across my shoes. His loud sigh holds no truths for me.

"Why the fuck didn't I stop her?" I stroke George's head as I stare into the inky black night.

Of course my partner-in-crime has no answers for me.

Nature offers a certain peace—a stillness that I've always craved. My eyes shut as I drink in the campground noises. In the distance, someone is playing what sounds like a Bob Dylan song on the guitar. I can only catch certain notes as the wind shifts. There's a smell of smoke in the air—someone's grilling chicken, I think. This place came well recommended. It's been cut out of a forest with rather private camping spots. I like it. If I weren't here tonight, I'd be in San Diego with the guys, Veronica, and the rest of the touring staff that follow us around. Let's see. It's a Thursday night. I bet the guys are having dinner with a large money donor to either the Democrat or the Republican Party. He or she is trying to influence their perception on a particular subject that is near and dear to their heart.

It's so damn hard to stay above the influence when you're in the bubble. This trip will be a good reminder as to why I started the Sons of Liberty. The lady who checked me out at the grocery store had such a kind smile that I asked her about her day. This was her second job. She worked at the fast food restaurant on the corner until five o'clock, and then went straight to the grocery store until close. Her husband had been laid off and was having a hard time finding steady work. Katelyn was her name. I need to remember to tell the guys about her. She's who the Sons of Liberty were founded for.

The night air brings me a certain level of clarity. It helps me see my relationship for what it is. This has to stop. Right now it feels as if an extension of the torturous past four months, instead of a fresh start as I was hoping for. The cleansing of the wine glass was supposed to represent a new beginning, but today it has felt like going twelve rounds with a professional boxer.

The conversations that we had today needed to be had. After a lot of reflection, I come to the conclusion that I may not have handled everything correctly during the last twenty-four hours, but we're at a better place for it, even though the evening didn't end as I had hoped.

Tomorrow is a new day. We will begin focusing on the future instead of being trapped in the past.

As if the universe agrees that this is a good plan, a tan squirrel scurries across a tree branch overhead. The rustling sound draws my attention, and I look in his direction. The moon which had been hidden by thick clouds, slips away, finally able to illuminate the tree as if it's filling in for the sun. The squirrel pauses long enough to nibble on something grasped between his tiny paws. He doesn't disturb George, and I just watch him with interest. He scampers into a tangled mass of leaves, twigs and other nature treasures. He drops the bit of food into a nest and then looks back at me before he runs off.

Okay, that's the second sign I've been shown today. I get it universe. I'm doing the right thing. I smile and toast the squirrel's good parenting skills before I stand up, walking a very lethargic George back to The Cougar. Tomorrow is a new day. I just hope that I haven't fucked things up too badly.

Chapter Eleven

Rachael

My eyes open, feeling as if I swam in chlorinated water without goggles. Sunlight is filtering through the brown-stained faux-wooden blinds in the tiny bedroom in the tin can. My quilt that Caroline's sister made is pulled to my chin, but that's where any resemblance of home ends. The bird calling to its mate outside of the thin walls instead of car horns blaring reminds me I'm not in my bedroom in my townhome. It's not four o'clock in the morning, and I don't have to get dressed so I can work out with Malik. I have no job that is expecting me. In fact, no one in my old life knows where I am. I'm not sure that I know where I am. What I do know is that I'm alone in a bed in the middle of nowhere with a man who says that he wants to take care of me yet won't take care of my most basic need.

I turn towards the built-in nightstand and see a plethora of different types of crackers next to a lone bottle of water and the latest issue of *People* magazine. Odd. I've never read a copy before. Leaning up on my elbow, I grab the saltines and prop my head on my pillow while I begin the precarious task of not getting sick. Looking back at the nightstand, I have to smile. There are one, two, three, oh my goodness. There are seven different types of crackers. He might be a moody asshole, but that's kind of sweet. I smile and lie back on the pillow, concentrating on keeping the contents of my stomach in check.

When I'm feeling better, and only then, do I allow myself to think about last night. I'm mortified. At the time it seemed like a good idea to relieve the ache that I'd had all day, longing for Graham. After I was finished, it occurred to me that he most likely heard what I was doing. Even though I tried to be quiet, I don't believe that I was. There's a part of me that says *fuck him. He should be taking care of me.* The other part is mortally embarrassed.

Ugh.

I decide to rip off the Band-Aid and hold my head up high. I have nothing to be ashamed of. I'm an adult. I have needs that have to be met. *Why didn't I put a pillow over my face?*

Here I go . . .

Climbing out of the bed, I take a deep breath, reassuring myself that I can face him. I mean, masturbation is natural right. Nothing to be ashamed of.

I pause on the doorknob. Facing him shouldn't be so difficult, but my rapidly pounding heart begs to differ.

Here I go . . . again . . .

I grip the doorknob and turn it with force. One of my cardinal rules is *fake it until you make it.* My shoulders are back. My chin is high. I've got swagger.

The door flies open and . . .

The room is empty except for George who is resting by the door, but all he bothers to do is cut his eyes in my direction.

Where I presume that Graham slept last night has been turned back into a dining table. The door to the studio is open, but he's not inside. It's not his job to tell me where he's going. I'm not his mother, his wife, or really even his girlfriend. Nevertheless, I scan the counter for a note, but it's empty. I check the table next. Nothing. The place isn't that big. No note.

However, it seems like a common courtesy would be to leave a note. Right?

Opening the door to the camper, I check for the truck. It's still here. That means that he couldn't have gone far.

I busy myself in the kitchen. Not that I'm some sort of amazing chef, and I hate to cook, but right now it's a mental distraction. The fresh vegetables that I requested make for a very tasty omelet. I decide to fix two. I'm not sure what Graham likes in his so I just duplicate mine.

When his is ready, I place it in the small microwave and carry my plate to the table. Just as I'm pouring a glass of orange juice, the door opens and Graham fills the entryway, casting a shadow on the tan linoleum floor.

My face flushes seven shades of red at the thought of last night, and I busy myself by putting my full attention into using the side of the fork to break off a bite of egg.

"Good morning," he says, as if nothing happened.

He's in grey running shorts, a black long-sleeved workout shirt that defines his chest perfectly and a headband to keep his wavy hair out of his eyes while he's running. A thin sheen of sweat makes his face glisten. Dear God, I could seriously get used to this vision every morning.

He walks over and plants a sweaty kiss on my forehead, and I finally find the courage to look up from my plate instead of continuing to stalk him through cut eyes. The kiss was unexpected and quite nice.

I take his cue and pretend also that he didn't hear me masturbating through the paper-thin divider. "Morning. I made you an omelet. It's in the microwave." I could just die.

"Who knew you could cook?" He teases—or maybe not—as he grabs his plate and a fork to join me at the table. "How are you feeling?"

"Good. The seven different choices of crackers helped." I don't miss the proud smile that plays across his full lips. How funny. He's trying and wants me to acknowledge it.

He cuts a bite and shoves it in his mouth. "Damn, this is good, baby."

"I never said that I couldn't cook." I sigh. "I just despise doing it. I had a nanny for a short time that would give Caroline and me cooking lessons. We still make her sugar cookie recipe every Christmas Eve." I actually taste my omelet for the first time and it does exceed expectations.

"How'd you sleep?" He swallows another huge bite and an odd expression misshapes his face.

Instantly, I begin to wonder what he's fishing for. Is this a way to discuss what he most likely heard last night? Is he wanting me to ask why he didn't sleep with me? Or is this simply a question like 'was the mattress soft enough?' I decide to ignore the strange look and go with the flippant answer of "fine."

His eyes drop to his omelet as silence descends over The Cougar, ending our morning conversation. It's so awkward. My stomach is in knots. As much as I pretend that I'm faking it until I'm making it, I'm still slightly mortified that he caught me in the act. My cheeks are burning with heat. When I finally have the courage to peek up at him through my lashes, he's staring at me, with a little smirk.

I finish about a quarter of my breakfast before my stomach informs me that it's time to quit eating. I stand up and walk to the garbage can, disposing of the rest of my omelet.

It's not a matter of if I'm going to be sick, it's how nonchalant can I be about it. I'm going for Agreeable Rachael, not Sick Rachael. These nerves mixed with hormones are killing me. I step into the bathroom and shut the door behind me, making sure that the lock is engaged. The last thing that I want at the moment is Graham's pity. I'm the one who got us into this situation by not mentioning that I was off the pill the last time we made love. Fucked? I deserve this nausea and this awkwardness between us. Honestly, I don't deserve to have him. This is my penance for my one very foolish mistake—but a mistake that we're both insanely excited about. Each contraction of my stomach muscles reminds me that I did this to myself and to him. That he would be on tour dealing with his thousands of problems in person instead of receiving them on his phone.

After I'm finished, I clean myself up and brush my teeth. It always surprises me how much better I feel after I've gotten sick. It's like a restart button for my body.

I open the door and walk out to discover that Mr. Grumpy has returned. "What were you doing in there?" he demands.

"Geez, Graham." I tease. "Can't a girl get some privacy?"

I walk over to the sink and turn on the water, preparing to do the dishes. Before I can register what's happening, he has me scooped in his arms and is carrying me to the bedroom. Tenderly, he places me on top of the quilt. "You were sick. Lie here. I'll do the dishes."

"You're being ridiculous," I reply as I sit up, reminding myself that I'm Agreeable Rachael. "I mean, I'm not going to turn down the help in the kitchen, but I'm not bedridden. I honestly feel fine."

With his arms crossed over his chest, his legs spread and a defiant look on his face, he's hot. Brooding Graham could be an Armani model. *Especially if the glasses make an appearance again.* I lick my lips, hoping that he will take the hint. I have needs. Right now they're pressing needs that haven't been addressed by dry humping a leg or a vibrator.

"Don't look at me like that, Rachael," he warns, cocking his eyebrow.

"How am I looking at you, Graham?" I scoot further down on the comforter while his sweater stays in place, exposing more of my thigh.

The word "rejection" flashes like a neon sign inside my brain. Before he leaves to join his tour, I want him to make love to me, but I don't know if I can stand another rebuff.

He turns his head away and looks at some spot on the wall that must be pretty damn interesting. Maybe it's just my hope that believes he's struggling with ignoring my subtle advance. The bulge in his shorts says that he's affected by me. But that really doesn't mean anything, as I learned yesterday. He had a fantastically hard erection in his kitchen, and he still told me no. *Why can't he get over whatever issue he's having and make me come?* Is that too much to ask? He's a male, for goodness sake. In my experience, men don't turn down an invitation.

"Like you want me to do kinky shit to your body," he replies in a raspy voice, still avoiding eye contact.

If I'm reading him correctly, I don't think that he can deny me again. Deciding to be bold and praying that I'm correct, I slip my hand in my panties. "We could begin with kinky shit."

He still doesn't look at me, but he adjusts his eyes from the wall to what must be a particularly interesting spot above my head. "I'm using every bit of willpower that I have, Rachael." His Adam's apple bobs up and down before he adds, "Please don't do this. I fucking ache to be inside of you."

He uncrosses his arms and rakes his hand through his hair causing the damp tendrils to fall haphazardly around his face, his headband long forgotten. After a pause, he sits down on the edge of the bed, and finally his blue eyes find my green. I guess he's being careful to avoid locating my hand. "We've got to learn to communicate with words instead of sex. Yesterday we made progress."

My index finger begins to toy with my slit. I'm so wet and ready for him. My desperation must make me bold, because I reply, "Would that great communication yesterday be when I was forced to use my vibrator?"

"Jesus Christ, Rachael," he says through a tense jaw. "Were you intentionally trying to kill me?"

When his eyes finally travel down my body, I spread my legs and slip my panties to the left, showing him my wet, swollen vagina. My finger slips inside the folds as I play with myself. "Communication is not necessarily verbal. I'm showing you how you make me feel." I swipe my finger through my wetness and hold it out for him to see. "This is how much I need you. Don't deny us how we communicate best."

He pulls his shirt over his head, depositing it on the ground. I watch in sweet anticipation as he pulls off his workout shorts and underwear. Naked Graham. My favorite. I reach out and grab his burning hot, throbbing cock as I position myself in front of it.

There are no words. Graham's face twists as if he's in pain as he slides into me. The fullness is almost orgasmic. I clench around his hardness as if I'm trying to entrap him. He doesn't move, and I revel in the feeling of him inside of me.

I wrap my legs around his waist and begin to twirl my hips on his cock. His forehead wrinkles deepen and his eyes squeeze shut. He's behaving as if it's some form of torture to make me come.

"Fuck me, Graham," I plead. "Give me what we need." I stress the word *we* because this is something that will make both of us feel euphoric.

"What you need is to be spanked. You know that we aren't ready for this, yet you spread your legs and finger yourself to drive me crazy. Do you like seeing me this conflicted?" he asks, without meeting my eyes and the trench between his eyes deepens.

I ignore everything after the word "spanked" because yes. That's what I need. I loved it the last time he spanked and then fucked me. "Spank me," I moan as I continue to move on his still erection.

His face morphs from one of anger to resolution. His forehead relaxes, but his eyes remain tight and jaw set. He looks more as if he's doing a chore than making love to me. I don't care. An orgasm from him is what I need.

He unwraps my legs and pulls out, leaving me feeling bereft. There's no way he can reject me again. He was already fucking me. What would be the point of leaving us both frustrated? But before I can protest, he has me positioned on all fours. This time when he enters me, he begins to move back and forth in a pounding motion.

My only thought is *thank God.*

"Graham," I yell, as he slams against my cervix over and over again. This is rough, unapologetic sex, and it's exactly what I've been craving. "Spank me."

His right hand connects with my butt check. The sting of the slap is extinguished by the thrust against my cervix.

His left hand connects with my other butt check. Again he follows this up with deep penetration.

He does this over and over again in the ultimate mix of pleasure and pain. It's dirty and kinky, and I love every second of it.

"Why do you make me do this to you?" he asks, as if he doesn't want to be bringing me this much pleasure.

"I love it. More," I say, gripping the quilt. "More. Harder . . ."

With one final slap and thrust I find the orgasm I've been craving. My pussy grips him so tightly that he yells out something incoherent and warm sprays of him flood me as I continue to pulse on his throbbing cock. His arm wraps around my waist and pulls me to him so my back presses against his chest. With his dick softening inside of me, he takes my lips with such brutality that I can feel the sweet ache that accompanies a bruising kiss. I don't care. I kiss him back with the same ferocity.

I wrap my arms around his neck, angling his mouth towards me so his tongue can reach deeper down my throat. I want more of his mouth—more of him. We continue the devouring of each other even after his semi-erect cock pulls out of me and falls towards his hip and the essence of him runs down my inner thighs.

The kiss begins to change to one that is more tender. Instead of him biting my lips and sucking my tongue, he licks my teeth and trails kisses along my jaw line. With one hand, he reaches up and taps my arm, indicating that he wants me to drop them. I obey and am rewarded with his sweater being removed from my body.

"Lie down on the bed, Rachael. I want to look at you." It's the dominant voice that I love and obey. I recognize this for what it is. He's finally quit the battle with himself and has given in to our shared pleasure. Secretly, I congratulate myself for wearing him down. I wasn't just using a line on him when I said that we communicate best through being physical.

I fall back on the mattress and spread myself open for him to examine. He starts at the heel of my foot, and runs his index finger over the bump of my anklebone and to the inside of my calf. In slow, languid strokes, he traces my rounded calf muscle and up to the knee. His eyes are hooded and his lips are swollen but in a neutral line. Graham's shoulders are relaxed. His shirt is off but he's somehow managed to put his shorts back on. They hang low on his hips, revealing his perfect abs. A dark smattering of pubic hair that has been neatly trimmed peeks from the top. It's so damn sexy that I'm already up for a second round with Mr. Jackson.

His finger runs up my inner thigh and catches some of the liquid. He rubs it over my bump. He continues to collect more of the wetness from my thighs and massages it into the evidence of my pregnancy. When it has been completely covered by him, he leans in closer to admire his work. His eyes flash to mine. "I did this to you."

I nod, not wanting to speak for fear that I'll say the wrong thing. This is the possessive, dominant Graham that I've only seen on a few occasions—just enough to keep me wanting more.

"Mine," he states again, as his finger makes its way up over my navel and to my breast. He takes one nipple between his fingers and gives is a tug.

The nerve impulse goes straight to my core, and I cry out in delight. My eyes close. I can't look at his expression any longer. It's too much. This is the Graham that I want, and I want it again—now, soon. And I don't know if he will fulfill my needs for a second time.

He reaches over to the other breast and squeezes the nipple. I cry out again and come very close to begging for more. Instead, I savor the attention and see what else he has planned.

He rolls my nipples between his fingers, as he begins to talk. "You want me, Rachael. I can smell your need."

"Yes," I cry, as my head rolls back and forth.

"Yet you denied me what's mine." He pinches my nipples.

"I love you, Graham. I was stupid. I'm sorry." My voice is high-pitched and throaty. It's more of a cry than an apology.

The mattress dips with his weight as he crawls on to the bed, straddling my hips. "Open your eyes."

I obey and look into his clear, Caribbean blue orbs. He bends down and sucks and nibbles at my left breast while he continues to pinch and roll my right nipple.

I'm swollen and aching for him to enter me, so close to another orgasm. My hips begin to rock forward and back, simulating the moves that I would like him to make with his dick inside of me.

His mouth pops off my nipple with a smacking sound. He catches my eyes and holds them hostage with his. "Did you get pregnant on purpose? Was this your way of justifying a relationship with me?"

The first question is legitimate and one that I had planned on addressing with him when I told him, if he hadn't freaked out so much. The second question just pisses me off. Horny as hell or not, I will not be treated like this. I roll away from him and off the other side of the bed.

Protectively, my hand crosses my bump, and I feel the dried evidence of his orgasm. "Listen, you bastard. I didn't get pregnant on purpose." My other hand balls into a fist. "I stopped taking my birth control because I thought we were over, and the idea of sleeping with another man disgusted me. You . . . you showing up that night was a surprise. I should have made you wear a condom, but I didn't. Now we're faced with the consequences of my shitty mistake. But don't you dare ever think that I did this on purpose."

Swallowing hard, I stare at the floor, the ceiling—anything to avoid looking at him. "After you left that night, I knew I had to find a way for us to be together. I knew that I still was crazy in love with you and it wasn't going away with time. My plan was to let you get settled in your new public life, then to reach out to you and see if there was still a place for me in your heart. Fortunately or unfortunately, however you choose to look at it, the unplanned pregnancy moved up the timeframe."

Before I can truly register his movements, he's crossed the mattress and has me pinned against the bedroom wall in front of the bed. "Quit protecting the baby," he growls. "I'm not going to hurt either one of you."

He takes both of my arms and pins them over my head with one hand. He leans down and kisses every centimeter of my protruding abdomen. His other arm grabs my waist and I wrap my legs around him, using my toes to push his shorts down. In some act of physics, his dick enters me as my body welcomes him.

"Don't call our baby a mistake," he growls into my ear as he impales me over and over again against the paper-thin walls of our new home. "He isn't a mistake. You aren't a mistake. We're not a mistake."

It becomes his mantra and I love it.

His eyes are clamped shut and his body is tense. He's using me to exorcise whatever demon has been plaguing him and I'm more than happy to let this play out, but I'll be damned if he brings up the idea that I somehow trapped him into a relationship. He got to ask once and hear my response. It better never be mentioned again.

I come long before him, but I do my best to not let him know. I want to be used and this still feels so right. Continuing his sweet torture, I tug his long locks and scratch his back. When he swells inside of me, I lean forward, biting his shoulder and instead of the mantra, he yells, "I love you."

Now, with his words and actions, I'm finally sated.

Chapter Twelve

Graham

"Where is she?" Max demands under his breath as I arrive at our meet-and-greet just in the nick of time. There's a line of people out the door of an auto parts store that has paid a shit-ton of money for us to do a public appearance.

"She's in Virginia with George," I reply through gritted teeth and a fake smile as another fan approaches me with huge balloon-like tits spilling over the top of her toddler-sized tank top.

They have a long table set up near the tire section. Our banner hangs behind us, advertising our radio show and tour. The radio station has two smaller banners that are freestanding on either side of the table. Kids who are probably the station's interns hover around, trying to look busy and handing out crap for us to scribble on.

Max is first in line. I'm seated in the middle, and Jake is lounging lazily to my right.

"I love you guys so much," she gushes as she hands me a newspaper to sign. I've autographed stranger items. I always scratch my radio name, Revere. No one really cares who Graham Jackson is anymore, except the pixie back in Virginia.

"Thanks." I smile and hand her back the newspaper.

Max leans over. "Still not wanting to be seen in public with you. She's a winner."

"Shut the fuck up," I say through my clenched jaw and tight fist that I hide under the table. "You don't know the first thing about us."

In the parking lot, a radio station is broadcasting live and giving away miniature foam radios with the call letters imprinted on them. I could use one of those stress balls right about now.

"Oh my gosh. I'm so glad that you're single," some grandmotherly type beams as she hands me a koozie with the radio station's call letters printed on it, and one of the stress balls. Our demographic is men between the ages of eighteen and thirty-five, yet only the women seem to show up at these events. It's rather baffling to me. Our show is very locker-room humor. I ponder if the grey-haired, frumpy, wrinkled lady with perma-set curls in front of me gets the jokes. "My granddaughter is single. She's really pretty. You want to see?" She fumbles with her five-year-outdated phone, trying to show me a picture. I smile pleasantly and count the minutes until this is over.

Max, ever my wingman, leans over and says to Grandma, "Graham's taken."

Grandma looks somewhat apologetic, and then shuffles down the table to begin her spiel about her granddaughter to Jake.

I'd like to say that I took pity on him and helped him out, but I didn't. I kept my head down, attempted to ignore Max, and smiled prettily for the line of people stretched out the front door of the business.

The hour goes by faster then I'd originally thought it would. When the final item has our signatures scratched on it, the auto parts store ushers us to the back where they keep the extra stock items while security clears out the remaining fans.

David, the Sons of Liberty Manager, has spent the last hour lurking off to the side with a scowl on his face. There's no mystery why he's mad. One of his money-makers has been MIA for the past two days and completely ignored his emails, calls, texts and probably airplane sky-written messages. I decide to head this conversation off at the pass as we enter the backroom.

"David," I greet as I walk towards him, a gigantic smile plastered across my face. "Pyro taken care of yet?" I know that this is Hank's job, but it's always a tad fun to poke the bear. He has a pointy nose that hooks toward the ground and gelled, shiny black hair that looks either oily or wet, depending on the light.

"You didn't respond to my email," he states, as he crosses his arms over his nonexistent chest. I've got a good seven inches on him, and he's heard from the guys that I've been known to throw a punch or two.

I laugh and slap him on the shoulder just a hair too hard, jerking his body forward. He sways for a split second and then recovers his balance.

"Didn't think that it needed a response other than the delete button. You're my agent, right?" *My* is the operative word here. I shift my weight to my toes and lean in so just he can hear me. "You work for us. Just remember that."

As I turn to walk away, he yells, "Quit telling fans that you're not single. It's bad for your image."

I could reply, *"It wasn't me that said that. It was Max."* But I don't. Out of the corner of my eye, I see Jake and Max jump to attention and move in a little closer. They're gauging my reaction to his statement. It's no secret that my relationship with Rachael is a touchy subject.

Slowly, I spin around and walk towards one of the best agents in the business. Honestly, we're blessed that he chose to represent us. I grab him by the collar and pin him against the wall. His mouth gapes open like a fish and his eyes grow wide with fear. "Let's get one thing straight. Whether or not I'm in a relationship is none of your God damn business. What is your business is to make sure that the best interests of the Sons of Liberty are being represented. *Capisce?*"

I release him and stroll nonchalantly out the back door of the building, letting the thick metal door slam behind me. The auto parts store backs up to an open field of sea grasses and wild flowers. It's actually kind of pretty.

The door squeaks open, but I don't turn around. I pray that it isn't him. He really shouldn't push any more buttons at this moment.

To my relief, Jake asks, "You okay, man?"

I don't respond because the truth is, I'm not the least bit okay. I said that I wouldn't sleep with Rachael until we had our shit together, and I fucked her every which way to Sunday this morning. Then I left however-many-weeks-she-is pregnant and alone in an RV park in the middle of nowhere. The word 'okay' doesn't even exist in my vocabulary.

Jake continues, "Look. I've never felt about a girl like you do. I don't understand, but you're my bro, right?"

I nod and kick a rock that's resting near the door into the field. I watch it soar up into the cloudless sky and be swallowed by the field of wildflowers. It speaks to me.

"Look, Jake, I appreciate the support. My heart's just not in this right now. It's back in a tin can called The Cougar with my girl and baby. Just be patient with me. I'll get it together. I'll pull the tour together. I'll make it work like I always do," I try reassuring him.

He remains silent.

My phone beeps in my pocket, and I check it like the crazed fool that I am. It's probably one of many messages from others that I receive every day, but when I'm not with Rachael, I check every one of them hoping that it's her.

Rachael: *Reason #??? that boxing is better than MMA: I don't have a clue anymore. I miss you. I feel like when you left we weren't in a good place, and I hate that. You seemed so upset. I just wanted to tell you that what you did earlier was okay with me. Please don't ever doubt how much I love that. I'm being cryptic. Sorry. I don't want anyone else to read this. Call when you can.*

"It's her, isn't it?" Jake askes.

I turn around and look at him for the first time. "Yeah. It's Rachael."

"You're actually smiling again. It looks good on you."

"Thanks, man. It feels good." I pause for a second and look up at the bright blue sky. I've told the guys how I feel about Rachael, but it was more of a justification for my actions. "I love her, Jake," I state emphatically.

He looks off in the distance and then back to me as he uses his hand to clear the hair from his eyes. "I've got your back. Find your happiness. Then come kick ass again with the Sons of Liberty."

***

"What are you up to, Rach?" I ask when I call her after arriving back from another steak dinner. Another night. Another expensive evening with someone hoping to buy our influence.

She yawns into the phone. I feel guilty for a second for calling her so late, but I don't dwell on it. I need to hear her voice. "Remember how I told you that I had signed with a book agent?"

No. But I don't tell her that. I think that she mentioned it when I was too busy thinking with my other head. "I know you're writing a book. You mentioned something about the agent over dinner, right?" *I was enjoying mentally fucking you against a wall while you rambled on about mundane things.*

"Yeah. Well, I opened the laptop that you bought me and spent the day making notes. Nothing fancy or spectacular. I just jotted down thoughts. More like brainstorming."

I flop down on the too-large-for-one-person hotel room bed and stare at the black TV screen. "Tell me about it."

For the next twenty minutes, she fills my ear with her ideas for a book. It's an autobiography of sorts, but it's raw and honest. It definitely has a self-help sort of twist. She says that because she was able to open up to me about her childhood she wants to include a chapter on why it's important to be a hands-on parent. That leads us into a conversation on how we want to parent our child. We both agree that he or she will have love and attention from both of us.

"Hey, can I ask you a question?" I ask sheepishly. I don't know why this particular question is so hard to get out.

"Anything. Shoot," she replies emphatically.

I swallow. "Why didn't you come with me?"

When I'd told her that I had to leave for San Diego, I didn't ask her to join me. I just assumed she would. I threw a few things in a bag, took a shower, and walked George. When I came back, she was cleaning up the breakfast dishes wearing nothing but my sweater. My cab arrived fifteen minutes later. She kissed me like there was no tomorrow, and I told her that I would see her on Sunday.

Max's question, as much as I hate to admit it, is nagging at me. Her traveling with me to San Diego would have gone a long way in the eyes of the guys to proving that this relationship is legit, and I'm not being played.

Before she can answer, I continue, "I mean, if you didn't want to come with me because of the being-seen-in-public-thing. Just tell me. At least I'll know why."

"Graham," she says my name with authority. "The last twenty-four hours have been a lot to . . . to process. You need to focus on the Sons of Liberty—your baby that you built. You and the guys don't need me to be a distraction."

"I wanted you to come." There. I said it. I'm not sure why those words were so difficult to express, but they were.

"Next time," she replies, but it's not convincing. Then she changes the subject. "Want to watch an episode of *House Hunters* together for old time's sake?"

I, of course, agree. We each choose the same one on our laptops and watch it together. She's particularly quiet and doesn't throw out any catty comments. Before it's over, I hear the soft rasps of her breath. "Rachael. Rachael, baby."

"What?" She groans sleepily.

"Hang up the phone and go to bed."

"'Kay. Love you," she mumbles.

"You too, angel. You too."

I hit end on the call, more homesick than when I went to summer camp for the first time at age nine. I'm three hours behind her. It's still relatively early out here. I stare at the phone for a moment. Do I text the guys to see if they want to have a beer in the lobby or just go to bed?

Just about the time that I decide that bed is the best choice, my phone dings. I dive for it, hoping that it's Rachael again.

Veronica: *Up for a bourbon in the bar?*

Me: *Who's coming?*

Veronica: *I texted you and the guys.*

My body aches with exhaustion and my mattress is awfully comfortable, but after how terrible the signing went, it would be probably do us all some good to have a beer and talk about things non-related to the tour, Sons of Liberty, or pregnant girlfriends. Veronica and I haven't had any face time and after Rachael's reaction to her it might be better to meet in public with the guys present.

Me: *Sure. Be down in ten.*

I throw on a pair of jeans and a green sweater, and grab my room card and phone, but leave my wallet in the room.

The elevator descends slowly, taking my mood with it. I know Rachael said that she loves me. Her reason for not joining me tonight seems legitimate. But there's just something about the way she agreed to coming with me next weekend to Phoenix—I think. It might be Scottsdale. Hell, I don't remember where the show is next week, but wherever it is, I don't think that she wants to come. I think that she's just being agreeable— amenable—because it's what she believes that I want to hear. Although that's really kind, I want her to want to tour with me. I want the Rachael that I know and love and not this sugary saccharine version of Rachael. Maybe that's asking too much at this point. *At least she's still in The Cougar* . . . but that doesn't go far to making me feel better.

Self-doubt is a bitch. By the time the elevator doors open in the lobby of the hotel, I'm questioning if the last forty-eight hours were even real. Maybe I never left San Diego. Maybe this has been a dream or an alternate universe happening. I shouldn't have spanked and fucked her. Even though she sent the text telling me she liked it, maybe she's having second thoughts. Maybe I overestimated her enjoyment of me dominating her during sex. I could have scared her off.

Graham, why do you think so poorly of yourself? I can answer that question. Rachael Early is the only woman that I've ever wanted and cared enough about to fight for and put everything on the line and that's pretty damn scary.

As I walk into the bar, I vow to keep our sex life as "normal" as I can. That's if there's still a relationship left after my epic kinky fuckup. *But she asked for it.*

Veronica is all alone at the bar. I groan hoping that one of the guys is in the bathroom. She's dressed in a figure-hugging bright red dress that reminds me of a mummy wrap. Her dark hair is down and draped over one shoulder as soft curls tuck under her over-inflated chest. She looks more like she should be at an expensive nightclub than lounging in the casual hotel bar lit with neon beer signs and papier-mâché fish decorating the walls.

She springs to her feet and hugs me. I give her a polite hug back and pull her driftwood bar stool out for her before I take the seat to her right.

"Are the guys down yet?"

She gives me a dismissive wave, "Oh. Max said the baby is fussy and Marissa would have his balls if he left her. Jake's out with a waitress who slipped him her number at dinner." Fucking figures. "I took the liberty of ordering for you," she says, motioning to the amber liquid in front of me. The bar is made of surf boards that have been lacquered together in a puzzle like pattern.

I mumble a thanks as I take a drink. It tastes funny to me—bitter. I don't know. It's not good, and my mouth contorts into a sour face. "What kind of bourbon is this?"

"Don't know. I just asked the bartender to choose a good one." Either the bartender is an idiot, or their bourbon has gone rancid. Is that possible? I must Google it when I get back to my room *by myself*.

I get the guy's attention and ask him to take the drink back and just give me a beer.

Veronica and I casually discuss work. She fills me in on the last couple of days. Fortunately, I haven't missed anything critical except for the stuff that I already know about. I politely ask her to not refer to Rachael as "the cougar" ever again, and she has the decency to look ashamed. She even apologizes and explains that it was a slip up. She texted Rachael an apology that evening. Whatever. It's now been dealt with.

Around one in the morning, I give her a goodbye hug. She has to pull down her dress because it's ridden up to her thong panties that I couldn't help but see when she recrossed her legs.

When I get back to my hotel room, I'm so exhausted that I barely have the energy to change my clothes. I uncharacteristically leave them piled in the middle of the floor and crawl into bed naked, but not before I remove my contacts and brush my teeth. *Thanks, Mom.* For the first time, in a very long time, I sleep without the awful dreams.

Chapter Thirteen

Rachael

"I'm sorry to bother you on a Sunday," I say when Candace answers the phone.

"No problem, my favorite client. Aren't you supposed to be on a beach somewhere? What can I do for you?"

I have to remind myself about her odd voice, or I would believe that I had woken her up.

"I've been working on notes for the book. Brainstorming ideas, if you will. Working on a structure. I was wondering if there's a format that it should follow. Could you give me some suggested books to read? I'm rambling. I'm sorry. I guess I'm just enjoying this process more than I thought that I would." George lies down at my feet, and I use my toes to scratch his belly. We've really bonded the last two days.

"Ever the perfectionist," Candace teases. "Generally what happens is after we've chosen a publisher, they will assign a ghostwriter to you. Your name alone will appear on the cover, but the writer will be the one who organizes the book and wordsmiths your ideas."

"Oh. Well, I was looking forward to telling my own story." I try not to sound too disappointed, but I am.

"Silly girl, everyone uses a ghostwriter. Who has time to write their own book?" She laughs.

Me. I'll have plenty of time while I watch a baby sleep.

"Give me an hour or two, and I'll send a list of what are considered the best autobiographies. Read those while you soak up some rays. There's no need to rush. We still need a publisher."

I hang up with Candace feeling the same way that I do when I believe that someone is minimizing my abilities. This is my story on how I conquered Washington D.C. politics. I don't like the idea of someone else telling it for me.

Reaching into my laptop bag, I take out the notebook that I've begun taking notes in about my time in Washington. I've already filled up about forty pages. Once I started brainstorming, the ideas flowed from the tip of my pen. I wrote about how I got my job with then Senator Jones. How I refused to take no for an answer and how he had to give me a life lesson on paying my dues.

I called Evan, and we spent two hours on the phone laughing about some of our craziest moments in the White House. I hung up with him and then jotted those notes down.

My next call was to Maggie. I shared with her that I was going to be writing a book, and she excitedly agreed to help. She pulled my calendar for my time serving the White House and emailed it to me. Just reviewing it was a scrapbook of the past seven years of my life.

Although I may have agreed to write this book out of desperation, it's beginning to feel like a new life passion, and I must admit, it feels pretty damn good.

Plus, the President called this morning to discuss an issue with the immigration policy. Yes! Being needed and feeling busy has greatly improved my mood.

I move my laptop and notebook to the side and decide that I should get a shower before Graham arrives back at The Cougar. When he left on Friday, he seemed a bit off. I thought he was feeling some sort of self-imposed guilt over giving me exactly the kind of sex that I asked for. He seems to be engrossed in an internal battle, and I can't figure out what the problem is. For someone who is so confident, he's always second-guessing himself with me. I sent him a text reassuring him that I liked what we did.

Then he sprang the question on me about why I didn't come to San Diego with him. Frankly, I didn't know it was an option. He didn't invite me to join him. I assumed that I was a distraction, so I thought it best to stay with George. It is so damn hard being Agreeable Rachael.

The bathroom in The Cougar is small but functional. The shower is built into the corner and sort of looks like a triangle. I fit in it just fine. However, I would be surprised if Graham has enough room to turn around and wash his back.

I turn on the water to hot, steaming the bathroom before I step inside. Checking my phone for the thousandth time, I have a message from Graham.

Graham: *Landed. Be home soon.*

I love that I'm his home. He could have typed *be there* soon, but he didn't. The use of the word *home* is telling. A smile crinkles my eyes as I stare at my phone screen. Even with all the doubts and difficult conversation ahead of us, I know that this was the right decision—all of this.

I strip off my clothes and leave them just outside the bathroom door. The steam from the shower creates a fog in the bathroom that envelops me, clinging to my body. Hot water pours over my head, burning my skin. The sting feels fantastic on my sore muscles from my morning jog with George and workout from Graham before he left. I'm reminded of his warning that the hot water tank is small so I should keep my showers short.

With that in mind, I shampoo my hair first and give it a good rinse. Next, I pour a dollop of conditioner into my hands and work it through the ends. While I let it set in my hair for a couple of minutes, I grab the body soap and pour some of the sweet lavender scent into my palm. I begin spreading it over my baby bump. It's getting more prominent. I'm once again reminded how thankful I am that I don't have to wear the constrictive hose any longer. As I massage the tight skin, I think about Graham rubbing his come over my bump. God, that was so hot.

I work my way up my abdomen, spreading the soap. When, I reach my chest, I feel something odd. My breath catches in my throat and my eyes grow wide. I press my fingers into the soft flesh, making sure that I'm not imagining them. *It can't be. This isn't happening.* There's no way. I throw open the shower door and stand before the vanity mirror. I use the hand towel to wipe the condensation off the reflective glass. My fears are confirmed. Right there in front of me—no place to hide. I'm getting boobs at almost forty.

I haven't wanted boobs since I was twenty-two and realized how great being flat-chested was. I can put on a padded bra and make my clothes fit right, but around the house, I don't have to wear anything. There have been plenty of days when I didn't wear a bra to work. Here they are—two rounded mounds of flesh topped with pink perma-hard nipples.

I hate them.

Because I'm a hormonal mess, I step back in the shower as the tears slide down my cheeks. It's time for another pity party. I let it all out before Graham arrives home and I have to be easy-going, perky Rachael again.

I don't want boobs, and I don't want to get fat. Graham will no longer want the Tinker Bell that looks like a bowling ball. I cry harder at the uncertainty of my future. Even though things seem to be going better with Graham, we haven't even begun discussing what a future will look like. Then I think about my book. It's been my sanity, giving me a future and hope that I can have something that is still mine, but now Candace wants someone else to write my story.

The tears turn into wails. Rationally, I know that I'm being ridiculous. If I take my problems and put them all in a stack they barely register on the "who cares" scale. But, right now, they are my problems, and I can't stop the waterworks.

I slide down the shower door and bury my face in my palms, letting the hot water beat on my back. My new breasts press against my knees, reminding me that they're there, making me cry harder.

Suddenly, the bathroom and then the shower doors fly open. "What's wrong?" Graham's booming voice yells as he shuts off the water.

I swallow and try to get my breathing calmed down enough that I can respond, but he doesn't give me a chance. I'm lifted from under my armpits and placed on the toilet lid like a ragdoll. He grabs a towel and begins drying my hair. "So help me God, Rachael. Tell me what's wrong." The towel pauses. "Look, if this is about the pictures, I can explain."

Pictures? What pictures?

"Are you okay?" he demands. The bathroom is still steamy, but the worried wrinkles spidering from his eyes are clear as day.

Through sniffles, I manage to tell him, "I have boobs."

The towel stays wrapped around me as he steps back and gives me a perplexed look. The worry lines are replaced with a twisted look of confusion as he reaches up and hangs his hands behind his neck. "You're crumpled on the shower floor over boobs?"

I wipe my nose on the towel and look down at the floor, very ashamed of myself. "Well, when you say it like that I feel stupid."

He starts laughing. It's a howling, crazy laughter that shakes his whole body. He grips the doorjamb and rests his forehead against it as his laughter turns into hysterics.

It really annoys the hell out of me. I stand up, wrapping my towel tightly around my new boobs and squeeze past him. He can laugh at me all he wants, but I don't have to sit there like a bump on a log and take it.

The sound of my stomping feet echoes throughout The Cougar, and I slam the bedroom door behind me, turning the lock. His laughter still fills the tin can as I reach for a clean set of clothes. Out of habit, I grab one of my gently padded bras. It's a razor back that hooks in front. To my horror, it will no longer latch. I step in front of the full-length mirror that's mounted on the back of the door and for the first time in a couple of days really look at my body.

It's not just my chest that is changing. My baby bump is noticeably larger. Instead of being just above my pubic bone, it now extends halfway to my bellybutton. And my waist—it's disappearing. I've never had curves per se, but I've always had a defined waist. I look fuller, thicker. I reach up and use my three middle fingers to massage the new bumps on my chest. What used to be rib bones under my nipples is lumpy tissue. It would be fascinating to see these changes if they were happening to someone else's body. Instead, I feel as some body-snatching alien from one of the horror flicks that Graham and I have watched has hijacked me.

I slip on a pair of thong panties that feel too tight and choose one of Graham's T-shirts. The bagginess hides my breast and the other changes to my abdomen, making me look more like I'm used to seeing myself. This gives me a sense of comfort, peace, knowing that I can still be the old Rachael.

Next, I grab my favorite pair of yoga pants and pull them up. The elastic band presses against my bump. Simultaneously, I feel both claustrophobic and nauseous. I begin gagging as I roll the pants off of my stomach and down below my hips. As soon as the elastic is gone, the feeling subsides and I'm able to lay back on the mattress to catch my breath.

Oh my God. This is awful. So awful. I can't wear pants. Graham thinks that this is funny. *What am I going to wear for the next thirty weeks?*

Before I can slip too far back into my pity party, Graham's banging on the bedroom door. "Let me in, Rach. I'm sorry I laughed." He knocks again, as if I didn't hear him the first time. "I wasn't laughing at you. I was just so relieved that you and the baby were okay." He pauses for a moment and tries the doorknob. "I think your body is gorgeous. Come on, babe. Open the door."

I'm still thinking about his picture comment earlier. Even in all of my body-morphing drama, I didn't miss that he's anxious about some pictures. My phone and laptop are in the other room so I can't do a quick Google search. I decide to play it cool, even though I'm anything but. "We still need to discuss the pictures. I want us to look at them together." That's a good answer—vague, yet still authoritative.

"We can do that, baby, but please let me in. I've flown all night to get here as soon as I could. I've missed you. Open the door." He's pleading with me now. "I was an asshole for laughing at your tears. I was just so relieved that you were okay. I mean, the thoughts that raced through my head . . ."

I don't respond.

"And you know that those pictures don't mean anything. My life is taken out of context. Come on, Rach. Please. Let me in."

I can't stay mad at him forever. And I've missed him too. These pictures that he brought up seem bothersome, but I decide to assume they're innocent and table the thought until we can Google. This was not the homecoming that I had planned, but it doesn't matter. He's here right now with me instead of traveling with the Sons of Liberty tour to the next city. This is a huge sacrifice that he's making, and I need to not be difficult. *I'm Agreeable Rachael.*

Standing up, I unlock the door. He fills the doorway, looking a bit sheepish, but he's the most beautiful thing that I've ever seen. I tell myself to play it cool. He's just a stupid boy, and I'm a dignified, sophisticated woman who's writing a book about my time in Washington politics. I've accomplished something that no one else in the world has. I'm a badass, kick-ass, fantastic female. So what do I do? I run and jump into his arms like a lovesick teenager. He kisses my hair and forehead, not saying a word, just showing me his affection. When he steps back, he has an examining look in his sparkly eyes. He brushes the wet strands of hair out of my face. "You sure look sexy in my clothes."

I sigh and look at the floor. "I have a problem, Graham."

He grabs my hand and leads me to the bench seating around the dining table. He sits down first and pulls me on to his lap. His nose nuzzles my neck as he kisses along my shoulder blade. "I solve problems."

His unshaven, prickly beard tickles, and I wiggle in his lap, feeling the hard bulge in his pants. Ignoring it for now, I continue, "None of my clothes fit any longer."

"So we buy new clothes," he replies as he works his way up to my ear, leaving a trail of tiny nibbles behind.

"It's not that simple," I moan as his denim-clad erection rubs along the top of my behind. "I need maternity things."

He grasps my hair and throws it over my left shoulder. As his arm reaches between my legs, he slides two fingers inside of me.

"Hmmmm . . ." he replies, as he scissors his fingers back and forth while the other hand moves to my chest. He whispers in my ear, "We'll find a maternity-clothing store and purchase whatever you need."

His hand grabs my new flesh and he says, much louder, "Oh my God. You do have tits." His fingers leave me and I'm placed on my feet in front of him. With careful consideration, he removes my pants first and the T-shirt next. I stand before him nude, except for my barely there panties.

He gasps, and a huge smile raises his apple cheeks. With wonder, he says, "Your body. It's changed in two short days." I go from minutes earlier feeling unattractive and depressed to all of a sudden feeling beautiful. He reflects his admiration for my new curves in his heavy-lidded eyes.

His hand brushes over my larger bump. "This wasn't here before." I shake my head and smile. "Gorgeous. You are so damn sexy."

He stands before me and removes his shirt and pants. His body is every girl's wet dream—defined abs, sculpted pecs, and perfect V-cut hips. I've seen it all before, but it still amazes me that this beautiful man wants me.

Sliding his boxer briefs over his erection, I let them fall to the ground. He sits back on the bench and fists his dick in his hand, and he strokes it up and down. "Come wrap your legs around my waist and ride me, baby, while I play with those new tits of yours."

I obey him because that sounds about as close to perfection as it comes. The space is tight between the back of the bench and the table, but as always with Graham and I we make it work.

My knees squeeze his ribs as I sink down on his very firm cock. He holds me in position until I have a rhythm and feel secure on his lap.

It's awkward, and I wrap my arms around his neck more to hang on than to hug him. Finally, he places one arm under my behind and, without breaking our contact, carries me into the bedroom. I kiss his chest, his neck and along his jawline in appreciation.

"Still on top," he instructs me as we tumble to the mattress. Underneath me, he spreads out horizontally on the bed. I mount his hips again, sliding him back inside of me.

"God, that feels fantastic," I groan as he fills me completely. I relax my thighs, letting my body fully accept him.

He reaches for my pillow and tucks it under his head. The dominant

Graham that I've come to know and like is gone. The man under me has a soft smile on his face with relaxed features. He looks happy and content. Although I like Graham when he takes charge, this is nice, too.

I find a slow, lazy rhythm of rocking back and forth and up and down. His gasps and moans spur me on. I'm enjoying controlling his pleasure.

"That's it, Rach. Come for me," he instructs, when I lean back and place my hands on his rock-hard quads. My finger travels southward as I play with my clit. My body floods with warmth and liquid at the fantastic sensation.

I close my eyes and move, letting my body dictate my passion. My orgasm builds slowly as I succumb to the euphoric sensation.

"I want to watch you come all over me. Use me," Graham repeats. Then, he turns up the dirty talk. "Your pussy is so hot, baby. So fucking wet. I love how tight you get right before you come for me."

As I feel myself building to the release that I crave, my finger massages my clit with more intensity, and then Graham does something unexpected. He leans up and sucks my breast into his mouth.

My slow, lazy orgasm that I was building towards turns into an explosion. I grip his back and shove my breast deeper into his mouth. Oh my God! Is that what I've been missing out on all my life?

As I slowly, mentally return to the bedroom, he's holding me to his chest while he still fills me. "That's it, angel," he coos. "I love your new, beautiful sex toys."

I giggle and grip him tightly. "I guess they can hang around for a while."

With such tender care, he moves me off of him and tucks me against his side. "What about you?" I ask as I reach for his still very hard penis.

"What about me?"

"You didn't come?" I catch a drip of pre-come and spread it over the head of his penis.

He moans. "Hmmm . . ."

I spend countless minutes stroking and sucking his cock. It's not enough pleasure to bring him to orgasm—more of a fact-finding mission. I discovered an area under his balls that makes him gasp every time I push on it. I also found out sucking and licking the head of his penis at the same time makes him yell dirty things about what he wants to do to my mouth.

Finally, I give him the release that I've been denying. The thought of swallowing come makes me sick to my stomach so I run to the sink to spit it out.

"I'm sorry," I apologize when I come back from the kitchen. "I just couldn't swallow it."

He pulls me to him. "Baby, you never have to apologize for that."

This feels too good to be true.

Chapter Fourteen

Graham

We got a bit of a late start on Sunday. I didn't complain one bit. In Knoxville, Tennessee Rachael found a maternity store. Between Target and the specialty shop, she now has enough things that fit her new body and she's happy. If she's happy then I'm ecstatic. Bra shopping was traumatic, more so for me than her. I felt like a pervert in Victoria's Secret, standing outside of the dressing room while two women brought her different bras to try. Thanks goodness she didn't ask for my opinion.

She was a trooper and has the first bra that she can fill without padding. I wouldn't allow her to buy pajamas. New rule. She sleeps either naked or in my shirts.

It's Monday, and we're driving through Memphis. With a little bit of luck we can catch up to the tour, which is in Phoenix this week.

"Hey. I thought we agreed to the phone rules," I scold when I see her grabbing her phone from the center console.

"Chill out, Graham," she says. "I need to see when my next doctor's appointment is."

I roll my eyes, but keep quiet.

She fiddles with her phone for a bit. "Looks like it's on Friday. Should I cancel? I mean, I had intended to cancel it because I was going to find a new doctor near Caroline's place, but I kept getting distracted with work and I obviously couldn't ask Maggie to do it for me."

"No," I reply adamantly. "You keep your appointments."

It's this part of her pregnancy that makes me anxious. I can make sure that she eats correctly and avoids stress, but all I can really do is tag along to her doctor appointments and be the supportive new dad.

She napped yesterday in the car. I'd glanced in her direction every chance that I got, making sure Rachael looked peaceful. Her soft little sleeping sighs were music to my ears. I'd reached over and stroked her forearm, convincing myself that she wasn't a dream. There's not a doubt in my mind that she is my future. We just have to keep all the bullshit from plaguing our lives.

"Well, I guess this time is as good as any," she says, as she turns towards me and adjusts the volume on the radio. "What's your plan for me having this baby?"

"What do you mean?" I'm honestly confused by her question. She'll go into labor and we'll head to the closest hospital. It seems simple enough.

Then she pulls out a long sewing needle and pops my bright red balloon. "I'm not just having this baby at any hospital." She's using her lecture/preachy voice and is drumming her fingernails on the armrest. I sit back and prepare to be educated by Professor Early. "One of the reasons that I was moving to Texas was to start a relationship with a new doctor who would deliver the baby. I hate to point out the obvious, Graham, but I'm about to turn thirty-nine, and I'm pregnant. It's not the same as being twenty and pregnant."

"Why not?"

"I see the doctor more than someone who is younger. There's a higher risk of diabetes and something called preeclampsia which is caused by high blood pressure. And not to mention the higher risk of genetic—"

I cut her off, because I can't listen to her ramble on about all the things that might be wrong with our perfect baby. "Okay. So what should we do?"

"I don't know." She sighs, and her voice turns to a whisper. "Not being settled when the baby is born has not been something that I've ever considered."

Silence fills the truck except for George's snores. I didn't plan past the part where I convinced Rachael to travel across the country with me to meet the tour. In my utopian world, us being together would solve all of our problems. The baby would be born in whatever city that we were in, and we'd travel from hotel suite to hotel suite like Max and Marissa have and just make it work.

The longer the silence rests between us the more that I sense her getting restless. She's begun rubbing her thumbs over the tips of her nails, which I've seen her do in the past when she's getting worked up. That's not good for her or the baby.

Think, Graham. Come up with something . . .

"We can fly back to D.C. for your appointments, if you like your doctor." I know that she had wanted to flee Washington because she didn't want anyone to know about the pregnancy, but that was before I made her understand that she was mine. Now, who cares? I'd take out an ad the *Washington Post* if she would let me.

"Okay," she begins tentatively. "So does that mean when I'm about thirty-six weeks along that I'll leave you and move back to Washington?"

Her words are like a knife to my heart. Leave me again? That will not do. This whole 'road trip' thing has been great for communication, but it sucks when I can't take my eyes off the road long enough to completely read her body language. Her voice doesn't give me any clue as to where her head is at.

"Marissa and Max set up a crib in their hotel room and Marissa hasn't missed a tour date." I hope that doesn't sound like I'm throwing Marissa in Rachael's face as a perfect example of how to be a mom on the road, but it does seem to be working for her.

"That's great for them, Graham," she snaps. *Fuck! I must have hit a nerve.* "But I'm not a nomad. That's not my personality. I've never been a mom before. I'm quite terrified of having an infant. I don't know how to feed it, or change its diaper."

"Quit calling our baby an 'it'," I growl. I'm not mad at her. I'm just frustrated that there doesn't seem to be a good solution here.

"Fine." She sounds defensive and moves toward the passenger door, as if she's trying her hardest to get away. It kills me, and I'm half tempted to pull the truck over and explain with my body why she shouldn't ever run from me. "What should we call him or her?"

I think about it for a moment. "Sam. The baby will now be referred to as Sam. It's a girl or boy name. And Sam Adams was one of the original Sons of Liberty members." I hope that the reference doesn't annoy her.

"Okay. When *Sam* is born." She stresses the name Sam, which makes me smile. "I want it to be in a hospital that I'm familiar with and with a doctor that knows my medical history. I want to bring Sam home to a house where everything is in order and prepared. I want to figure out how to be a parent before I entertain the idea of bringing Sam on the road."

All of that never occurred to me when I was making this plan. I know that she's right. I can understand why she wants those things, and I don't fault her for it. Hell, I've never been a parent before either. I guess all of that makes sense. I know that babies need a lot of stuff. When my sister had my niece, she looked as if she was moving into a restaurant when we did family dinners out, instead of just borrowing a table for an hour.

The longer this conversation goes on, the more my chest tightens. "Okay. Let's agree to cross that bridge when we come to it. Let's worry about a doctor first."

"Don't you see, Graham? If I'm going to be in Texas—"

"God dammit, quit talking about running away to Texas!" I yell as I slap the steering wheel. She jumps, and I feel like a real asshole. "You aren't going to hide with Caroline and Colin. They aren't going to take care of you. I am. I will figure this out."

Apparently everyone has a breaking point, and I just found mine.

I glance in her direction and see her eyes widen with fear. That makes me sick. I don't want to scare her. I just want her to quit making contingency plans that don't include me in them.

"I'm sorry." I sigh, as I reach for her hand. My fingers interlock with hers, and she's like a grounding force. Touching her reminds me just how much I have to lose if I fuck this up. "I'm not mad at you. It just makes me crazy when I think about you cutting me out of your life."

She squeezes my hand and it's the most reassuring feeling in this world. "I'm not cutting you out. I never said that you couldn't be a part of my life in Texas. I just want to be near someone who loves me and can help me be a mom. Caroline and Colin are good parents. They have experience. If Sam has a fever in the middle of the night, they can tell me what to do. I don't have friends in D.C. that I can lean on. I don't know anyone on your tour, and I just don't want to be alone."

The cab of the truck fills with thick silence as I process her words. I know that she's probably right. There just has to be some way to keep her with me. I'm not willing to admit defeat.

There's a truck stop up ahead so I change lanes, pulling into the parking lot.

"I don't need to use the restroom?" she asks, not dropping my hand.

"I need some fresh air," I reply as I bring our locked hands to my lips, kissing her knuckles. "Reality can be a bitch." I try to joke, but it falls flat.

I grab George's leash and walk him in the grass. She goes inside to "try" and buy us a couple of waters.

When I see her disappear through the double doors, I decide to break our No Phone rule and give Max a call.

He answers on the second ring. "The prodigal son. You ready to come home?"

I laugh. He's been calling me that since I decided to take a sabbatical, as I've come to call this little trip. "We're still in Tennessee, but getting much closer to Arkansas. How's everything?"

"You know our radio show this morning sucked goat balls, right." It's not a question. It's a statement.

"It'll be better when I record with you guys. We have better on-air chemistry when we're in the same room." I know that's a part of it, but not the entire reason. I'm so distracted. I feel as if the radio show is becoming more of a chore than something that I live for.

Max, of course, doesn't let me slide. "You've lost your kill-shot, Jackson. I served you up a perfect line about a stripper's tits and you dropped it like a hot potato. Weak, man. You also backed off criticizing the President's immigration plan that we all know is shit at best. That's not the Graham that I know and love."

He's so right. The stripper's tits comment reminded me of Rachael's new breasts, and I just couldn't go there. It felt as if I was betraying Rach and being an asshole to the stripper. Maybe I have lost my kill-shot.

George flops down at my feet, unwilling to walk around the prickly grass any longer.

"It's not," I acquiesce.

"We agreed when we started taping this show that we would never pull punches." I give a rueful laugh at his boxing metaphor. "You're not only hurting the show, but you are cheating on your soul. That's fucked up."

"You're right," I agree, as I nudge George to his feet. "Thanks for keeping me in line."

"That's what I'm here for." He sounds so cocky that I have to laugh.

"In other news, how is it being on the road with the new baby?" I'm fishing here. I need a success story—some nugget of knowledge that I can drop on Rachael. Basically, I need some hope.

"Tons more luggage, but Mar is handling it like the pro that she is. She . . ."

I see Rachael stomping in my direction, holding a magazine in her hands. Her blond hair swishes back and forth behind her, and her face is a deadly shade of fuchsia pink. I've seen this look before. It was when she rang my doorbell to confront me about being one of the Sons of Liberty. As she draws closer, I see her normally large eyes are slits and her mouth is tight. "Uh . . . sorry, Max. Gotta run."

Ending the call, I walk towards the truck. I have a sick feeling that Rachael just saw the pictures that I've conveniently managed to distract her from. This conversation reminds me of old fish in the refrigerator. I know that it's in there, and I'm reminded of it every time I open the door to grab something, yet as long as it stays there, nice and cold, I don't have to deal with the stench of removing it.

This conversation is going to go about as well as rotting fish.

I open the back passenger door and give George the command to get inside, as Rachael rages towards me like a bull seeing a red cape. I have a feeling that I'm going to need both hands and my undivided attention to keep Rachael from killing me.

"What's this?" she asks, slapping the magazine against my chest.

Slamming the truck door, I snatch the tabloid rag out of her hand and roll it into a cylinder. "It's a bunch of pictures taken out of context," I say this rather flippantly, but my heart is pounding so hard against my ribs that it's painful.

"Explain," she demands, stomping her foot.

"No," I counter, tucking the magazine into the waistband of my jeans while I cross my arms defiantly over my chest. "Do you think that I'm sleeping with Veronica? Better yet, let me ask the question this way." I lean forward and growl in her ear. "Do you think that there is anyone else in this world that I want besides you?" My tongue runs along the shell of her ear, causing her to shiver.

For a moment I think that we've come far enough that this is it. She trusts me. I've underestimated Rachael once again.

She steps out of my embrace and crosses her arms over her chest, accentuating the new perks of pregnancy and mimicking my own stance. "I need to hear you explain why you were hugging and touching your assistant inappropriately in a tacky, themed bar in San Diego. And said, and I do quote 'I'm seeing someone' at one of your signings, which the magazine has clearly been led to believe is your assistant. Is that why you didn't invite me to join you?"

Invite her? She didn't need a fucking invitation to stand by my side like some sort of kept woman. "No." I stomp around the truck and climb in the cab. The line in the sand has been drawn.

This is going to be one of thousands of false rumors. We establish trust now and fight this out, because I'm not doing it every week when I'm sleeping with the production assistant, or the waitress, or whomever our agent decides to leak to the press.

She throws open the passenger door and yells, "Fuck you! Explain this to me."

I grip the steering wheel until my knuckles painfully cramp, praying for some divine intervention to make this woman realize how important she is to me. I've told her and shown her. If she can't come to her senses and see this for what it is, then there is truly no hope for us. I shift in the seat so I can see her. "Rachael, am I in love with anyone else besides you?" I demand.

She stands there with her hands planted on her hips, staring holes through my soul. I'm not backing down.

I fly out of the truck, slamming the door behind me and walk back around to her. When I reach Rachael, she spins around with a defiant *bullshit* look on her face. Her chin is cocked up and her arms are crossed again. I grab her by her shoulders and hold her so she can look in my eyes. "Is there anyone else besides you?"

"That magazine sure thinks so," she replies tartly.

I pick her up and place her on the passenger seat. She cuts her eyes towards the windshield. "I don't give a fuck what the magazine believes. I only care what you believe. Answer me, Rachael." I swallow hard, realizing the gravity of the situation. This is really a make-or-break moment for us. My blood is boiling, and I feel as if we're teetering on the edge of a cliff. We either establish trust, or I contact the paternal rights attorney that Max has mentioned more than once. "Answer the question. I'm only asking it one more time. Is there anyone else but you?" My voice drops a couple of octaves to a deep growl.

Defiantly, she refuses to look at me. I let go of one arm and grab her chin, turning her lips to mine. A deep *V* has formed between her eyes, and her jaw is locked. Her shoulders are tense and raised uncomfortably close to her ears. She has every right to be angry. But I need to know that I have her trust.

Staring into her eyes, I wait for her to tell me the words that I desperately need to hear.

Time passes . . . seconds . . . maybe minutes . . . It's irrelevant. I'm prepared to stand like this for the rest of my life until she acknowledges that I'm hers every bit the way she's mine.

Her mouth parts and her pink tongue darts out, licking her lips. It gives me the entry that I need. Gripping her head in my hand, I bring her mouth to mine as I study her eyes. Her green orbs grow larger as the lines stretching from her eyes begin to relax. *That's my girl.*

She opens her mouth again, probably to tell me to fuck off. But before she can get the words out my tongue slides over her plump, pink lips. Cherry Chapstik has never been so tasty. At first she refuses to participate. I growl and suck her bottom lip until she reluctantly begins to kiss me back and wraps her arms around my neck. "That's my girl," I moan into her luscious mouth.

I press my hardness into the warmth between her thighs. "Answer me," I demand, as I rub against her.

As she nibbles on my jaw, she timidly says, "There's only me."

"Tell me who I love," I demand, as I mark her neck with my teeth.

"Me and only me," she says in a high-pitched voice, as she drags her nails down my back.

I use my body to shield hers from any prying eyes of the truck-stop patrons. Her hips grind against my erection, making me crazy. I unbutton her pants and reach my hand inside of her low-rise jeans letting her ride my fingers, taking what she needs.

As she comes, I pull her close to me, reveling in her sweet juices that flood my hand. "That's right, sweet girl. I've got you."

Her orgasms are so beautiful to watch. I'm the one who makes her head drop back and inspires the soft moans that exit her throat. It's me who causes a purple vein to pulsate against her alabaster skin. She's my *rest of my life.*

Her eyes grow wide with shock when I slip my hand from her pants. She opens her mouth to speak.

But I anticipate the shame that she's about to succumb to. "No one saw. I hid you."

Her shoulders fall in relief. I kiss her forehead and shut the car door for her.

As I open the driver's side door, she says, "I'm still mad at you," crossing her arms, a smirk on her face.

"No, you're not," I reply as I slide into the driver's seat and start the truck.

***

The next day, I have a chance to study the pictures in the magazine when Rachael requires one of her many rest-stop breaks. I slide the tabloid out from under my seat and gaze at the article written about me. Revere? Are we one and the same? I don't know anymore. The media calls us by our show names. I'm really okay with that. Revere is my stage name—my persona. Graham is the guy who is a brother, son, and whatever the hell I am to Rachael.

The pics are raunchy. I'm pulling Veronica's bar stool out for her. Our hug looks much more than platonic. When I sent the drink back, it looks as if I'm ordering one for her. There's a picture where it appears that I'm touching her knee. The article is scandalous. My assistant and I are hooking up every chance that we get, according to multiple sources. I even told someone at a signing event that we are a couple.

I sigh, feeling sick. This is what I signed up for when I agreed to put a face with the voice of the Sons of Liberty. Would I still have agreed to give up my anonymity if Rachael and I met a month earlier? I don't know. Maybe. Maybe not. The Sons of Liberty and our cause is important to me, but obviously not as important as Rachael and the baby, since I've put my professional life on hold for them.

I'm so tired of feeling as if I'm failing at everything. The term "white-knuckling life" definitely defines me right now.

Next, I check my phone. Hank has sent me numerous messages with the same problems. Someone dropped a ten thousand dollar light, shattering it. Insurance doesn't want to pay to replace it. The Phoenix facility that is hosting us this week is concerned about the immigration groups that have asked to set up booths. They feel they're too militant and are requiring that we provide more security. It's the last message that forces me to break our phone rules.

The Sons of Liberty accountant has also left a message, stating that we have "funds that are unaccounted for." That sounds like theft to me.

"Bryan, Graham. What's going on?" I reply when he picks up his phone.

Fortunately, he doesn't beat around the bush. "Look, I hate to tell you this, but we conducted an audit of the Sons of Liberty accounts and you're missing a substantial sum of money."

I reach up and drag my hand through my floppy hair, noting that I need a haircut. "What's substantial?"

"It looks like someone has been siphoning money from the tour—not a lot at one time, so it took us a few months to notice."

I sigh. "How much?"

"Around forty-eight thousand dollars," he replies regretfully.

"Fuck!" This is because I've been so distracted with Rachael and the baby. This is my fault. I've allowed someone to steal from me and my two best friends—my brothers.

"I've hired a woman that I've used before when I've discovered issues like this. She's good, Graham. She'll find out who it is and uncover the depths of the theft."

I thank him and hang up the phone.

As Rachael exits the building, I shove the magazine under the seat and put my phone back on charge in the center console. I do my best to relax my shoulders and jaw. I'm not sharing my tour problems with her. She doesn't need any stress. I told her that I would take care of everything else. She's only supposed to be growing our child.

My forced relaxed face slides in place as she climbs into the truck.

"I got you a treat," she says, as she buckles her seat belt. "But you have to guess what it is." Her bubbly mood works wonders to improve mine.

A plastic bag dangles from her wrist, and she looks a bit mischievous.

I start the truck and steer us back on the highway. "Is it bigger than a bread box?"

She giggles at my reference to the game Twenty Questions.

"Smaller than a bread box."

"Is it something that I can eat?"

"Nope. Not possible." She's smiling ear to ear and is almost bouncing with excitement. I don't want this game to end.

"Is it something that I can wear?"

Her finger rests against her chin as she ponders the answer, and it's the cutest damn thing I've ever seen. "Hmmm . . . maybe. I'm not sure how to answer that one."

"It's a koozie with a crude saying on it," I guess.

"Nope. Try again."

"It's a T-shirt that reads 'Someone in Arkansas Loves Me.'"

She giggles and reaches into the plastic bag and brings out a CD. Proudly, she shows it to me. It's titled *Greatest Road Trip Songs of All Time.*

"Remember when I asked you what kind of music you liked, and you went Mr. Grumpy on me? Well, I decided we needed road-trip theme music. We're going to listen to this CD and choose our song from it."

She removes the cellophane and hands the CD to me. I slide it in to the slot in the radio and soon the truck fills with the sweet sound of Ray Charles singing "Hit the Road Jack."

I reach over and grasp her hand. "Thanks for my gift. It's awesome."

We stop at a campground on the Arkansas and Oklahoma border. She walks George while I get The Cougar set up for the night.

After midnight, I slide between the sheets, not wanting to disturb her sleep. She's lying on her side with her knees tucked up—perfect for me to wrap myself around. In the dark, I ponder how I thought that I could ever get over her. She makes me crazy. She may drive me mad but there is no one more right for me than her.

"I love you, Rachael," I breathe into her hair. "Sleep well, my angel."

Chapter Fifteen

Rachael

"What are your real thoughts on the President's immigration plan?" Graham asks as we pass through the middle of nowhere. There are fields of nothing as far as the eye can see.

"Why?" I lean over and turn down our road-trip music. "So you can quote the former White House Chief of Staff? No thanks."

Then the light bulb goes off over my head. "Oh my God! You're trying to make me one of your Betsy Rosses. Well, no thank you Mr. Jackson. That does not fly with me."

"Okay. I promise not to list you as a source, or even as a Betsy Ross. I'm legitimately curious as to what you think." Then he adds, "And not the White House's party line."

This is dangerous territory. I never discuss what I personally think about anything. Yes. Graham and I have talked policy, but I always felt as if I was giving the counter opinion to his, and not expressing my real beliefs. I've been trained since I accepted the job in then Senator Jones's office to not have my own opinion.

"Well . . ." I start tentatively, "I think that it's a very diverse problem that isn't going to be solved by President Jones or his successor. There's no one solution to the problem. It's multi-faceted."

"That's it?" Graham goads. "That's all you've got, Rach? I'm disappointed in you."

Silence fills the cab of the truck, with only the sound of the tires rolling over the asphalt. I contemplate how I actually do feel about the President's plan. It's a great first step. Yes. That's what it is.

I add, "I think that the President is brave to introduce the plan that he has. It gives illegal immigrants who can prove a two-year work history the ability to become citizens and it doesn't penalize the employers who gave them a job." I swallow. "Once again, it's very controversial. I get the argument that they're taking jobs away from American citizens and the employers are technically criminals, but the President knew he was going to have to take some punches to make a change."

"Yeah . . . yeah . . . yeah . . . that's the party line. I want to know how you feel." He stresses the word "you."

The sun is setting in front of us and the sky is bathed in shades of corals, blues, pinks and yellows. It's really stunning. "Have you noticed that the sunsets out here in the middle of nowhere are so much prettier than in D.C? I always heard that smog makes sunsets brighter, but I think the experts are wrong."

"Quit changing the subject. But yes, I do think the sunset is gorgeous."

Laughter erupts from my belly as I spy the look on his face. Usually Graham looks relaxed and calm, as if he could be posing on a sailboat wearing Ralph Lauren faded red shorts and a white polo for one of their many ads. When he talks politics, he reminds me a bit of a Doberman. His jaw becomes set and he leans forward a bit, as if he's ready to pounce. The juxtaposition between the different versions of Graham I find really hysterical.

"What's so funny?" he asks as his forehead crinkles.

"You. You actually really want me to debate immigration with you? Why, Graham? Why does my opinion matter?" I say through giggles.

He relaxes a bit and smiles at himself. "I guess I take this a bit seriously." He pauses for a second and then continues, "I don't know, Rach. It's just that I remember so clearly how passionately you talked about President Jones when you visited the campaign headquarters while I was an aid." Ahh . . . yes. The elusive visit that changed his world, and the one I can't remember. "And I just want you to talk that passionately about something that doesn't involve you putting me in my place."

His words strike a nerve. I guess he's right. I've really tried to be on my best behavior this road trip—being amenable, not complaining too much, keep my thoughts to myself. I want this relationship to work so badly that I haven't really been Rachael Early. Hell, I even admitted that I trusted him and let him finger me in a truck-stop parking lot like some kind of ten-dollar whore after seeing very incriminating pictures. Who am I, anyway?

I suck in a deep breath, and say, "Okay. Here's the deal. Immigration in this country is a shit show. You have those people that deserve to be here, because let's face facts—we're all immigrants. At some point, someone in our family tree decided that they wanted to try their luck somewhere else and made the hard decision to leave everything they knew to cross the expanse of ocean or river or wherever and make this country their home. Yet somewhere along the way, someone decided that our country is too crowded." I gesture toward the giant expanse of nothingness around us to demonstrate my point. "And put unrealistic expectations on becoming a citizen, forcing people to sneak in illegally. The loopholes in the laws are causing pregnant woman to come to this country to give birth so their children will be citizens. I mean, how desperate is that? Or people are paying an American citizen to marry them so they can get their citizenship. It's a great Hollywood movie and all, but it's shitty that people are being forced to do this."

Graham opens his mouth to interject, but I don't let him. He wanted Opinionated Rachael? Well, he's getting her. "Furthermore, we have to do a better job securing our borders because we've got a real problem. Our border with Mexico looks like Swiss cheese. The amount of illegal drugs, weapons, and humans being smuggled across is staggering. I don't know if we should put a barbwire fence up that spans the entire border or hire more agents, but I do know that the amount of human life lost trying to cross from Mexico to the U.S. is staggering.

"And while we're on that subject, someone must improve the relations with Mexico. We treat them like they're our ignorant stepbrother instead of embracing them as our partner in this. . ."

Graham interrupts, and I let him this time. "So I have this idea . . ."

"Oh no. Your last idea was a radio show that talked about the smell of girls' vaginas. No thanks, G."

Now, it is his turn to laugh out loud. He cocks his eyebrow. "Crude, baby. I like it when you talk dirty."

I punch him in his arm, which makes him laugh harder. "Vagina . . . vagina . . . vagina . . ." I scream like a petulant ten-year-old.

Once he's calmed down, he reaches over and takes my hand. "So I've had this idea for a while. I'm not sure how it's going to work yet, but here's what I want to do." His Adam's apple bobs up and down before he continues. "I want to start an organization of sorts. Something where the Sons of Liberty find politicians that are making a difference in this world, and we throw our support behind them to run for a higher office. Like, how I see this working is we get recommendations, take nominations, whatever, from citizens who see their elected official as doing good deeds for their community. Then, we financially back that candidate when we encourage them to run for a higher office. Make sense? Like we're grass-roots backers that actually have a platform for getting them elected."

I'm quiet for a moment while I contemplate his idea. It's not novel. The Tea Party is a perfect example of a group who tried to do this. The difference is Graham does have the platform. Their radio show is extremely popular, and we saw in the last election just how much impact they truly have. Their tour is selling like hotcakes. They have enough clout that this might actually work.

He must interpret my silence as negative because he continues justifying it. "We have dinners in every city where we meet with all these loaded dudes. They're trying to buy our influence. Anyway, so we ask them to donate to our organization. We can give these candidates not only money, but publicity and support."

Silence fills the car again while I think. Now the night sky is dark, and we need to begin searching for our campgrounds.

Thoughts ping-pong through my brain faster than a NASCAR race. It's a great idea, but it's very difficult to execute. They would have to choose the perfect test candidate and put all of their faith in him or her that they could pull it off. That level of trust takes a lot of cahoonas. On the other side of the coin, it absolutely gives the Sons of Liberty an opportunity to put their money where their mouth is. They want real changes . . . well, backing candidates to inspire that change is highly impactful.

All of sudden, he yells, "Say something Rachael."

I jump and grasp my heart, causing me to laugh. "Sorry. Lost in my own head. I think it's a fantastic idea. I'm just trying to process it all. My MO is to hear the great idea, and then I figure out how to make it work." I reach over and rub his shoulder. "Calm down, Hoss. It's all good."

Once we're tucked in for the night, as Graham calls it, I have a chance to contemplate his idea a bit more. It's a good one. I pull out my trusty notebook and begin making notes on how we can make it work as Graham softly snores to my left and George lies on the floor to my right. I'm sandwiched between my boys, and there's no place that I would rather be.

Maybe Graham's passions can become mine also.

Chapter Sixteen

Graham

It's Thursday and we're stopping in Harmon County, Oklahoma, somewhere close to the Texas border. Here's the deal. We could have made it to Phoenix this week. I didn't tell Rachael, but we made a slight detour—purposeful wrong turn—on the Arkansas and Oklahoma line. I read ahead in my calendar and realized that Lubbock was next week's stop. I made the executive decision to give us this full week together before the realities of touring begin.

The land here is pretty barren. There aren't a lot of trees, but there are miles and miles of nothing that looks the same. I'm sort of regretting choosing this as our place to leave the travel trailer and George before we travel back to Washington D.C. tomorrow morning for Rachael's doctor's appointment.

All of this is rolling through my mind when we pull up to the campgrounds and are greeted by a lady who looks like she does meth instead of eating Cheerios for breakfast. I try to not judge people based on appearance because they can be deceiving so I park the camper anyway and follow her inside the pop-up camper that she's using as an office.

The place smells like someone spilled a bottle of honey and didn't bother to clean it, and it's so warm that sweat beads along my temples. I have a bad feeling about this—real bad.

"Ma'am, do you—"

She interrupts. "It's Darlene. Don't call me ma'am. I ain't old enough to be your mother. Just look that way 'cause my teeth are bad."

"Darlene." I flash her my winningest smile. "I'm going to need to leave my dog, George, here overnight for a few days. Would you mind walking him and feeding him? I'll pay you, of course."

"What kinda dog is it?" she asks, leaning against the dining table. I get the distinct impression that she might be asking to see if there's enough meat on his bones for dinner. She's so thin that her body seems to have curved into the shape of a *C*.

"Labrador."

"I useta have a dog. His name was Buddy, but the stupid dog just wouldn't stay home. Probably got ranned over or starved to death. He was that dumb." She snickers and sucks off of a bong.

I'm thinking that Buddy might just have been a genius. Hopefully, he has a great new life on a farm somewhere where he gets to rest on a front porch stoop during the hot summer days and swim in a lake.

Warning sirens are going off like crazy, and I'm just about to make a polite excuse as to why we will be staying somewhere else when Rachael walks into the tiny trailer. The look on her face says it all. She's not impressed. Our eyes lock, and I silently implore her to get the message that I'm not comfortable staying here.

"My sister just called. She's in Oklahoma City, and she really needs us to take care of the baby." Message received loud and clear. "Do you mind if we head back that way? It's a two-hour drive, but I think we can reach there before too late?"

"Sure, babe. Call your sister back and tell her that we'll be there," I lie through my teeth.

I turn back to Darlene. "So sorry to have bothered you, but it looks like we've had a change of plans."

"Suit yourself," she says, and turns on the little black-and-white TV that rests on the kitchen counter before the door closes behind me.

I slide into the driver's seat and start the truck so fast that you'd think my hair was on fire. "Oh my God, that was brilliant," I congratulate

Rachael. "How did you know that I was looking for a way to politely decline staying there?"

"George," she replies confidently, with a shoulder shrug.

"Huh?"

"Well, he's usually so chilled in the backseat. When you walked in to that tiny trailer, he began to whine. I seriously think he's smarter than most people, so I decided if George wasn't happy, neither was I. I thought I would use the sister line since you know that I'm an only child."

I reach into the backseat and pet whatever part of George that I can reach. "Good boy, big guy," I coo.

When I've given him enough accolades, I grab Rachael's hand. "Smart thinking. That place and that lady were way scary."

This will work better anyways. We'll be closer to the airport in Oklahoma City and can still join the tour in only a day's drive—if that.

We break the No Phone rule near Oklahoma City when I have Rachael Google campgrounds and read the reviews. She selects a nice place about twenty minutes from the airport and the man who lives on property likes George and even has a dog for him to play with.

***

After I have The Cougar set up and Rachael is happily reading notes from her notebook and transcribing them into her documents program on her laptop, I give her a kiss on the forehead and tell her that I'm taking the truck. She looks perplexed, but I explain that I need to pick up some reading material for the show this weekend.

I like to grab the local newspapers and magazines when the tour arrives in a new location. It's fun when we can extrapolate our talking points for the show down to local issues. First of all, the crowd loves it, and secondly, placing an issue squarely in someone's backyard gets their attention.

"Okay. While you're out, will you grab some more crackers? The baby seems to prefer the bagel chip kind."

She looks gorgeous. She's changed into my lacrosse coaching T-shirt. It's a shade of royal blue that makes her complexion glow. Her hair is piled on top of her head with two pencils crisscrossed holding it in place. For a moment I consider skipping out on my homework trip and pinning her to the bed.

My dick and my brain have a quick rock, paper, scissors battle, with my brain winning. I've neglected the Sons of Liberty enough. Rach can wait to be taken care of for another hour. Although my cock wonders if it can.

I promise Rachael that I will not be long and head for the truck. Once I'm back on the highway and I know where I'm going, I give Max a call. He's all too eager to answer.

"How's my favorite traveler?" Max greets me.

"In Oklahoma City for a few nights. I think on Monday, we'll catch up with you guys in Lubbock."

"Great news. And George?"

"George saved us from certain death by cannibalism, so he gets extra kibble."

"That George is a smart boy."

"Yes. He is." I decide to cut to the chase with why I called. "How's Phoenix going?"

I've been scared to ask. Every update has been bad, but I can't get a read on Hank yet. Is he a glass half-empty kind of guy, or is everything really going to hell in a handbasket?

"Well," Max begins. But his "well" is more drawn out, like "w-e-l-l-l-l-l." That's not good. "The sponsors are happy. Our appearances at their stores have brought them a lot of traffic. Like we did a signing at some local restaurant and they couldn't keep up with the food orders."

"That's great. We like happy sponsors." I see a drugstore up ahead and take the exit. "What about the venue? Have you been there yet?"

"And Graham, right there is the heart of the problem," he says this in his game-show announcer voice. "Like, the people love us. Old. Young. They're showing up at the sponsor events and gush over our awesomeness. It's behind the scenes that's a nightmare."

"Elaborate." I pull into a parking spot, but don't get out of the truck.

"I mean, I'm trying to take a more active role in what you used to do." I don't like how he says "used to do." It makes my stomach tighten and I feel a bit sick. I'll be there on Monday and this shit will be fixed. "I went to the venue today, and it was like watching monkeys at the zoo fuck a Nerf football."

I'm so glad that I had not just taken a sip of water or I would have sprayed it all over my windshield. Even after all these years, Max's comments still tickle my funny bone. "Fuck a football?"

"Yeah. I remember standing outside of the monkey cage at the zoo when I was a kid and watching this monkey hump a football. It was so damn funny, and I laughed hard enough that I pissed my pants. Mom was annoyed and dragged me to the bathroom. When we came back, the bastard had passed it to another monkey who was humping away. Absolutely pointless humping, but damn it was funny to watch."

"Makes sense. I'll file that one away for future use," I reply. "Okay. Now back to the tour." Sometimes Max gets a bit distracted and I have to walk him back to the original question.

"Yeah. So. I get there and it's chaos. No one has a site plan for where the organizations should set up. They're hot, tired, and pissed because their time is being wasted. Some militant bitch is screaming at the poor girl whose job it is to assign locations. It's really not the girl's fault. She says that Hank hasn't finished the site plan yet."

"So what did you do?"

"Well, I did what any great leader does and jumped on the brick wall built around a tree and gave an *Independence Day*-quality rally speech, which calmed the masses down. Then, I went and kicked Hank in the nuts until he gave me the site plan."

"What was Hank doing that the site plan wasn't ready?"

"Great question, Mr. Jackson. You're one smart cookie. I'm so glad that you asked." Max pauses dramatically. "He was . . . wait for it . . . doing nothing!"

"Nothing?"

"Not a God damn thing." He quickly backtracks. "Doing nothing might be a tad of an overstatement. He was eating a fast food burger with the crew and discussing a scene from *Sons of Anarchy.*"

My forefinger taps a beat on the steering wheel in frustration. The saying, "when the cat's away, the mice will play" leaps into my head. "Did you call him out on it?"

"Of course. How long have you known me, man? Sheesh . . ." Having a conversation sometimes with Max is draining. "His excuse was that he bought the crew lunch to boost morale."

"Okay. I'll talk to Hank when I arrive tomorrow night. We don't have enough cash to buy the crew lunch. They already receive a per diem food stipend as part of their contract."

A dad and little boy use the Red Box in front of my truck to select a movie. The little boy must get the movie that he was hoping for because he bounces up and down with excitement, and when the box spits the movie out, he hugs it against his chest. I smile at the image and imagine introducing Sam to my favorite movies. *I get it universe. You don't have to keep reminding me why I'm on this journey.*

"Speaking of money, when is the tour going to actually yield me a dollar for my bank account? Because if I'd quit our radio show, I would be dead broke."

I file the mental list of movies that I've been making away in my head and focus back on the conversation at hand. "Well, we knew that the radio show was our bread and butter until we'd paid back the advance from the tour production company. It's not happening as fast as I had hoped, but merchandise sales should help."

"Well, I . . .,"

"I know that me not being present is a strain," I say, not letting Max cut in. "I know that Hank would be doing a better job if I was managing him every day. This is the last show—I promise. Next Monday, we'll meet you guys in Lubbock and I'll spend every waking moment busting Hank's balls until we have him back in line. I'll also spend some serious time with Bryan, making sure that our finances are in line. I'll be the CEO again just like I agreed to."

"Those words are music to my ears. Good luck with the doctor's appointment tomorrow. And tell Rachael hi for me."

When Max hangs up, I stare at my phone is disbelief. Wow! He actually acknowledged that Rachael's pregnant and asked me to tell her hello. I don't know what caused the change of heart, but I'll take it.

Then, I remember that I forgot to mention that I talked to Rachael about our candidate support organization or whatever we should call it. We've made changes so far in the way politics are being run. This is a way where we can truly work to get the right people elected.

I shoot Max a quick text telling him that Rachael is on board with the idea. Her position so closely tied to the President gives us the legitimacy that we need. His response is a positive one.

There's a spring in my step as I walk through the glass double doors of the drug store. A pimple-faced kid working the checkout counter bids me a welcome. It's about as enthusiastic as I was to be at Darlene's campground.

I grab Rachael's bagel crackers first so I'm sure not to forget them, and then head for the magazine aisle. It's not nearly as robust as it was when I was kid. I guess we can thank the Internet for that.

They have all the political magazines that I read so I grab a copy of each. Then, I head towards the local section and pick up the latest edition of *The Capital Beacon*, which appears to cover Oklahoma politics, *The Journal Record*, and *The Oklahoman*. That should do.

As I make my way back down the aisle, I spot a cover of one of the Hollywood gossip magazines. Guess who is on the cover? Me, along with a picture of Max and Jake. The cover reads *Tour in chaos . . . Radio show numbers slipping . . . Is it over for the Sons of Liberty?*

I grab the rag and add it to my pile of other purchases. The same pimple-faced kid that greeted me when I came in, checks me out. As he runs the magazines over the scanner, he attempts to make small talk. It's painful. I'm polite, but anxious to get back to The Cougar and read if the media believes that the tour is done for.

As he scans the offensive magazine, he recognizes me on the cover. His mouth opens and his eyes grow wide. "You're Revere."

"So I've been told," I reply.

"Can I get your autograph?" He pulls out a Sharpie marker and hands me the magazine cover to sign. It's a bit surreal. He wants my signature on a magazine cover that is predicting my demise. Instead of defining irony for him, I sign the magazine and politely hand it back before I go back down the aisle to grab another copy.

By the time that I make it home to The Cougar, Rachael is asleep and George is curled up on his bed. I slip my pants and shirt off and shove them in the dirty clothes basket. Next, I find my running shorts and put them on. I do all of this without disturbing Rachael. This is a bit disappointing. I would have loved for her to have woken up so we could make love, but I know that she needs her rest. She is growing a human being, after all.

Walking back through the trailer, which is about five steps, I grab my loot and open the recording studio. The nasty gossip magazine rests on top of the pile taunting me so naturally I choose to read it first.

I flip through a bunch of articles about who is dating who and who is breaking up. Then there's a fascinating article about a nightclub brawl between two pop divas. The magazine offers me great skin care tips and the hottest nail-color trends for summer. It's enlightening. Then, finally I find the article that interests me the most.

After giving it a good skimming, my stomach begins to relax. The headline was more scandalous than the content. However, this is a huge wakeup call. I've got to get this tour back on track. Our problems are no longer being contained to the three of us.

The magazine is discarded on top of my small desk and I turn my attention to my homework.

Chapter Seventeen

Rachael

"Thanks for coming," I say for the thousandth time as I grip his hand. He's supposed to be in Phoenix today, but I had a doctor's appointment back in D.C. and Graham insisted on joining me. If I let my mind think about his responsibilities to the Sons of Liberty that he's neglecting, I could get terribly worked up. So I don't. I trust that Graham is doing what's best right now for both of us. He's asked me to trust him, so I am. Although the nagging questions about how we manage a new relationship, baby and his tour weigh on my mind if I let them.

I've become good at telling myself to not plan so far ahead. Instead of me filling my calendar with dates six months out, I'm working on focusing on the here and now. Is there a twelve-step program for this? I might need to join. The lack of structure makes me feel useless and lazy, but even I can admit that it's a tad liberating.

To settle these feelings, I drop Graham's hand and open my bag, pulling out my ever-present notebook. I open it to the section that I've labeled "SAM." This is where I'm taking notes on my pregnancy.

"You're including the baby in your book?" Graham asks, clearly reading over my shoulder.

I hand him my notes so he doesn't get a neck strain. "Yes. I think this new journey that I'm on is as important as my path to the White House. Don't you?"

His lips turn up in a sweet smile and he leans over, kissing the tip of my nose. "You know I do."

He scans through what I've written, then he bursts into laughter. I lean over his thigh and see that he's reached the part where I discover my new breasts. "It's not funny." I laugh and ball up my fist, hitting him in the shoulder.

His smirk kills me. "Babe, it was really funny. Here I thought something terrible had happened and it turns out that you were upset over something that every woman wants and every man enjoys playing with."

"Well, obviously not everyone," I reply tartly.

"Have you thought of a title?"

"Yeah. I think I have." I pause, scanning the waiting room to make sure that no one is listening. The other couple waiting for the doctor is preoccupied with a little boy of about two years-old, who is making a mess of his animal crackers. We're safe. "*Anything, But Not Everything.*"

"Hmmm . . ." he says, and seems to be toying with the idea for a moment in his mind. "Explain."

I've been test driving it since I signed the contract and returned it back to Candace, but finally saying it out loud gives it power. I like how my heart flutters when I hear it. Yes. I think the title is perfect. "Caroline's mom had this quote cut out of a newspaper, and it hung on their refrigerator as long as I've known her. It read, *I can do anything, but not everything.* See, she was a single mom to four girls. I think it was her reminder that she couldn't do it all, but it didn't make her a failure."

Graham grabs my hand and tucks a strand of my hair behind my ear. The look on his face makes me want to weep with happiness. He is beaming with pride. He's actually proud of me. For what? I'm not sure, but I bask in his glow. No one has ever looked at me this way. Not my parents. Not the President. A smile forces my cheeks to meet my eyes. "You like the title?"

"It's the most perfect title ever—*Anything, But Not Everything.*" He kisses my knuckles. "You amaze me, Rachael."

I amaze him. Someone is amazed by me. How does he always know exactly what to say to endear him more to my heart?

I could possibly be the luckiest girl in the world.

The nurse that I've become friendly with, Betty, walks into the waiting room and politely says, "The doctor is ready," ending our moment. It's okay. It is one that I will replay for the rest of my life. It's the first time that my actions made someone that I love feel proud—and it had nothing to do with my career.

I tuck my notebook back into my bag. Graham and I stand at the same time without dropping hands. "You ready?" I ask.

He smirks. "I was born ready."

We're settled into an examination room with an ultrasound machine in the corner. I point at it. "The first time I came in, we saw the baby using that."

"Will we get to see Sam today?" he asks Nurse Betty.

"Oh. I'm sure that Dr. White will take a peek." She hands me the dreaded blue and grey gown and points to the curtained dressing room. "You can leave your bra on, but remove everything else."

The door shuts behind her as I step inside the tiny privacy room and pull the curtain around me. From the other side, I hear "Seriously, you let me handcuff you to the bed, but I can't watch you undress? I mean, come on, Rach, give me a show."

Giggling, I peek my head around the curtain. "A peep show . . . hmmm . . . let me see what I can do about that."

I close the curtain back and slide off my jeans. My right bare leg wraps around the curtain as I make bass beats to a burlesque-inspired song.

Graham catcalls my silliness and yells, "Show me more."

I remove my panties and sling-shot them around the curtain to him. He catches them and stuffs them in his right front pocket, with a dirty smile.

Next, I remove my blouse and hang it neatly on one of the provided hangers.

I walk out from behind the curtain, draped in the sheet/dress that brushes along the top of my ankles. In my sexiest voice, I say, "Hey big boy. Care to tie this for me?"

His full lips turn down in a sexy pout. "I'm much better at removing clothing than putting it on."

He ties the strings around my neck and I wrap the extra bulky material around my waist. It drowns me. When you're barely five feet, one size doesn't come close to fitting all.

Just as I'm scooting back on the table, the door opens and Dr. White enters. She's rather mousey and is the same age as me. Caroline went to Harvard with her. I like her. Her bedside manner leaves a lot to be desired, but I need a brainiac more than I need a cheerleader.

She walks straight to Graham and introduces herself.

He flashes his broad smile, and replies, "Graham Jackson, Sam Jackson's father."

"Name already? You don't know the sex of the baby."

I chime in. "Graham had issues with me calling the baby 'it' so he chose to refer to him or her as Sam. It's kind of stuck."

She doesn't bother to respond and immediately motions for me to lie back on the table. "No one checked your weight," she comments.

"Her breasts have added at least two pounds."

Graham could quit contributing right about now. I shoot him a dirty look. "Ignore the peanut gallery."

"Okay. Let's check the heartbeat."

My eyes meet Graham's while she busies herself opening drawers, looking for the heart monitor. His face is lit up like fireworks on the Fourth of July. The thought that I could have ever hidden this pregnancy from him makes me feel ashamed. Although both of us can agree that the timing of Sam is not good, there's no doubt that we both are already head over heels in love with this baby.

He walks to my side and holds my hand while his foot taps eagerly against the almond-colored tiled floor. We both wait for the sound of Sam's heartbeat to fill the room.

The doctor runs the wand over the bottom of my protruding abdomen. There's a whooshing noise that sounds promising. "Is that Sam's heartbeat?" Graham asks, giving my hand a squeeze.

"No. That's Rachael's. The baby's heartbeat sounds more like a thud, thud." She moves the wand back and forth over my stomach, looking for the elusive sound. The longer it takes, the tighter I grip Graham's hand.

I glance up and see that he's beginning to look worried also. He's no longer smiling and his shoulders are tight. It feels like hours, but I'm sure that she's only been searching for the heartbeat for a few minutes.

"Everything okay?" Graham asks as a passive look masks his face, but the way his voice cracks at the end of the question tells me he's anything but. I don't have to see his face again to know that he's anxious. His return grip on my hand borders on painful.

"I'm sure everything is fine. Let's just grab the ultrasound machine and make sure." Doctor White walks to the corner and rolls the machine by the examining table.

I lie there in stunned silence. The pregnancy checklist begins scrolling through my brain like the stock quotes at the bottom of CNBC. I've been so nauseous. The doctor said that was a sign of a healthy pregnancy. I've watched my diet and tried to get enough rest. Caffeine hasn't touched my lips.

This can't be happening. For the first time in a long time, I close my eyes and pray. *Dear God, I've made some bad choices. For those, I'm sorry. But, I want this baby so much. We'll be good parents. Let him or her be okay, and I'll bring him to church every Sunday. I'll do anything. Just let this baby be healthy.*

Five minutes later, I get the most devastating news of my life. "No heartbeat."

***

The rest of the day is a blur of activity. We're forced to make horrible decisions and discuss choices that I wouldn't wish on my worst enemy. Graham tells everyone that will listen that I'm his number one priority and to do what's best for me.

He never lets go of my hand. He repeatedly reassures me that we're going to be okay. This is going to be okay. I want to scream that no, it's not going to be "okay." Our baby is gone. I'm not going to be a mom and you're not going to be a dad, but I'm too devastated to speak.

The reason that I left my beloved job is gone. And Graham will soon be gone also. There's no reason for him to be absent for the tour if we're no longer going to be parents. Sam was our future. Sam was who encouraged us to try so hard to make this work. Sam is gone.

We arrive back at Graham's house long after dark. I drop my bag and jacket by the front door and head straight to the couch. My legs are so heavy that I'm surprised that I can drag them and that they're still supporting me. As my head falls against the armrest, I'm quite sure that this is what near-death feels like.

My face is swollen from tears and a vicious headache pounds behind my eyes. I don't have enough energy to position my arms, so they rest haphazardly against the cushion. Graham picks up my legs and folds them on the couch. Next, he grabs a navy woolen blanket and tucks it around me. I would like to thank him, but the words are stuck in my throat.

He takes a seat on the floor next to me. His fingers comb through my strands of wild hair. "Today has been the worst day of my life," he states.

I stare blankly at him.

He continues, "And I have to leave tonight for Phoenix." He swallows hard and looks down. "I'm so damn sorry, Rach."

I'd like to comfort him, but my well is dry. I have nothing left to offer anyone, and I'm no more than a shell of a human being. My soul exited my body when I heard those terrible words—*no heartbeat*. I wish the world would stop turning and for time to stop so I could process today's tragedy. I want Graham and me to mourn together. Selfishly, I don't want the sun to shine or music to play. My baby is gone. I want the earth to cry with me.

"Caroline is on her way," he continues.

With that news, I lift my eyes. "Caroline's too busy. You shouldn't have called." My voice is flat, lifeless. There's no fight left in me.

"Of course I should have. She loves you. . ."

"She has her own family. She doesn't need my problems." I pull my knees to my chest.

The silence descends over both of us like a fog. What's there to say? Life is shitty. My heart aches for our loss. My eyes burn from all of the tears that I've shed today. A dull throbbing ache is present behind my left eye, and I honestly don't know if it's possible for me to put one foot in front of another to make it to bed.

But I'm doing well compared to Graham. Sure. From the outside, he appears fine. He looks as if he could use some sleep, and his usual bright eyes are a hazy grey. But where I look like a haggard mess, he still appears to be a model for Ralph Lauren. He's been such a rock today. God bless him, he asked the questions that I couldn't formulate. He made the decisions for me that I couldn't bear to make myself, and he signed the paperwork that I couldn't.

While I get to spend time grieving our loss, he has to put a smile on his face and entertain everyone in Phoenix that have shelled out their hard-earned dollars to see the Sons of Liberty, live. He has to keep going, and I don't know how that's possible.

"Let's get you showered before Caroline arrives," he says.

I'm too tired to respond, so I just shake my head.

"Pain? Do you need one of the pills?"

I shake my head again. "I just want to go to sleep."

He scoops me up in his arms, and I bury myself in his chest. Emotions wash over me again and tears slide down my cheeks as he carries me to his bedroom. How it's possible that I have any water left inside is really beyond me. These tears are not for our loss. I'm just overwhelmed with how thankful I am to have Graham here with me to deal with this. Thoughts that I could have done this alone make me feel shameful. If there was any doubt in my mind that Graham and I were more in lust than in love, they've vanished. This is love. This right here and right now. This man carrying me to bed without me asking because he knows that most of the time, I can walk beside him as an equal partner, but other times in a relationship that set of four footprints must become two.

He places me on the comforter while he folds the sheets back on the side of the bed that I slept on the other night. I crawl over to the pillow and slip under the blankets. I'm surrounded by the scent that is uniquely Graham, which brings a marginal degree of comfort.

"Need anything?" he asks, tucking the sheet under my chin.

Yes. I need you not to leave. I need you to hold me all night long and reassure me that one day we're going to be okay, even though I hate the world right now. That one day that we will smile again and maybe even laugh. The sun will shine and the pain in my chest will fade with time. Instead, I reply, "No. Go on. What time is your flight?"

"Colin booked Caroline on a private plane. I'm taking it to Phoenix," he says this nonchalantly, but I know that Graham, Colin and Caroline have gone to herculean efforts on my behalf to make this happen. Not to mention the cost. He missed his commercial flight long ago. "And before you say anything, Colin said to tell you to shut up."

A small smile turns up my lips. I can just hear him going into planning mode—making phone calls and barking orders. Colin isn't doing this for me or Graham. He's moved earth and sky for Caroline because, well, that's just what he does.

"There's a bit of my girl," Graham says as he runs his pointer finger over my mouth. I'm not smiling, but the pleasant thought has caused my frown to fade. "I'm leaving right after the show and flying to Oklahoma to pick up George. Then we'll be home. Should be back by noon on Sunday at the latest."

"Graham . . ." I begin to protest, but he leans down, kissing me, I assume to shut me up.

"You have to promise me that you're going to take the antibiotics and medicine if you're in pain. Caroline is a doctor. That's about the only reason why I'm leaving. Listen to her," he lectures. I don't point out that she's an orthopedic surgeon not a gynecologist.

A doorbell chimes, and Graham leaves the bedroom to answer it. I know how busy Caroline is, and I know how hard it is for her to get away. She runs a lab, is mom to three kids, and doesn't like to leave Colin. Her jumping on a plane and leaving all of that behind was a sacrifice, one that she made for me, and I love her desperately for it.

Caroline and Graham do a terrible job of whispering about me behind my back. I can't make out all of their conversation, but words like "silent," "traumatic," "worried," and "fragile" are clear. I want to yell at them to have the conversation in front of me, but I don't have enough energy to pick my head up, let alone tell either one of them that I don't appreciate their rude behavior.

Caroline walks into the bedroom looking like the angel that she is, even though I'm slightly annoyed with her. Her long hair is twisted up in some sort of messy knot on top of her head. She's wearing a baggy maroon sweater and jeans. I've always admired her effortless, bohemian style. "Hey chica," she says.

I scoot up in bed, leaning against the headboard. "Hi," I reply, biting my lip.

Then the crazy chemistry thing happens—the one where you've been such a part of each other's lives that no words need to be exchanged. It's where you live inside each other's head, and you're so grateful that you have the connection so you don't have to say the words out loud. Just a knowing look from her and I begin to sob.

She drops her suitcase and runs towards me, wrapping me in her arms. She holds me while any semblance of strength that I've clung to for Graham's sake collapses. Wails that I don't recognize as mine exit my body.

The only thing that she says is, "I've got you, babe." Only my best friend would know that they're exactly the words that I need to hear. Not "you're going to be okay," because right now I don't think that I'll ever be. Or "God, doesn't give you more than you can handle," because obviously, he does. She just allows me to melt and then scrapes me off the bed and later will reassemble the new version of Rachael.

At some point, I give into the exhaustion and fall asleep in her arms, surrounded by the comforting scent of Graham.

***

I wake the next morning—could be afternoon—to the smell of bacon. When I open my eyes, I feel happy and hopeful for about one-point-three seconds. Then, the realities of yesterday crash around me. My hand instinctively covers my pubic bone, but my baby isn't there to protect. Instead of getting out of bed and spending time with my best friend who has dropped everything to help me through this, I roll over and go back to sleep.

The next time that I emerge from the dark abyss, Caroline is on the phone talking to someone.

"I'm sorry, but she can't take a call at the moment. May I take your information, and she can call you back on Monday?" Caroline says.

"Wonderful. I'll let her know."

There's a faint stench of bacon that lingers in the air. I roll over and look at Graham's alarm clock. It's almost four. Wow. *I must have needed the sleep.* Scooting out of bed, I take care of my bathroom needs, avoiding looking in the mirror, and shuffle into the living room.

Caroline has her back to me. Her laptop is open and she's sitting at the bar, working, I guess. I don't want to bother her, so I turn around and go back to bed.

I'm not physically tired enough to sleep, but lying in the dark room, under the warm covers, feels right. Staring at the ceiling, I intentionally force my brain to think of nothing. My mind is empty. I note that the quiet and stillness of Graham's house has a faint ringing or maybe buzzing noise. Is it the sound that electronics make? Electricity surging through all the things that I thought that I needed before yesterday?

Now, all I want is morning sickness, a rounded abdomen, full breasts, and Graham.

"Whatcha thinkin' about?" Caroline asks, jarring me from my dark path.

"How when bad things happen, you're reminded of what's really important."

She walks over and sits down on the foot of the bed, crossing her legs. I bend my knees so she has room. "You feel like eating a late lunch? I made BLT sandwiches."

I shake my head and try to come up with something to say. "How are the kids?" That's normal conversation.

The blinds are closed, but light is still seeping through the slats. Enough light that I can see my best friend's face light up. "They're great. Ainsley is preparing for her dance recital. She plays the part of a ladybug. Colin's been working with her to 'think like a ladybug. How does a ladybug move?' You know me. I roll my eyes at his nonsense, but it's very cute to see." She smiles and shakes her head, as if admonishing the memory. "The twins are hell on wheels. Always getting banged up on something. Usually it's falling out of a tree. They caught frogs the other day and hid them in drawers in the kitchen. Every time I opened a cabinet or drawer, something was jumping out. I must have screamed a hundred times. I yelled for Colin. I don't think that the boys got the message that they shouldn't do it again because he was chastising them through tears of laughter."

My limbs relax into the pillow as Caroline regales me with stories. I know how hard Colin and she have worked to build this little slice of love and happiness. I also know all that both of them have sacrificed. It has paid off. One day, I want what they seem to have perfected.

She goes on and on, gushing about her family. I don't have to talk, which works for me, and I get caught up on all the details of Caroline's life. Her happiness is balm for my ragged, torn, threadbare soul.

"Okay. Enough about me. Why don't you take a shower, and I'll find us a good bottle of wine to drink until we're smashed."

That's my best friend in a nutshell. "No wine. Let's head straight for the tequila."

"Like how you think," she says, with a wink. "I'll go raid Graham's liquor cabinet."

With that, she leaps off the mattress and heads out of the bedroom. Tequila has always been our drink. As I've told her at least a hundred times, "When the going gets tough, the tough take shots of tequila."

After I shower, I check my phone for the first time. The missed calls from the White House don't even spark a bit of interest. Ignoring the voicemails, I head straight for my text messages.

Graham: *Reason #10,763 that MMA is better than boxing: Fighters go to the mat in takedowns. The great ones learn to turn this into an advantage and ultimately dominate their opponent from such a vulnerable position. That's you, Rachael. You are so strong. I love you, and I'll be home as soon as I can.*

I read his message a couple of times. I get what he's trying to communicate, and I love him for it. But this time, I don't know what the positive is in losing our baby. There's nothing good that can come out of this.

Instead of responding, I toss my phone back on charge. At the moment, I don't care whether or not I win our stupid texting game. It seems pointless anyway. But everything right now seems pointless. I'm also in no mood to talk to him. I don't need a pep talk or sayings like "the glass is half full." I want to get completely obliterated with my best friend.

Chapter Eighteen

Graham

"What the fuck?" Max growls as I walk into the hotel lobby bar, dropping my duffle next to an empty bar stool. Jazz music plays softly in the background of the dimly lit room. Jake barely looks up to acknowledge my presence and Max bounces in his seat like he's a three-year-old that needs to go to the restroom.

"You were supposed to be here seven hours ago," he lectures. "You do remember that you promised to return to the tour on Thursdays? I believe there was a rather loud conversation where we discussed this. Time was the ass crack of dawn." He pauses, as if he expects me to acknowledge his statement. I don't and decide that attempting to put holes through the thick wooden bar in front of me using only my eyes is a challenge that I'm willing to accept. "It was bad enough that you were missing today or yesterday's—fuck, I don't even know what time it is—meet and greet because of Rachael's doctor's appointment, but you also skipped our Friday night dinner with one of our biggest sponsors that you assured us you would be at." He draws in a deep breath to continue his verbal ass-kicking. "That one was fun to explain. Yes, Mr. Corporate Sponsor, Revere will be at the tour tomorrow. We know that you give us lots of dollars, but one of our members is too busy burying his head in . . ."

My hand slaps the bar hard enough that pain shoots to my shoulder. It doesn't bother traveling to my heart because that's just an empty hole.

The glasses near me rattle and bar patrons reach for them to ensure that a precious drop isn't wasted on the unclean surface as the bartender shoots me a warning look. He must assume that I'm about to start trouble. I raise my chin and nod in the universal sign that there are no problems here. Well, not problems that he has to concern himself with. He picks up a glass and runs a rag over it before placing it back on the shelf, but he doesn't stop glaring.

In different times, I would be insulted that he didn't offer to get me a drink, but well, today it's probably for the best.

I guess I got Max's attention because his mouth is open, but words have stopped vomiting out.

Jake picks his head up and looks at me as I would imagine one must stare at their alcoholic parent who once again didn't show up for their little league baseball game. *You can't make me feel worse.*

"We lost the baby." Like shards of glass, the words slice and cut my throat as I spit them out.

I don't want their sympathy, and I don't need their support. What I do need is to pretend that today was one of my many nightmares, wake myself, and not mention this horrible dream to anyone else. I need for this not to have happened to Rachael and me. This could be like one of those choose-your-own-adventure books that I used to check out of the library as a kid. Oops! I chose the shitty path that leads to heartbreak and despair. I'll just back up twenty pages and go down the road that leads to a healthy baby and a happy life.

Tomorrow, we have a live performance. I have to compartmentalize this loss and focus on making sure that the people who attend our show don't feel as if they wasted their hard-earned dollars. The show must go on, and all that. My brain knows that, but I have no clue how I'm going to convince my heart.

Max reaches out to touch my arm, but I jerk it back. The only touch that I need is Rachael's. "Look, man, I'm so sorry."

Standing up, I reach down and pick up my bag. "I've just had the worst day of my life, and I had to leave the only other human being on this planet who can sympathize with my situation at home." The guilt eats away at my insides. "I'm going to my hotel room and pretend to sleep while I look at the ceiling until I'm bored and then turn my stare to the wallpaper."

Max spits out the first syllable of what I think is another apology, but I hold up my hand. I've heard enough apologies to last me a lifetime. Jake's features have softened, but he doesn't say anything, which is a blessing.

These guys have been my ride-or-die brothers. We met when we were eighteen-year-old kids. We all have the same tattoos on our calves that we got together after completing our fraternity pledge year. I thought up until this point that as long as I had them in my life, I had everything that I needed. That's changed. I still need them, but Rachael has become more important.

***

"Revere . . . Revere . . . Graham," Hank yells. I got lost in my own head— again—which lately has been a scary fucking place to hang out. He's obviously been trying to get my attention for a while by the way that he's waving his arms over his head.

"What?" I ask, looking up from my phone. I was mindlessly scrolling through some political blog, not reading a single word.

"The guys are ready to record."

"Yeah. Okay. Give me a minute. I'll be there."

As I stand up, I feel every muscle and tendon in my body. It's Sunday, and we're hoping to record a couple of shows before I head back to D.C. I don't know the last time that I've slept more than a couple of hours. My eyes feel like kernels of sand are scratching my corneas. I took one look at my contacts this morning and laughed. Today is a glasses kind of day. Usually, I can go like this no problem. Sleep is something that I can do when I'm dead, but today—well, today? It's caught up with me.

Last night's show was a nice distraction from real life. I had a long talk with my soul and found a way to push through the heartache to give the people what they wanted. For the first time since we lost the baby, I didn't think about Rachael, or heartbeats, or futures, or stolen money, or a tour that's degrading around my ears. I didn't ponder what was next for me, or the pixie fairy who I had to abandon after the most devastating few hours of my life.

I drag my pathetic ass into the studio and pull up a rolling chair. "Let's do this," I declare to Max and Jake, with as much enthusiasm as I can muster.

"You look like hammered shit. Just go home." Max turns away from me, shaking his head.

"No. I'm good. I'm ready," I reassure my fellow Sons of Liberty as I slide the headphones over my ears.

I do a couple of tests with my voice while I adjust the controls, finding the right volume. Next, I grab my phone from the front pocket of my jeans, just in case Rachael or Caroline call, when Max yanks the earphones from my head. "Go home, fucker. We're recording without you."

My stomach plummets. I've never missed a show. We've aired reruns when the guys and I decided to take a vacation, but it's always been the three of us on air. Never a substitute. Never just two. "No," I state firmly as I reach for my cans.

He holds them out of my reach. His face is neutral. He doesn't look pissed. If anything, he looks resolved. "I'd rather that you spent the next three hours fixing the rat's nest that we're calling a tour than record another half-assed show."

My head drops. Max has always been the one that has called me on my bullshit.

He must sense my surrender because he says sympathetically, "You just lost your baby, man. Go take care of yourself and Rachael. We've got this." He gestures between Jake and himself. "What we can't do is fix the tour fuckups. That's your department." He sets the headphones down on the table in front of me. "Look. We can't keep going on like this. Someone is stealing money from us. Hank is at his wits end with the tour. He's clearly overwhelmed. Before every show, we're holding our breath to see if it's actually going to happen. We've never been on time once, and we're paying huge fines for it. The lighting and sound guys think our cues are suggestions instead of facts. We either need to fix the tour or cancel the rest of the shows."

His words are like a punch to the gut. I know it's bad. I just didn't realize that everyone knows that it's this bad.

Jake walks over to me and slaps my back. "This is an opportunity that we've worked hard for. I don't like seeing you this way. Take the time that you need to fix your shit at home. Then, join us again as the three Sons of Liberty, not the two and a quarter that we've got happening now. Make our tour what it should be. But you can't keep burning the candle at both ends."

"Thanks," I reply, hanging my head. Grabbing my bag, I rise to my feet and drag my pathetic ass out of the recording studio and to a waiting town car. I'm sick to my stomach. This is not what I had imagined success feeling like.

I toss my duffle into the trunk and sink into the black leather seat. "Airport, please."

***

Caroline must have been watching for me because as soon as George and I exit from the cab, my front door flies open and she meets me halfway between the curb and the house.

It always surprises me how tall she is. I guess I just assume that Caroline and Rachael are the same height, which is crazy. I can't imagine the two of them ever being able to share clothes in college.

"Hi," I greet her, as I bend down to unlatch George from his leash. He looks up with huge, round, thankful eyes. He runs around the yard, hot on the trail of some creature that dared to cross his domain.

"Good trip?" she asks. Her long hair is blowing in the breeze, and her face looks clean, fresh. She's pretty, even without makeup.

I don't bother to go into the details of just how shitty my life is, so I reply, "I could get used to flying on a private plane. Please thank Colin once again for me. George also appreciated having his own couch to lounge on."

She waves me off. I've gotten the impression from Rachael that Caroline is still not one hundred percent comfortable with Colin's wealth, acquired from his football career and smart investments. She told me once about how they've shielded their kids from Colin's former life. To them, Colin is just their dad—not the star athlete and former endorsement king that I watched on TV every Sunday. "We need to talk about Rachael."

"Does she know that I'm home?" I ask, nudging a stick with the tow of my loafer.

Caroline crosses her arms over her chest. "No, because she hasn't gotten out of bed yet today."

My watch says that it's three o'clock in the afternoon—not out of bed yet. That's not good. "Maybe her body just needs time to recover. I mean, it's only been two days." I'm making excuses for her. It's my job to defend her.

Caroline is having none of it. "I know my best friend. This is mental, not physical. Last night we got plowed on tequila."

My mouth falls open in shock. I've seen Rachael drink wine, but never tequila.

"It's our thing," Caroline says, once again waving me off like my reaction is silly. "Usually, we pull out tequila for important life chats. Last night, she just drank shot after shot. I tried to get her to talk, but she wouldn't. I asked her about the book that she's writing and got nothing. But, when I asked her about you, she said that you were only with her because of the baby."

Caroline leans forward and pokes me in the chest. I step back, surprised by her reaction. "Let me make one thing clear, Graham. If that's the case and you don't wish to have a relationship with her any more, then you're a real asshole. She is a wonderful, amazing, smart woman, who has maybe made some mistakes and not handled things well, but if you walk away from her, you're a fool."

Her fists are dug into her hips, and her eyes are slits. Frankly, she's a bit intimidating.

"Noted," I reply. "However, I'm not sure why Rachael would think that. I don't know what else I can do to show how much she means to me." I throw my hands up in defeat. A dam inside of me breaks. Maybe it's the exhaustion. Maybe it's that the candle that I've been burning at both ends has finally met in the middle. I don't know, but I can't take another second of her doubt.

I thought we had moved past this. It seemed as if her accepting that the magazine pics were a fabricated story finally gave me the reassurance that I needed that we were good. One step forward . . . two steps back.

I walk past Caroline, leaving her standing there open-mouthed. George runs in the house in front of me as I beeline for my bedroom. The door is shut. I throw it open and it bangs against the wall, ricocheting as I use my right hand to block it. I barely notice.

She's lying on my side of the bed with the covers pulled up to her nose. The blinds have been opened, I'm assuming by Caroline. I feel her presence behind me, but I don't turn around and acknowledge her. My blood is boiling. My eyes are trained on one person and one person only. It's the pixie lying in my bed, who *still* doesn't believe that I'm crazy in love with her.

"You. You get out of bed," I yell.

She pulls the covers down to her chest but doesn't respond. Her hair is pulled up into a tight knot on top of her head, and her eyes are red rimmed and swollen. Rachael doesn't look like any version of the fairy that she favors. No. She looks more like a limp dishrag.

I feel schizophrenic in the way my emotions keep shifting. Instead of yelling and demanding that she acknowledge all that I've done to prove to her how devoted I am to her, I crawl up the bed, leaning against the headboard and cradle her in my arms. She molds against me and I lean down, kissing her forehead, nose, and hair.

When I look up, Caroline is gone.

Rachael sobs into my chest. "I'm so sorry Graham. I'm so sorry that I couldn't carry our baby. You gave me one job and I failed." Her little body trembles in my arms as I clutch her to me even tighter.

"You didn't fail, baby," I try to soothe. "You didn't do anything wrong. Sometimes really shitty things happen, and we don't know why."

"We deserve happiness," she says. "Why us? Why, after all of our sacrifices, did we have to lose the baby? We didn't give enough, Graham . . ."

Fortunately, she doesn't finish the thought and I don't let her. I kiss her lips, silencing the nonsense that she is spewing. She wraps her arms around my neck and I hold her against me, hoping that she'll see just how wrong she is. I honestly don't know why terrible things happen to good people while others always seem to come out unscathed. Why did my sister have to get breast cancer? She did nothing wrong. Yet there she was, a mom with a young daughter facing her own mortality. In hindsight though, I can see how it pulled our family together. It wasn't just Kelly's fight. I was by her side, and our parents, and my niece. Her husband became the mom and dad, but he did it with grace and courage. He's a wonderful man and so devoted to his family. Would he have been this way without the diagnosis? Who knows?

After a long time, her tears subside and she stops shaking. I still hold her, not ready to end this connection.

Finally, she looks up at me with big, swollen eyes. "I have to use the restroom."

I laugh and it feels so damn good. She even gives me a little smirk. "I've learned that even when you're so dehydrated from crying that your mouth feels like sandpaper, you still have basic needs."

I think that might have been an attempt at a joke.

She slides off my lap, and I feel empty without her weight. I was holding and consoling her, right? Or was it the other way around? As she walks into the bathroom, I watch her petite hips move side to side. Even in my old college lacrosse T-shirt, she looks gorgeous.

At some point in the evening, we move from the bedroom to the couch. Caroline had left a note telling us goodbye and to call if we needed anything. I find some old horror flick on NetFlix and click play. Neither of us, I think, actually watches it. We just cling to each other, seeking solace from the raging storm of problems surrounding us.

***

The rest of Sunday and Monday were more of the same. It's Tuesday and the house feels like a morgue. Even George has noticed our solemn moods. I leash him up. "Hey, buddy, let's go for a jog."

He doesn't bother standing up and looks up at me with an expression that says "You've got to be kidding me."

I bend down and stroke his head. "Will you do it for me?"

George stands up and stretches his long black legs behind him before he reluctantly agrees that this is somewhat a good idea.

"Rach," I call. "George and I are going for a run."

She's lying on the couch, wrapped in my flannel plaid bathrobe that my mom bought for me when I went off to college. It swallows her, but she's comfortable in it so I leave her alone. Frankly, just the fact that she got out of bed this morning at an hour before noon is progress. Whatever Rachael drapes around her small frame might as well be an evening gown if it means that she's conscious for the morning hours.

"Okay," she replies flatly as she stares at another episode of *House Hunters*. How many do they play a day? I swear HGTV performs some sort of magic trick where they manage to cram three hundred and seventy-two episodes into one twenty-four hour period.

The front door closes behind George and I, and we turn west, heading for the park. Exercise is a byproduct of this outing. I really just want to talk to my mom without any danger of Rachael overhearing the conversation. I've reached the point where I need to call in the big guns—my wise, quirky and fabulous mother.

George and I run for about ten minutes before I spot a park bench that isn't occupied. It's in a somewhat obscured location, nestled between two cherry trees. Its chipped green paint with initials and names carved into it tells of better days, but there's something about the permanence of the scarred wood that I like. Yes. It's beaten up, but it's still functional. Its place of importance between these two trees—heavy with pink, red, and white blooms—makes it dignified and purposeful. I do something that I normally don't do—I pull out my cell phone and snap a picture of the scene.

As I'm taking my seat, I pull up the photo and make sure that the lens captured the colors and image as I'm seeing it now. After studying it for a few moments, I make it the background on my phone. I don't think of myself as an artist, but I've come to discover that I have a strong affinity for the outdoors. This is another moment that I've found solace in Mother Nature.

"Hi Mom," I reply when she answers the phone.

"Graham, honey, how are you?" Her voice isn't sappy or overly sympathetic. She's my mom. It's her "I'm worried about you, but I'm not judging or making you feel uncomfortable" voice. This is one of the many reasons that I adore her.

"Shitty." One word, but it's the best way that I know how to express my state of mind.

"It's only been a few days. Of course you're still struggling. How is Rachael?"

"Shittier."

She gives a rueful laugh. "Do you remember when Kelly was diagnosed with breast cancer?"

"What does Kelly being sick have to do with us losing the baby? Come on, Mom. I'm calling to hear your wise words. I don't need a more depressing trip down memory lane right now."

George walks over and sniffs a blossom that has fallen to the ground. He looks at it curiously, picks it up with his mouth and lies down at my feet.

As I'm opening my mouth to tell him to drop it, he spits it out and it rests about an inch past his nose. I bend down and stroke his back for a being such a good dog and not eating it.

My mom continues as if she hasn't heard a word that I said. "We were all so distraught over her diagnosis. I mean she just had become a mom. She was so young. As a family, we cried and spent the days and nights mourning the diagnosis." She pauses for a beat. "You remember, Graham. You were in D.C. interning for the presidential campaign. We talked every night on the phone. I saw a real change in you after that summer. I think it made us all face some of our worst fears."

I don't bother to tell my mom that my change happened before Kelly's diagnosis when a certain fairy named Rachael Early steamrolled my life.

"About five days after the diagnosis, I was over at Kelly's house, helping to pack her for the surgery. She looked like death warmed over—grey skin, lifeless hair, hollow cheeks and dead eyes. As you know, your sister doesn't leave the house without her full makeup." Boy, do I. I think we were late every Sunday for church because Kelly couldn't quite get her eye makeup right. "I looked at her and asked, 'Kelly, do you want to live?' She got so angry at me. She screamed at me, 'Of course I do.' Then, I replied, 'Well start acting like it.'"

That's my mom in a nutshell. She says the words that no one else is willing to say.

She laughs. "Kelly was so angry. She cried, and dramatically threw herself on the bed. After ten minutes of letting her scream at me, at the world and finally at herself, I drug her into the shower and made her wash her body. Then, I took her to the neighborhood spa and paid to get her hair fixed, nails painted and an hour massage. On the way home, she asked me why I did all of this when she was about to lose her left breast and her hair. I replied because we are not a family where we lie down and die. We fight, and when we do, we must look the part."

The sun is beginning to set behind the trees, which turns the normally pink blossoms to a Creamsicle orange. I run my hand through my hair. "Mom, where are you going with this? I need help with Rachael, not a trip down memory lane."

"I'm getting there, boy," she replies. "I believe that half the battle is attitude. It's okay to cry and scream and be mad at the world. You guys suffered a loss that is immeasurable, but you have to mourn while still moving forward. Even if it's something simple like making a goal to do one normal thing a day. For Kelly, it was getting up with her little girl every morning. No matter how sick she was or how miserable she felt, she made breakfast and watched cartoons every morning with your niece. Then, as she adjusted to everything, she found a new way of being a mom. Help

Rachael find her normal again."

"Thanks, Mom," I reply, not really sure that she helped me at all, but just hearing her voice is comfort enough.

We change the subject and I fill her in on the Sons of Liberty. In a couple of weeks, the tour will be in Houston. There are no words to express how excited I am to be home and for my family to catch a glimpse of what I do.

"Well, Mom, I should get back to Rachael. Thanks for everything. I love you," I tell her to end the conversation.

"Before you go, love, one thing. You've suffered a loss, too. Don't expect everything to be sunshine and roses so quickly. You both need time to heal. As long as you're moving forward."

And that's why I adore my mom. Lots of love mixed with a dose of reality. In a roundabout way, she gave me an idea. Funerals are one way that people mourn their loss and move forward. The ceremony is part of the beginning stages of healing for the loved ones. Rachael and I need to do something that tells the world that our baby mattered, and I think I know exactly how to do that.

***

"Where are you going?" Rachael asks as I pull a pair of old, tattered jeans over my hips.

It's Wednesday morning and Rachael made it out of bed before ten o'clock. Progress.

"I've got an errand to run, baby." She looks at me with those same sad eyes that make my chest too tight to expand. "I won't be long."

I walk over to where she's curled up on the couch and kiss the top of her head. "Call me if you need me."

Turning toward my dog that's positioned close to the couch as if he's guarding Rachael, "George," I instruct. "Take care of our girl." My words feel redundant.

He just sighs and rolls on his back—his way of begging for stomach scratches.

Walking towards the row of stores at the end of my street, I notice that it's beginning to warm up. The cherry blossoms are out, creating a rainstorm of pink buds as the wind catches the blooms. Spring is a beautiful time of year in the D.C. area.

I'm surrounded by renewal and rebirth, which contradicts the black mood at my house. Hopefully this is a way to bring some color to our tragedy.

When I reach my destination, I don't bother getting sidetracked. I head straight for the back of the store to find Frank. He's a surly guy with a wiry grey ponytail. We met at the dog park. He has a bulldog named Butch which George likes to play with.

"Graham," he acknowledges me without looking up from the plot of earth that his hands are submerged in.

"Morning, Frank," I reply. "I'm looking for a cherry tree to plant in my yard. You have any in stock?"

"They're in high demand this time of year, but I think I might still have one at the greenhouse. Could deliver it by five today."

"That works. I'll pay the cashier and leave my address with her."

Frank doesn't say anything further. Conversation is over. Strange guy. I think he gets along better with plants and animals than people.

When I arrive back home, neither Rachael nor George have moved. Rachael is staring blankly at HGTV and George is snoozing. I bypass both of them and head through the sliding glass doors to the backyard. Doing a quick survey, I find the perfect spot for our new tree. There's a sunny part of the yard near Rachael's office window.

Finding the shovel hiding with my infrequently used yard tools is not difficult. I carry it to the perfect location and dig a hole about three feet deep by three feet wide. The rich smell of earth fills my nose, and the soft skin on my hands stings with the fruit of my manual labor. My shoulders burn and my back aches. It's a good, therapeutic feeling as if I'm my sweating out my demons.

I realize while I'm in the middle of my dig that planting this tree will mean that I can never sell this house. It gives me pause for only a brief second. No. This feels right. I want to leave some mark on the world, acknowledging that Sam was real and loved and existed. I want something beautiful to bloom out of our loss.

"Graham," Rachael calls from the sliding glass door. "There's some guy here with a tree."

I slam my shovel into the ground near the hole and follow her into the house.

Frank is standing at the front door loving on George, who instantly recognized someone else who would pet him. "Meet you in the driveway," I call to Frank.

There's about a six foot tall cherry tree in a black pot sitting near my kitchen window.

"She's all yours," Frank says, shoving a piece of paper for me to sign towards me.

I sign my real name, which feels odd. Revere flies out of my pen easier these days. I shake his hand. "Thanks for the help. I appreciate it."

"You know, Graham," he begins and stops, as if he needs to collect his words. "I didn't know that you were one of the Sons of Liberty until someone at the dog park told me. But I'm just real proud to say that I knew you when. You're doing good, boy."

With that, Frank turns and walks towards his old, rusted pickup truck.

I shake my head. What a surreal moment.

Now, back to the task at hand. Planting the cherry tree.

I carry the tree through the back fence gate and rest it near the hole that I dug. Next, I walk into the house and ask Rachael to come outside and join me. She looks perplexed but walks outside without asking any questions.

I've been rehearsing in my head the words that I planned on using to convince her that planting this tree in Sam's memory is the right thing to do. Fortunately, I don't have to say a word. She spies the tree. Then her eyes track to the prepared hole and the location by her window. Rachael turns to me and buries her head against my chest, and her tears mix with my sweat-soaked shirt.

We hold each other, acknowledging silently what this tree means to both of us. It's a chance at life after our loss. The cherry blossoms will be a reminder that Sam was a part of us and very important, if for only eleven short weeks. Hopefully, they'll be a reminder that no matter what happens in our future that like the cherry tree, we survived the cold winter of death and came out on the other side as whole people.

"You ready for me to plant it?" I ask as I rub her back.

She looks up at me with large eyes. "Yes. And thank you for doing this." Her choked up words echo in my heart.

I use the shovel to knock the roots from the black container and place the tree in the hole. Rachael steps back and gives me direction on how the tree should rest in its home. A little turn to the right . . . now straighten it more . . .

When the tree is perfect in her eyes, I begin to fill in the dirt around the roots. Rachael gets on her hands and knees and packs the earth solidly around the base. We work silently, a perfect team without the need for verbal communication.

Once we have a rounded mound, I grab the hose and let Rachael nourish the tree with water. She painstakingly makes sure that it doesn't wash away the earth. She cleans the trunk and scrapes the soil from the base, exposing a bit of the roots.

The tree seems to have given her a purpose as well as a beautiful memorial to our baby. This was the perfect remembrance.

"Would you like to say a few words, Rach?" I ask, as I use my thumb to wipe a bit of soil from her cheek.

She looks up at me. "No words to be said. They'll just cheapen the moment. We both know how we feel and what this tree signifies. It's our whenever and wherever."

I scoop her up and carry her to the bedroom. *Yes, baby, whenever and wherever.*

***

"Can you hand me that shirt?" It's Thursday evening and I have to leave her again. She's sitting on the bed with the laptop resting against her legs.

"Sure," she replies, as she tosses me my blue and white striped dress shirt.

We haven't done much of anything for the last four days except watch movies, eat takeout, and snuggle on the couch. I've missed recording the radio show, but the mental break has been needed. Our loss still weighs heavy on my heart. I think that it always will, but my concern remains for Rachael. Her phone is still turned off and lying on the kitchen counter. She hasn't checked it once.

This is the first day that she has shown interest in her book. This morning, she got up before me and made coffee. When I walked into the kitchen, she was sitting at the kitchen table and had her notebook opened in front of her. She seemed to be writing. I turned around and went back to grab a shower and give her a few more minutes to finish her thoughts.

Today. Today has felt a little more normal.

Now we're in the bedroom preparing for me to leave again.

"What are you typing?" I ask, as I fold some tan slacks and place them in my duffle.

She peers over the screen and replies, "I'm doing some research."

"Research on what?" I grab three pairs of underwear out of the drawer and some navy socks.

"Do you honestly want to know?"

I turn around and toss my stuff in my bag, then walk over to her. She scoots over, giving me room next to her. I lean against her side, draping my arm over her shoulder. The words on the screen cause my breath to catch in my throat. The headline reads "Miscarriage: Now what?"

My eyes cut to the side, and she's biting down hard on her bottom lip. "What have you learned?" I decide to ask an open-ended question and see where this conversation leads. We haven't discussed it after her breakdown on Sunday. I know that she told the First Lady, because Caroline told me that she made the call before they hit the bottle of tequila. Caroline said that she was so poised. She listened to the conversation just long enough to know that she is okay.

"Well," she says, placing her laptop on the bed beside her. She takes a deep breath and then lets it out. "I've learned to listen to my body, and that it's okay if I feel like I'm emotionally all over the map. That some women need months to recover mentally and physically while others bounce back quickly. I found out that miscarriages are much more common than I realized, and it doesn't mean that we can't have a healthy baby." She pauses and swallows hard. "But most of all, I've read that I have to forgive myself. But that might take some time."

I turn to face her, expecting that she will need comfort and reassurance that losing the baby wasn't her fault. Instead, I see the Rachael that touched my heart so many years ago when I was a young college graduate and in desperate need of direction. She has a determined aura about her. Strong. Beautiful. I brush a piece of hair behind her ear and raise her chin with my finger so she's staring me in the eyes. "Every morning I marvel that I can love you more than when I fell asleep the night before. But, right now, my heart is swollen with so much love and pride that you are mine. You, Rachael Early, are the most amazing woman ever." I kiss the tip of her nose. "Thank you for being you."

For the first time since we lost the baby, she smiles. Her cheeks are flushed red like candy apples. Her eyes twinkle, and my heart does funny things inside of my chest. "Go. Leave. I want to savor this moment before you say something to screw it up."

I smirk and kiss her goodbye without speaking. Don't want to ruin whatever emotion made her smile like that.

***

I jerk awake, flailing for my phone in the unfamiliar hotel room. "Hello?" I answer, not recognizing the number. Normally I would send it to voicemail, but it's after midnight. Usually the only time the phone rings this late is because someone died or is in jail.

Bryan, our accountant, clears his throat. "Sorry to call so late, Graham, but well, we have a problem."

I flip on the bedside table lamp in the hotel, as if the light will help me listen better, and slide my glasses on. "I'm all ears."

"Well, we've completed the audit on the bank accounts and it seems to be far worse than we thought."

"Wonderful," I reply sarcastically, as I sit on the edge of the bed and slip my glasses on. For some reason, I need my glasses to take a late-night call.

"Best guess is that someone has been siphoning off funds from the accounts for a while. It's not huge amounts. Fifty dollars on a five thousand dollar deposit here, or five hundred dollars on an eight thousand dollar deposit there. They're small amounts that add up to a huge theft."

I run my hand through my hair. "We already knew this, right? You told me a couple of weeks ago."

"Yes. That's true, but we've just discovered that it's happened in more than one account. See, we set you up with multiple checking accounts. One for payroll, one for expenses, one for venue fees, etc. Whoever is doing this has access to all the accounts."

My stomach churns with acid. There are only four of us who have access to all the accounts. That's Max, Jake, Hank and myself. "Okay. Thanks. I'll take care of this first thing in the morning."

I hang up, feeling the sick ache of dread. Max and Jake might as well be blood. They wouldn't take a beer out of the fridge without asking. It has to be Hank, but I can't just come out and accuse him of being a no-good, stealing, rat bastard. I need proof. He's under contract. I can't fire him without having to pay it out, and frankly, there's not enough money in all the accounts combined to write him a check.

Maybe he knows this. Maybe that's why he's stealing. He knows that we're too much in the red to do anything about his thievery.

But, it's a crime. If I can gather enough evidence, then I can turn him over to the police and let them deal with him.

I'm too wound up now to sleep. I text the guys to see if anyone is awake and wait patiently while no one responds. Instead of texting Veronica to see if she wants a drink—I've stepped in that pile—I grab my laptop and place it on the glass desk.

While it turns on, I open the mini-refrigerator that's built into the dresser and peruse my liquor choices. There's a mini bottle of bourbon.

Perfect! I fix a glass and carry it to the desk.

I open a blank document and begin creating a procedure notebook for our tour. The ideas flow so easily from my brain, through my fingers and ultimately the computer screen. It's like placing the words on paper relieves my agitated mind. Yes. This is what needed to happen. We now all have a document that we're held accountable to.

Late into the night or early morning, I crawl into bed, feeling for the first time since the tour began that I might actually have a handle on what's going on.

***

"What needs to happen is for me to rejoin this tour full time," I tell the faces surrounding me. It's eight o'clock in the morning on the day of our show. Max, Jake, Hank and I are having coffee at the Starbucks in the hotel lobby.

I chose the location because the tables are small. I wanted to be very close to everybody when I revealed the depths of the theft. I wanted to read the looks on their faces. Max and Jake looked shocked. Hank looked nervous, but of course, that's not enough proof to fire him and then send him to jail.

"So what's the next step?" Max asks.

"Well, I created a handbook of sorts for this tour. Maybe call it a code of conduct. I sent it over to the closest print shop this morning. I'm requiring everyone on our payroll to read it, sign it and it's what we're going to use to hold everyone accountable for their actions." I pick up my paper cup and take a sip. "Then I'm going to fire their ass if they screw up."

Max's cheek rises in a smirk. "That's the Graham that I know and love."

This feels good. This feels real, and I love being back in charge of my tour—my Sons of Liberty. "I have a few things to finish sorting out back in D.C., but I plan on being back on tour full-time by the end of the week."

Jake reaches across the quaint table and gives me a fist bump. "Graham's back," but it feels forced as if he doesn't quite believe that I am.

What the loss of our baby taught me is that life is precious. Each day is not guaranteed. We've been given an opportunity that most people only dream of. Here we've turned my little idea over beers at a local Irish bar into an opportunity for us to change the way our nation's government is run. This is our time—the Sons of Liberty's time—and we must seize it.

Our meeting concludes with little fanfare. The guys and I have a meet-and-greet in an hour for the local sponsors. Hank? Well, Hank has an actual job to do—to maybe get our show started on time for once, while robbing us blind.

***

"Shit! Did you hear that crowd? We were on fire," Max exclaims in excitement after we're back in the dressing room.

It felt good. Damn good. We were all on the same page, firing on all cylinders.

"That was your best show yet," Marissa congratulates us as she wraps her arms around Max's waist. Marissa doesn't care that her man is a wet, sticky mess with crazy, wild hair. By the end of a show, Max resembles Sideshow Bob. His loud shirts cling to his fit physique. I'm a bit envious that his girl is here to congratulate him. A pang of sadness hits me, but I dismiss it quickly. I've learned to enjoy these brief moments of bliss for what they are.

All three of us are drenched in sweat. If we'd been thinking, we would have scheduled the northern states for the summer. Instead, it's the end of April and we're in Lubbock, Texas.

"God, the adlibbing was great," Jake chimes in, as he opens a bottle of water and pours it over his head. He looks as if he should be selling shampoo by the way he shakes the droplets from his long, floppy hair. "Did you hear the crowd when we went off script? They loved it."

I smile. These guys are so enamored with what we do. It makes me feel awesome that my idea has created this opportunity for the three of us to be business partners. "What about when you drew the comparison to all the presidential candidates using campaign funds as a twelve-month branding campaign?" I turn towards Jake. "Brilliant."

Jake beams. "I'm too pumped to go back to the hotel. Let's party. Like college. Hit up a club."

A female voice behind me says, "That sounds like fun."

I turn and see Veronica standing there. She's ever the temptress. Long, black flowing locks, clear blue eyes and clothes purchased from the pre-teen department. "We haven't all been out together in a long time."

Before anyone can object, Max has his phone out and has scheduled a car to take us to the local hotspot.

Two hours later, we're in a bar that is playing the hell out of country, pop and dance tunes on rotation by a half-assed DJ at best. Who cares? Max, Jake and I are partying like old times. When Marissa and Veronica went to the restroom about fifteen minutes ago, Max purchased a bottle of Fireball Whiskey. Tonight is going to be ugly.

"Did you see that stripper's ass tonight?" Jake asks, as he leans against the wood railing surrounding the dance floor.

"The one whose ass looked like two tiny piglets making love in a thong?" Max replies with a dreamy look in his eyes. He pretends to squeeze the imaginary behind and we all laugh.

"That's the one. Butt implants or good genes?"

Max holds his shot glass up, "God thanking us for being male."

I laugh as we all three toast fine asses. "How's Rachael's ass?" Max yells over the blaring bass.

"Her ass is much better," I shout back. *Much* might be a bit of an overstatement. I feel like I should cross my fingers behind my back, as if I'm six again. I haven't begun to discuss with Rachael the idea of her joining me on tour, and I just promised the guys this morning that I would be. I slam a shot of Fireball, hoping that it will make my dreams a reality.

"Will her ass be associated with the likes of us?" Max asks, motioning to all three of us.

I lie through my teeth, "Why not? She's ready to be a part of the Sons of Liberty."

I don't miss Max's frown, but I ignore it and pour us all another round.

It's not a total lie. Since the day in the car that I forced her to give me her opinion, not the White House's spin, she's been more forthcoming with discussing politics, which makes me hard. Smart and beautiful—she's a deadly combination. She also loved the idea of us backing candidates for more high-profile positions that have proven themselves already. I've just never come right out and asked her if she wants to play with the Sons of Liberty. She'd make a great CEO. *That would make her my boss? It would be Rach's job to take care of me.* It's a novel thought, one that I think I'm okay with.

Veronica and Marissa stop by our table long enough to do a shot and then head for the dance floor. The bar is packed tonight. Bodies are pushed tightly together and the smell of sweat and sex permeates the air. This feels like college—and damn it's awesome to feel normal again.

We've been recognized a ton, but the fans are being so respectful, only asking for a handshake or a high five, and someone even bought us a round of beers.

"Care to dance?" a female voice whispers in my ear. Her hot breath sends involuntary shivers down my spine.

I turn around a see a pretty, brown-eyed girl with long dark hair. She's probably in her early twenties and a student at Texas Tech. Her shirt leaves little to the imagination and her cut-off, fringed, shorts, make her legs look a mile long. Before Rachael, this girl was my type. Young, tan, with big tits.

Laughing, I reply, "No thanks," and turn back to my beer.

She presses her large boobs against my back as her hands make their way south. "Fine. We can skip the dance and just head straight back to your hotel room."

Oh! This girl was definitely my type. I turn back around and place my hands on her shoulders moving her back. "Not interested."

Her bright red lips turn down to pout and she crosses her arms over her chest, pushing her boobs up to her chin. "I don't take no for an answer." Then she does something that five years ago would have had me in a bathroom stall with her braced against the door. She pulls her breast out of the top her shirt and runs her long pink tongue around her light tan nipple.

I'm blaming it on the Fireball Whiskey, but I laugh. Not a chuckle or a smirk—I laugh out loud at how ridiculous this is. She stops paying attention to her tit and hauls back, slapping me across the face.

It's so sudden that it takes a moment for the sting from the slap to replace the shock of her actions. Reaching up, I feel my inflamed cheek. "What the fuck?" I yell.

She turns and stomps off, disappearing in the crowd.

The guys are looking at me like "Oh shit! What's he going to do next?" Instead of letting her ruin our otherwise fun night, I ignore the situation. "So what do you think about our thief?"

Apparently, I stepped from one bad situation to another. Max and Jake cut their eyes toward each other and then look at me. "Our problem is not the thief," Jake says. "I mean, it is the thief. Absolutely, it is, but our bigger problem is you."

I look around to make sure that I heard him right. Max is the confrontational one. Jake is, well, Jake. He's laidback. He doesn't talk a lot. He is our peace maker.

"My absence is more damning to this tour than a thief who is robbing us blind?" I said that I would be back on the tour full time. Why are we still discussing the past? I reassured them that I was going to fix everything. I thought the conversation that we had over breakfast was quite productive. Jake did seem a bit bothered, but hell, so am I. Our tour manager is stealing from us. I don't think we can be back in a good place until the bastard is out of our lives. But, I thought the three of us were united again. Apparently the air has not been completely cleared.

"Yeah. Yeah it is," he says, running his hand through his floppy, wavy hair. "Look, I don't want to ruin our evening or anything, but you're the leader. The CEO of Sons of Liberty. Sure, Max has the loudest mouth, but you're the one who was supposed to sail this ship. I get why you've taken a leave of absence. I'm so sorry that you guys lost the baby, but in a selfish way I'm glad that you can once again focus on us."

His words sting much more than the crazy bitch's slap. His words are an acid burn to my soul. "Shit, man, what else do you want from me? I get that the tour has faltered without me around, but I told you this morning that I'll be back full-time." I run my hand through my hair in frustration. "You can't mean that you think that us losing the baby is a good thing."

Jake takes a shot of the Fireball and replies, "Every damn word of it I mean." He slams down his glass and looks me in the eyes. "I hate that you guys lost the baby, and I'm sorry to see you upset. But I'm glad that we can become your priority again." He gestures around us. "We've got such a good thing going here. Do you even know that CNN said this morning that we might be the single deciding factor in this year's presidential election? When's the last time that you combed through our Betsy Ross leads? You've been so consumed with Rachael that you've checked out of politics. Your commentary is shit. You're recycling the same garbage that the cable talk shows spew. You've lost your edge. You've lost what makes you Revere and it's really shit to see." Jake's voice becomes softer. "Yes, we've had a good weekend. Bits of old Revere were present tonight, but I need all of you. I need you firing on all cylinders. You're the glue that makes this work. When you come back, come back and be Revere."

He throws down two twenties on the table and turns to leave. I grasp his arm, feeling like I've been gut punched. "I'm sorry that you feel that way. I said this morning that I'll be back soon."

His eyes are filled with pity. "And I want to believe you, man, I really do. Tonight was a taste of how good we can be. I want you not only here physically, but I want you mentally dialed in. I want what we had tonight every damn day." He shakes his head and walks towards the exit.

I turn back and look at Max. He says, "hurts more when it comes from the strong, silent type doesn't it?"

Staring mindlessly at the dance floor, I replay Jake's words over and over again in my mind. He's right. I know he's right. Max knows that he's right. I haven't been doing my research. Yes. I might have sat in front of my laptop and stared at a screen, but Rachael has been my priority. Hell, his accusation that I've been regurgitating cable news was kind. I haven't really even turned it on in weeks. I guess I thought that no one had noticed. Apparently, everyone has.

I reach behind me and grab a bar stool, pulling it to the table. Sinking down on it, I step inside the black hole of doubt. Can I recover? Have I thrown the Sons of Liberty away for Rachael? Maybe I can't divide my focus. Maybe I can either have the Sons of Liberty or Rachael, but not both. The thought is so depressing that the whiskey sours in my stomach.

Max's slap on my shoulder pulls me out of my own head. I look up as he shoves another shot of Fireball Whiskey at me. "Drink this."

We toast and down our shots. "You've got a great resource lying naked in your bed. She's only one of the greatest political strategists of our time, and she ran the White House. She might, just might, be able to throw the Sons of Liberty a bone."

Hearing Max talk so positively about Rachael again goes a long way to loosening the knot in my chest. He's right. I've gotten so lost in our world that I forgot just who Rachael Early is. Yes, she's who I want to spend the rest of my life with, but she's also the person who inspired the Sons of Liberty. She was my muse, who kept me focused on my goal. She's also a wealth of knowledge and skills, and Max is right. She's lying naked in my bed. Time to go home and get my girl . . .

Chapter Nineteen

Rachael

It feels surreal to walk these halls again. It hasn't been that long since the White House employees and interns lined the walls, clapping as I exited for the last time as White House Chief of Staff.

I'm not sure that I recognize that girl anymore. She was deathly afraid of the future—scared of becoming a partner to Graham, and a mother. She was unsure of everything.

Now, the girl who approaches the President's private office is changed in ways that she hasn't come to fully recognize yet. She'd trade everything that she could to still be expecting a baby, to be by Graham's side with a giant black Lab as her constant companion in a tin can in the middle of somewhere in the United States.

The secret service agents that lurk in the background of the White House each greet me with smiles. It feels right to be somewhere familiar. Nothing has been constant since I left this office.

I've spent a lot of time since Graham has been gone meditating on what's next for me—always the planner. I even ventured into my new closet and office, and spent some time trying out my desk. At first the idea of continuing with *Anything, But Not Everything* seemed hollow in light of losing the baby. Sam was my happily ever after. Sam was how I planned to end the book on a cheery, upbeat note. Success! See, world, I managed to have it all. I got the fantastically spectacular career and the baby that I've just recently dreamed of having, as well as the super-cute boy. Well, my happy ending isn't happy. My conclusion is no longer the same. I have no way to end my story.

The cherry tree blooming outside my office window has been a source of calm for me. And I love Graham so much more than I even thought possible for coming up with such an amazing tribute to Sam.

After hours upon hours of staring at the physical reminder of the life that we created, I came to the conclusion that I have to be my own happily ever after. It will not be the same joy as the idea of becoming a mother has brought to me, but I owe it to Sam to keep going. I have to. It's my tribute to the life that we created together and the journey my pregnancy has taken us on.

Today has been the first decent day that I've had. I found some hope that one day I will be able to move on—never the same and always with a scar on my heart—but Graham and I will find joy again.

Then, like things seem to happen in my life, I received a call from Evan this morning. He had been asked by President Jones to extend me a part-time job offer. The President wants to bring me on as an advisor. Apparently he misses our evening conversations and strategy sessions. The job pays well. It means being back at the beck and call of the White House. If President Jones needs me, I drop what I'm doing and take his call or race to his office. It would also give me the flexibility to continue working on my book while having a steady stream of money being deposited in the bank. Those are good things. My savings account is still somewhat padded because I haven't had much in the way of expenses, but I can't expect Graham to keep paying for everything.

We've never discussed our finances. I assume that Graham's radio show contract is what he uses to pay his bills. He certainly spends money. The truck and The Cougar couldn't have been cheap, and then he had it retrofitted with his recording studio equipment.

However, I've seen the magazine cover that Graham thought by leaving in his studio I would miss. I hadn't been spying per se, I just happened to be looking for something when I'd gotten up before Graham the morning that we'd left to come back to D.C. I was curious what had kept him up late. That was when I'd seen the headline. My stomach had dropped, and I'd known it was my fault.

"Miss Early," the President's weekend secretary greets me warmly. "Your absence has been noticed."

"Thank you, Regina."

She's a kind woman that's in her fifties and has served the President for as long as I have—well, I guess she's now been with him longer.

"He's ready for you. Would you like some coffee or tea?"

"You know, coffee would be great."

She smiles and turns to enter a small kitchenette near the President's office. Regina doesn't ask how I take my coffee, but it's perfect as usual.

I thank her and enter the space where I've spent most of my evenings for the past seven years. The President is sitting in his spot on the peacock blue sofa with a manila folder in his lap. As usual, I scan his hands to check for any signs of tremble. Fortunately, they look steady. The medicine must be doing the trick.

He's dressed casually in a tan pair of slacks and a pale yellow sweater. Today, he doesn't look as aged as he has in the past. Maybe Shelby and he enjoyed a rare private evening of movie watching.

Leaning against the doorjamb, I wait for him to invite me in. It doesn't take long. "Rachael." He beams. "Come have a seat."

Because I'm a creature of habit, I take the same chair that I used to sit in every evening. Normally, my bag would rest at my feet, filled with the items that we needed to discuss. Today, it's just my purse, and it holds nothing relevant to the President. The thought simultaneously makes me sad and relieved.

The President doesn't keep me waiting. "First of all, I'm sorry for your loss. Not that I'm going to pretend to know what it feels like, but please know that you are in my and Shelby's prayers."

I nod and take a sip of my coffee.

"Before I discuss the position that I had Evan call you about, I want to talk about you." I must let my face betray my unease, because he chuckles.

"Calm down. After our last visit you left me in the dark on certain areas of your life. I care about you personally, but I need to know before I offer you this job that you are focused and available."

In my head, warning bells sound. He's wanting an update on my personal life. President Jones is going to ask if I'm still with the baby's father. How do I answer that question? I certainly don't doubt Graham's commitment, but he's going to rejoin the tour full-time, and I'm not sure where that exactly leaves me.

Do I want to tour with him, focused on completing my book? There's a part of me that screams that it feels weak and dependent to follow a man. Then I ask myself the question—do I want to go days and probably weeks without seeing him? I know that that's not possible. Now that Graham and I have spent so much time together, the thought of not seeing him every day makes me already miss him.

"What have you spent your time doing since you've left the White House?" He crosses his legs and the image fills my head of him as a psychiatrist, probing my brain to see if I'm mentally fit.

You're losing it, Rachael. Just answer his question.

"Well, let's see. I spent the days before I lost the baby riding in a truck with a boy and his dog that pulled a travel-trailer called The Cougar. We ate in roadside diners and slept at campground sites. I did laundry at a washeteria." I pause for a second and study the expression on his face. His eyes are wide and his forehead is slightly wrinkled. I may have just shocked the President of the United States. "Oh. And we were almost eaten by a meth head in Oklahoma." I throw that tidbit in just for shock value.

He nods and is silent.

I don't think that there's any need to mention what I've been doing since we lost Sam. Lying on the couch and planting a tree aren't nearly as shocking.

I guess when he finally recovers from my story, he replies, "And you did all of that why?"

My cheeks pull up into a face-splitting grin. "Because I am head over heels in love with a boy."

"Best reason that I've heard." He leans forward, as if this story is getting better by the moment. "And the boy is?"

I take a sip of my coffee as a stall tactic. I'm going to tell him. I'm not ashamed of the man whom I love, and I find myself wanting to broadcast it to the world. Revere is just a fraction of who Graham Jackson is, and I hope that the President can recognize that.

Blue and orange flames dance in the beautifully sculpted fireplace. There's something so relaxing about a fire. I think of roasting s'mores with Caroline, Colin and their crew. Fires apparently also make me bold. "You know him. He's been to the White House a couple of times, and even been to your screening room for fight night. In fact, that's how I met him."

I pause, waiting for President Jones to make the connection. When he does, he shakes his head and looks away. His reaction is puzzling to me, so I ask, "No congratulations?"

He uncrosses his legs and leans forward with his elbows resting on his knees. His head moves back and forth, and I get the impression that he is disappointed in me. Anger tries to flare in my belly, but I tamper it. This man has been the biggest influence in my life. I owe it to him to reserve judgement until he has said what he needs to say.

"I was hoping it was Evan."

My hands slap over my mouth to keep the laughter at bay. "Evan. As in Evan Atkins? Are you kidding me? Why? Why would you assume him?"

He looks chagrinned. "Well, you two have a good friendship, and I assumed that you were resigning because it would look bad that the White House Chief of Staff was sleeping the White House Press Secretary." He has an embarrassed smile, complete with flushed cheeks. "Boy, was I wrong." Then he pauses. "Graham Jackson, really?"

"Really." Before he can interject, I continue. "Before I get the lecture, trust me when I say that I've warred with myself about the content of his shows. I'm not one hundred percent on board with what he's doing, but I love him as a human being. It makes it easy to overlook locker-room humor when you can reconcile that it's just a stage persona. He's a good man and treats me like I deserve to be treated." I don't mention the little refrigerator incident.

He holds his hands up in surrender. "You're happy? I'm happy." Then he shifts uncomfortably in his chair. "I know that this is a terrible question to ask just a week after losing the baby, but the pregnancy was unplanned?"

All joy and happiness exits the room in a whoosh. It's replaced by melancholy and angst. I stare at the Oriental rug that has been my mental escape for the past seven years. This is actually a question that I've toyed with over the last week. I'm a planner, and as a planner I'm always looking towards the future, trying to do less so.

After a bit, I swallow hard and reply, "I believe it would be a disgrace to the memory of the baby that we lost not to try again. However, as Graham told me once, I need time and space before that can happen again. But, yes, Mr. President, I do want to have another child one day."

He seems satisfied with my answers. Our conversation moves from personal to professional as he outlines the job responsibilities of being an advisor. I tell him that I will give it careful consideration and let him know in a couple of days.

***

I, Rachael Early, did something today that I've not down in ages—if ever. I prepared a meal for Graham and me, and not just something simple like an omelet. No takeout. No sandwiches. No boxed meals. I went to the butcher and purchased two lovely steaks. Next, I went to the fresh vegetable and fruit stand and bought a head of cauliflower, apples, tomatoes, and salad fixings. Graham's neighborhood is nice. George and I enjoyed our walk and just getting out of the house for a few hours.

Hopefully dinner tonight will be a congratulations of sorts. Graham doesn't have to worry about me any longer and can rejoin his tour full-time, and I'm employed. George and I can remain here in D.C. and I'll fly out to visit Graham on tour when the White House isn't needing me. My income can help relieve any pressure that he feels to support me, and his focus can be on fixing and rebuilding the Sons of Liberty tour. It seems pretty darn ideal.

I've showered, put on makeup, fixed my hair in one of my signature knots and slipped on a casual dress that's figure skimming and makes me feel pretty. For the first time since we lost the baby, I look a bit like me again. This is part of the façade. Fake it until you make it. You look the part until you can play it.

But my happiness isn't completely faked. Today is a better day.

"Hi honey. I'm home," Graham yells, as I hear the front door open. George, who has been resting since our morning trip for groceries, leaps to his feet and lumbers to greet Graham. I follow behind, not wanting to steal George's thunder.

Graham looks gorgeous—dark denim jeans, a grey sweater and a navy blue baseball hat. The sweater isn't tight, but it skims his muscular chest in a way that makes me jealous of the cashmere material. I remind myself that, much to my chagrin, we have five more days before we can be sexually active again.

He drops to his knees and gives George the attention that he requires, but he doesn't take his eyes from mine. "Rachael, you look gorgeous— radiant."

"Thank you." I blush.

He stands up and wraps me in his arms, taking me back in a deep dip and planting a lover's kiss on my lips. "I was a bit worried about you, but I'm glad to see that you're feeling better." He backtracks. "I mean, you seem to be. How are you?"

"Today I just decided that I had to find my new normal." His brows forming a *V*. "It's what Caroline always says. When something life-changing happens it's stressful, whether it's a good change or bad. Anyway, she always says that you have to give up trying to feel the way you felt before the event and focus on finding a new routine—a new normal."

"Makes sense. I know someone else who also preaches that advice," he says, pulling me into a tight embrace. I listen to the *thud, thud* of his heartbeat, grateful to have him, and grateful that he's a good enough man to have forgiven me for all of the hurt that I've caused.

"What smells so damn good?" he asks, after a bit.

I look up at him and don't have to fake my smile. "Dinner."

"You cooked?" he asks, with a cocked brow.

"Don't act so surprised. Just because the pots and pans in my old house went unused doesn't mean that I don't know to prepare food. I did make you an omelet. Remember?"

I take his hand and lead him through the living room and into the kitchen. I've set the table with Graham's white dishes and have fresh-cut spring flowers arranged in a beer mug, it was the only vase that I could find, and now it's resting in the center of the table. I cut three small branches of flowers off the cherry tree and used them as the focal piece for the flower arrangement. Two lit candles flank the glass. "Sit down," I order, as I pull out his chair.

He does, but has a perplexed look on his face. "You did all of this for me?"

"Nope. George." I don't miss a beat. "What can I fix you to drink?"

"Wine would work, if we have any." He places the cloth napkin that I purchased for this occasion across his lap. "Seriously, what's going on?"

I grab the bottle of Chilean Malbec that I found this morning at the market and pour us each a glass. "I have some exciting news to share, but not now. Let me plate dinner." I flit around his kitchen as if I own the place. "Tell me about the show."

While I finish broiling the steaks and making our salads, Graham shares news about the tour and adds a very interesting story about a girl who hit on him at a club. The pangs of jealousy in my chest don't go unnoticed. Briefly, I wonder if a wedding ring would keep the girls in their place, but I dismiss that thought immediately.

I know at some point we're going to have to discuss what happens to The Cougar and truck. Because I'm trying to not look too far in the future, I push that thought away also.

"Sounds like an interesting couple of days." I place the salad in front of Graham and take my own seat next to him. He reaches over and grabs my hand, placing our interlaced fingers in his lap. He chooses to grasp his fork with his left hand and eat that way. I don't complain.

We eat in silence, except for Graham's utterances of how good his salad tastes. It's a tad overkill. It's spinach, kale and lettuce with a lemon vinaigrette dressing. It's not spectacular, although, the fresh tomatoes are rather yummy.

When we're finished, I pick up both of our plates and take them to the sink. "What's the next course, Chef Early?"

I giggle at his dumb joke. "Steaks, cauliflower mashed, and stewed apples."

"My stomach growled. Did you hear it?" He jokes—I think.

I top off his wine glass and mine, and rest the bottle on the table.

He takes a sip, and asks, "What's your exciting news? Do you have a publisher?"

I tuck my hair behind my ears as I place his plate in front of him. My eyes lock with his and the chemistry between us is palpable. I don't know how it's possible to crave someone as much as I long for him. Before November, I would have said that our energy was something invented by Hollywood to sell movie tickets, but it's real. There are moments when I'm sure that the pull can be physically seen.

He grabs my hips, and looks up at me with those heavy-lidded bedroom eyes. I know what's on his mind because it's the same thing on mine. His need to own me, and my desire to let him is like adding gasoline to a forest fire. I bend down, for a pleasant change, and let him make love to my mouth. His tongue shows me what he wants to do to my body, and I reciprocate. My ass is cupped in his hands and I moan in appreciation of the massage.

"Dinner," I remind him, as he kisses down my neck.

"Fuck food," he replies, with a nip to my collarbone.

"Five more days." I gently wiggle out of his grasp.

"Five more days," he repeats, and looks down with pleading eyes at the straining bulge in his pants.

I grab my plate of food from the counter and join him at the table.

"Distract me from my nefarious thoughts. Exciting news?" he asks as he cuts into his steak. I wasn't sure how he liked his steak prepared, so I went with medium. Apparently, according to the moans of appreciation, I chose correctly. "This is fantastic, baby."

I try the cauliflower mash. It's really tasty. Thank you to Google and some nice lady who shared her favorite recipe on a blog, because until today, I could only order it from the corner restaurant. "I had a meeting with the President today to discuss an advisory role in the administration."

I look up from my steak, expecting to see Graham's eyes shining blue with pride, and a huge smile of happiness on his face. Instead, he looks as if I've kicked him in the gut. His fork tumbles out of his hand and crashes against the plate, making a loud clanking noise that startles George. Graham's eyes turn black and stormy, reminding me of a seriously angry ocean, and his brows pull together. "You had what?"

My appetite makes a run for the border so I set my silverware down next to my plate, unsure what in the world is going on. I mumble, "A meeting today with the President."

He motions for me to continue.

"To discuss an advisory role in his administration," I add, with trepidation in my voice. "Why are you so angry?"

He ignores my question. "Tell me what it entails."

"No. Answer my question first. Why are you upset that the President of the United States wants me to be an advisor? It's an honor." Honor sounds more like hon-or. I'm trying to keep the emotions out of my voice and handle this situation delicately, but for the life of me, I never expected my lovely home-cooked meal to be this derailed by my seemingly great news.

Graham throws down his napkin and replies, "I'm going for a run. I need to think."

"Bullshit." I yell, leaping to my feet. "You aren't throwing a hissy fit like a bratty pre-teen and then deciding to go for a run. You obviously have a problem with me accepting this job. Tell me why," I demand as I carry my mostly untouched plate to the garbage, scraping the food into the can.

"Why are you wasting food? Put it in the fridge and we'll have it later," he orders.

I like domineering Graham when we're making love. I don't approve of him outside of the bedroom, or maybe I do . . . But, I'm tired of being Agreeable Rachael. He can meet me in the middle. I'm tired of rolling over and playing dead to appease him.

The plate lands in the sink with a clank. "No. You've ruined my meal that I worked so hard on." I use my fork to scrape the remnants of the stewed apples that I didn't have a chance to sample into the garbage can, taking my frustrations out on the plate.

"I didn't mean to ruin anything," he says, sounding dejected. "You just took me by surprise."

I walk over and take his plate off the table, and wrap it in foil before placing it in the refrigerator. When I'm done, I grab the bottle of wine and fill my glass to the top. I sit back down at the kitchen table and say, "Spill it, Graham. I've worked my ass off today to make sure that you had a good meal. I fixed myself up and worked my hardest to ensure that I was as much like the old Rachael as possible so you would feel comfortable leaving me to rejoin the tour. I landed a job to help out with our finances. And instead of being proud of me, you're throwing a fit. What gives?"

"We need to talk."

My least favorite words in the English language are "we need to talk." It's never good. No one says "we need to talk" and then proceeds to tell you that you won the lottery. Those four words are always followed by bad news.

What little I had of dinner isn't settling well in my stomach and my heart begins to speed up. Thoughts race through my mind. *I'm no longer pregnant, so he doesn't want me anymore. He's seeing someone else. He's going to want me to choose between a career and him. He's ending our relationship so he can focus on his work.* None of my thoughts are positive.

"Quit looking like I'm about to tell you that your mother died," he quips, as he takes a sip of his wine.

In my mind, I think *this conversation would be more along the lines of losing Caroline or one of her kids—not my mother.* Of course, I don't say this. Graham doesn't need to know that I never bothered to tell my parents about the baby or that I was resigning from my post at the White House, and that they didn't call when it hit the news.

"So now you're a comedian, huh?" I match his sip of wine with my own. We might be drunk before this conversation actually happens.

"Look," he starts, before taking my hands in his. His are shaking. Not trembling like a leaf, or any other metaphor. No. But they're vibrating enough that I know that this is not an easy conversation for him to have, which piles on to the sense of dread that I'm feeling.

He drops my hands and grabs his glass of wine and downs about half of it before he begins again. "The tour isn't going well," he says this as if he's breaking news to a child that their elder dog didn't make it home from the vet's office.

I'm not totally surprised. Over the past few weeks, the thought has entered my mind as to just how he could take so much time away from the Sons of Liberty and they still be going strong. I learned at a young age that if the owner isn't present, then everything goes to hell in a handbasket. I also saw the cover of the magazine. Of course, he doesn't know that I've seen it. I try to keep my face neutral and just let him speak.

The man in front of me ages before my eyes. He doesn't have to communicate to me how hard this is for him to talk about; his face and body language speak more than words ever could. Even though I'm angry at him for his reaction to my news and for ruining my dinner, I reach out and place my hand on his knee. This is no longer about me and my anger, and is all about him.

"What's going on?" I ask.

"I'm pretty sure that our tour manager, Hank, is stealing from us, but I can't prove it." His eyes shift to the floor when he delivers this bit of news.

I gasp. Theft is such a violation of trust. It cuts to the core of our basic human need to feel safe. My dread over this conversation is replaced with anger and repulsion. "What do you mean Hank is stealing from you? Fire him!"

"I wish I could. I can't prove that it's him. He has a contract. If I fire him, I still have to pay him. That's theft on top of theft," he states. I watch his Adam's apple bob up and down, as if he's swallowing something that is rather unpleasant.

"Graham, I'm so sorry. I had no idea . . ."

He cuts me off. "There's more."

This time, I pick up my glass of wine and take a slug. More? How could there be more?

"Rachael, it's a shit show. We don't start the bands on time, so everything goes late, and we're paying fines out the ass. Then, our road crew keeps getting caught smoking pot, or not showing up, or just generally fucking off, so that's another set of problems." He pauses for a moment and then takes a deep breath before he continues, "You wouldn't believe the amount of extra security that we've had to hire to keep the different opposing view organizations from killing each other. It's like it was a great idea in theory, but actually it's a nightmare. We're barely making enough money to pay our bills. The only positive note is that people are still showing up to our sponsor events, and to the show." He pauses, taking a breath. "On top of that, our radio ratings are beginning to drop, and it's all my fault."

"Graham . . ." I say, wanting to crawl in his lap and tuck him tightly against me. I see this for what it is. I've watched a man want something so desperately that he would campaign when he was so tired that he could barely stand, or so sick that he was vomiting in a trashcan while a medic gave him an IV so he could go to the next rally spot. I know what laying it all on the line looks like. I've seen it before, and Graham is that desperate.

He holds his hand up, preventing me from comforting him. I'm not offended. He needs to say his piece. I've learned this about him. "That's not the worst of it." He looks at me with pleading eyes. "Please don't take this wrong, but I've been so focused on us that I've let my research slip. I've lost my edge. I've lost what makes Graham Jackson, a nobody, into Revere. Jake pointed it out last night and he's right. I've been dialing it in for weeks."

"Tell me what you need," I say. "What can I do to make this better? Let me help you."

I can fix this. This is what I do. My skill set is what earned me the title of youngest, and only female White House Chief of Staff. My heart is pounding at the thought of being able to right this for him. I silently plead for him to let me. *Graham, this is the same as you making me admit that I trusted you, and I know you wouldn't cheat on me—no matter what the world says. This is my line in the sand. Acknowledge that you want me as your partner.*

He stands up and begins to pace the kitchen. In Texas, there's a saying "a cat in an electrical storm." His behavior fits the metaphor. "Come on, Graham. I can help. I know that I can, but you have to tell me what you need."

Agreeable Rachael would quickly anticipate his needs. She would open with something like, Graham, dear Graham, man in our relationship, I'll gladly be the woman by your side and clean up your mess. But I'm no longer Agreeable Rachael. She died along with the life growing inside of me. I'm me—warts and all. Life is too short and too precious to try to be something that I'm not. He has to ask me for help. I like the new/old Rachael. She has the same drive and will-power to succeed, but she knows that she can be herself and have the support of her lover. He's proven his worth by sticking by my side through thick and thin. It's a novel concept.

He stops pacing and turns to face me. His face is twisted in anguish and I don't recognize where it's coming from. *Ask me. Ask me for whatever help you need.* In my mind, I'm begging him, imploring that he open up to me. He doesn't have to always be the hero. I can fill that role also. I just need him to ask me for help.

Graham walks back to his glass of wine and slams it. He then finds the bottle of bourbon and pours a glass over ice. That's when I start worrying that it's me. Am I so terrifying that he can't talk to me? Does he need for me to exit, stage left, from his life? I'm watching a man self-destruct and there's nothing that I can do to help him if he doesn't ask. It's maddening and terrifying all in one beautiful package wrapped in jeans and grey cashmere.

"Tell me, Graham. Tell me what you need," I implore.

"I . . ." He starts, then stops. "I need for you to . . ."

It's pulling teeth, really. I jump to my feet and wrap him in my arms.

This is part of being the new and improved Rachael. I can support him without losing what makes me, well, me. I'm all in at this point. Graham Jackson is my future. He's my warm place on a cold, stormy night. He's my rocking-chair buddy at the age of eighty. He's my partner-in-crime and my port in a storm. He's all that I ever need to feel like life is complete—if he'll have me.

"Tell me, Graham. Tell me what I can do to help you."

"I need you . . ." He sputters and swallows hard. "I need you to come on tour with me and fix it. Fix this mess that I'm in. Find a way to make it better, and in the black, and what it's meant to be. I need you to run this tour like you ran the White House and let me focus on what I do best, which is being Revere."

I'm humbled by his words and relieved that this isn't the end for us. No one has ever asked me for help. Sure, President Jones paid me for my knowledge and expertise. I've been asked to consult on many issues, but no one I love has ever asked me to help them out of a jam. *Doesn't he know that I would move mountains for him?* New Rachael has learned to love herself just as much as she loves Graham.

"That wasn't so hard now, was it?" I ask with burning cheeks.

"So?" He steps back with a curious look in his eye, as if he trying to read my body language.

Does he actually think that I would tell him no? "Yes."

"Yes, what?" His brows crease.

"Yes, I will lend you my incredible management expertise, don my Wonder Woman cape and swoop in like the superhero that I am to right your wrongs."

His chin drops as his eyes roll. "Seriously? That's your answer? A simple 'yes, Graham, of course, I will help you because you're the love of my life' would have been sufficient."

Now, it's my turn to roll my eyes. "That's an answer that Agreeable Rachael would have given."

Poor guy. His brows crinkle in confusion. "Agreeable Rachael? Who in the hell is that?" He mutters under his breath, "I need a fucking manual."

My cheeks flush as a smile reaches my eyes. "Oh. She's no one that matters anymore."

I walk towards him, because I can't think of any better place to be at the moment than in his arms, but he takes two steps back, almost bumping into the kitchen sink. Pausing in confusion, my heart sinks. Surely, we aren't back to the place where we have to be friends and can't touch each other.

Then, his left cheek pulls up in a side-ways grin, like he has the biggest secret in the world. His hands reach for me and I offer him mine. With a gentle jerk he pulls me next to him. My heart tries to beat its way out of my chest. This feels like a big moment—an epic moment! My body temperature rises and my face flushes with heat. Before I can stop myself, my lip is pinched in between my teeth. I look up at Graham in anticipation of what he is going to do next.

His dimple appears just under his eye and as he looks down, a piece of hair falls over his forehead. There's a slight edge to his voice when he says, "So while you seem to be in an agreeable mood, why don't you agree to marry me?"

It's three simple letters, and translates to every spoken language. Y-E-S. In Spanish it's *sí*. In French it's pronounced *oui*. In German, it's *ja*, and in Portuguese, it's *sim*. I speak all of these languages fluently. The first time I said yes, my heart knew it was the *only* answer, but the rest of me was still getting on board; the second time it was agreeing to a new career; and I have no doubt that this "yes" will hold just as much adventure as I become Graham's wife and partner. Well, as I told President Jones yesterday, I'm all in. I'm head over heels in love with a boy. There is no doubt in my mind— no second-guessing. So as I look Graham in his sparkly blue eyes and take his face between my trembling palms, I whisper the most powerful word in any language—yes.

Epilogue

"I mean, the bride wore white! What a joke. What happened to first comes love, then comes marriage, then comes the baby in the baby carriage? Is nothing sacred any longer? Values. That's what is missing from today's society . . ." The lady who looks like my wife spews this nonsense to the camera. The white blond hair and petite frame is where any semblance ends. She's a bitter, hateful woman who can turn our story into something that is ugly, and I will not have that happen today of all days.

I shut the TV off and slip the remote between the mattress and the box springs, hoping Rachael won't think to look there. She'll be curious to see how the world is reacting to our announcement, but I don't care. I, or should I say, the Sons of Liberty pay someone to worry about that kind of stuff so we don't have to.

No. Today is our day. Real life starts tomorrow.

"Rach, they're waiting on us," I call to my wife of thirty minutes.

"They're just going to have to wait. The baby can't feed himself," she responds in a hushed but serious tone.

I stand up and walk into the adjoining room in our hotel suite where I drink in the sight of my life. Rachael is snuggled into a coral and aqua striped chair with her feet propped up on an ottoman. Her long blond hair is resting over one shoulder. She's slipped out of her wedding dress, which is tossed over the back of the couch, and replaced it with a pale pink bathrobe. One small but firm breast is exposed and our son is attached to it, enjoying his evening meal. His chubby, pink hand reaches up and grasps a lock of her hair, twisting it around his fingers. He has a strong pull, but if it hurts Rachael, she doesn't let on.

"Hey, big guy," she coos. "You were so good during the ceremony. Mommy was so proud of you. You let Miss Shelby hold you and you didn't even cry." Her face is so soft, relaxed when she talks to him. Those that called her a ball buster would not recognize this version of the beautiful woman I call my wife.

I take the chair opposite her in our hotel suite and watch the two things that I love the most in the world have their moment.

When Rachael is able to take her eyes off of our son, she smiles a serene smile that matches her dancing eyes. "The ceremony was beautiful."

"Was it? I didn't notice. I was too busy pinching myself that the gorgeous lady in front of me was really mine."

She rolls her eyes and smirks. "You're so corny."

"And cute . . ."

"Yes. Definitely cute," she agrees, with a nod.

There's a knock on the door that breaks our shared moment of calm. "I'm coming," I yell as I walk toward the hotel room door.

When I do, it startles the baby, making him jerk in Rachael's arms. Immediately, she cradles him against her shoulder and whispers soothing words in his ear.

I open the door, completely annoyed at the interruption. "What?" I ask our wedding planner, Erin.

"Guests are seated and dinner will be served shortly. Can I get an idea of when you'll be down?"

She's a nice enough woman. Supposedly, she's the best wedding planner on the East Coast. Right now, she and the rest of the wedding guests can go to hell.

"We'll be there once the baby is finished eating and settled," I reply in a tight voice.

"I would just hate for you two to miss your party. Plus, Former President Jones and Mrs. Jones are on a tight timeline, and the President's assistant said that he can only stay another hour. They have to leave . . ."

I whisper, so Rachael can't hear me. "I don't give a fuck about Former President Jones's timeline, or the current President's, for that matter. My wedding. My wife. My baby. I wrote a very large check so every guest could enjoy lobster at my reception. We'll. Come. Down. When. We're. Ready."

I shut the door before she has a chance to respond.

Fortunately, Rachael seems too preoccupied getting our son ready for bed to have overheard the conversation I just had with Erin. Hell! It's a shame Rachael hadn't met her when she was in politics. The lady could have been her right-hand man—chopping off heads.

I locate Rachael and my son in the second bedroom off of our suite, which has a baby bed set up in the corner, and a hotel-provided rocking chair. The curtains are parted and moonlight bathes them in a pale glowing shade of blue-grey. I literally grab the doorjamb at the sight of them and gasp. I wish I had known twenty months ago, when she'd ambushed me in the Cracker Barrel in the middle of nowhere, Virginia, that this was how my life would end up. I would have done things so differently. It's a miracle that we've arrived in this place, and the enormity of the amount of work that we've put into this relationship and the sacrifices that we've made along the way are not lost on me.

"Is he asleep?" I ask in a hushed voice, while I walk quietly towards them.

"Yes, but I don't want to let him go," she says adoringly, as she runs her fingers over Hunter's thin, black hair. "I just love him so much."

"I know you do, baby. That was Erin at the door letting us know that dinner is being served." It's a statement—not a suggestion that we leave. The nanny is waiting for our call to come and stay with Hunter while we enjoy the reception. However, if it was up to me, Rachael and I wouldn't leave our suite again until the morning.

She doesn't reply with words. Her body language speaks volumes though. She leans over and dusts kisses on Hunter's head and cheeks, and then she hands him to me.

"I just can't believe he's ours," she says, in her lullaby voice that she discovered the moment she held him in her arms.

His footed pajamas are blue and have big black dogs on them. I know that she chose them in honor of George. Hunter's little body molds against my chest and I whisper into his ear, "Good night, sleep tight, don't let the bed bugs bite, Daddy loves you with all his might."

Carefully, I place him in the middle of the crib and kiss my two fingers before touching them to his head.

Rachael joins me, and I wrap her tightly with my arm pulling her against my side. "Thank you so much for trying again. I know it was hard, but you've given me him, and the only gift that I've received that is more wonderful is you." Then, after a heartbeat, I add, "Mrs. Jackson."

She smiles and replies, "We've been blessed beyond belief, haven't we?"

I'm not sure how long we stand there staring at our miracle, and it doesn't matter. I've learned what life is about by loving these two. Everything else doesn't hold a candle.

"I guess we should go say hello to the people that have traveled from all over the country to attend our wedding." She sounds about as excited as I feel.

"Or I could carry you into the bedroom, untie that robe and properly introduce myself to you as your husband."

She giggles and grabs my hand, dragging us out of our son's room. Once the door is shut, she says, "Dear God, Graham. Your lines suck. 'Properly introduce myself as your husband.' Come on. You can do better than that." She fists her hands and places them on her hip. When she does, her robe falls open, exposing her left breast. The milky white skin against the strawberry pink nipple drives me insane. The swell of her perky tits do funny things to me.

"Quit looking at me like that!" she squeals as she backs away from me.

I move towards her, stalking her as if she's my prey. "How am I looking at you, Rachael?"

Her back hits the wall of our bedroom. "Like a man with one thing on his mind, and it's not rubbing shoulders with the who's who of the political and entertainment worlds."

I reach down and fist my very hard cock through my tuxedo pants. Her eyes follow my hand, and a small puff of air blows out of her lips when she sees what I'm holding. Her mouth forms a tiny circle, and I know that she's mine.

Her robe falls to the ground, and she stands in front of me in her blue thong panties and nothing else. Her hair is over both shoulders, veiling her breasts, with just a hint of nipple poking through. And I know right now, in this moment, that if I'm not inside of her in about thirty seconds, I'm going to embarrass myself.

"Touch yourself," I order, as I begin removing my slacks.

Her hand brushes over her stomach as her fingers make their way down to her bare slit.

"Tell me how wet you are, Rachael." My fingers vibrate with such anticipation that I'm not sure I can unbutton my shirt.

Her head drops back against the wall, and she lets out a soft moan. "I've been slick for you since I saw you in your tux." Her teeth tug at her bottom lip. "You, Graham, you are all I need. All I want."

I kick my discarded monkey suit to the side and press my body against hers, rubbing my leaking erection against her stomach. Grabbing her hands, I pin them above her head as I stare down into the green orbs that strip my soul. "Forever, Rachael. Whenever and wherever," I demand from her in my strong, dominant voice that she loves.

Her knees buckle and I have to drop one of her hands to hold her up. Her pelvis rubs against my thigh as I press my weeping dick against her creamy skin. "Forever. Yes . . . always whenever and wherever," she confirms.

And I lose it. Thoughts of slowly consummating our marriage go out the window. Before I know it, I have her bent over the arm of the sofa and I'm balls' deep inside of her. It's like so many times before. The more compliant she is, the more savage I become. Grabbing her hips, I slam into her over and over again. Her whimpers of pleasure drive me mad.

"Play with your tits and tell me how good they feel," I order.

I can tell when her fingers begin to tweak her nipples, because she clinches tightly around my cock. I almost lose it, but I'm not letting this end—ever.

"Tell me, Rachael," I grind out between punishing drives.

"They're . . . they're . . . so tender," she whispers. "And heavy."

I look around her and see in the soft glow from a lamp her breasts shaking back and forth as she pinches her nipples. It's so fucking hot.

Without separating us, I pick her up and carry her to the couch. I sit down with her back to my front. Her moans at the change of our angle drive me mad.

I replace her hands with mine. "These are mine to play with now. Use me. Make yourself come on my hard dick."

She straddles me, sitting back on her heels. I'm so deep inside of her that this must be what heaven feels like. Slumping a little more into the couch, I adjust so I have better access to her clit. As she begins to rise and fall on my throbbing cock, I massage one breast, ignoring her hard nipples, while I massage her nub.

Her moans of pleasure fill our honeymoon suite and make me crazy. Pleasuring her is my life's desire. "Touch my nipples," she says through a strangled voice.

Her back is arched beautifully, and her hair is sweeping back and forth along the small of it as she rises and falls.

"No," I reply, as I give her right breast a twist.

"Please, Graham. Pinch my nipples, please," she begs, as her voice becomes more strained.

I know that she's close. Her wetness is covering my thighs. "No, Rachael. You don't get to decide what I do with your body. Only I do."

I drop one of her breasts and swat her rounded ass with my hand, leaving a light pink mark.

"Again," she begs. "While you pinch my nipple."

I take her eraser-long nipple between my thumb and finger and apply intense pressure. She cries out and begins a wild dance on my cock. I spank the tops of her ass cheeks while she explodes in a body-trembling orgasm. I hold her, keeping her upright until her body becomes pliable in my arms.

Laying her on the sofa, I enter her again, needing my release. She looks like an angel—hair splayed out around her, a content look on her face. My heart catches in my throat. *Oh my God! This is my wife, and I can do this to her for the rest of my life.*

I pull out, and use my hand to jerk off all over her stomach. I mark her with my seed that made this day, this moment, possible.

***

"Where have you two been all of this time?" my sister asks as Rachael and I join dinner, which is almost over. Erin was nice enough to have two plates left in the warming tray for us.

"Feeding my baby and fucking my wife," I swear. It never gets old. Shocking my older sister is one of my favorite hobbies.

Her face drops in horror, and she leans in so no one can hear. "It's your wedding day. Have some manners."

Fortunately, Rachael missed this exchange, or she would probably have my balls in a jar.

Rachael leans across me and gives my sister a polite hug. "Hi Kelly. It's so nice to see you again."

It's not lost on me that I married a woman who is the same age as my much older sister. Ha!

"Hunter was so good during the ceremony. What an angel." My sister directs the compliment to only Rachael while she shoots me a dirty look.

"Thank you." Rachael beams. "He really is such a good baby. Graham and I are beyond blessed to be his parents."

My niece, who has entered the snotty, I'm-a-teenager-now phase of her life is playing on her new phone that I bought her for Christmas. "Are you going to dance with your favorite uncle?"

She rolls her eyes and says, "You'll just step all over my toes."

Rachael laughs and replies smugly, "I happen to know that he's a phenomenal dancer. Makes even the worst dancer look like a star."

My plate is almost empty, and Rachael's has been barely touched. I lean over and whisper in her ear, "Eat. You'll need your strength tonight."

She smirks and takes a bite of her lobster.

My mother pipes up, and says, "Darling, it's such a shame that your parents couldn't make it today. I've heard that hip replacement surgery has a very difficult recovery."

I head this nonsense off at the pass. Rachael's parents were not invited to the wedding. Two weeks after Rachael joined the tour, we were in Houston. It was a great homecoming. She'd been finally introduced to my family as my girlfriend, and they'd gushed over her more than me. They'd treated Rachael as if she were their own daughter. I couldn't have loved them more.

Her parents, on the other hand, had penciled us in for an hour-long dinner at a restaurant near their office. They'd barely acknowledged my presence and spent the entire meal chastising Rachael for embarrassing them by not letting them know that she was resigning from her post at the White House. It had been uncomfortable and awkward, and I left very pissed off.

Instead of joining me in bashing her cold family, Rachael had apologized for their rudeness while her shoulders were hunched over, and she'd stared at the floorboard of the truck. That was when I'd given her permission to never ever let someone treat her that way.

She'd looked up and smiled at me. "I'm almost forty and they've been like this my whole life. How much more do I have to put up with?"

I'd replied, "No more, my gorgeous girl."

That was the last time we spoke to her parents. I honestly think her father's hip replacement surgery was scheduled around our wedding as their way of saving face.

"Honeymoon?" my sister asks.

Rachael laughs into her napkin. "Our honeymoon is staying home. Isn't that awful? We've been gone nonstop, living in a travel trailer with a new baby. We just want to introduce him to his beautiful bedroom and lay on the couch and watch TV."

Kelly nods.

"I mean I want to use my gorgeous office and closet that Graham set up for me, what . . ." She looks at me, and we both do the math in our heads.

"I guess that it has been over a year and half ago."

I lean over and kiss her cheek. "Time flies when you're having fun."

We give each other a knowing look. This journey could not be described as fun. Gut-wrenching, life-changing and epic are a few of the words that pop in my head, but we've walked hand in hand from the moment that we agreed to step foot in The Cougar.

Erin bends down between us and says that it's time to cut the cake. I tell her that we'd rather have our first dance.

She shakes her head and walks off looking cross, but she heads for the band and lets them know that we're ready.

Choosing our first song as a married couple was easy. It had to be "You Look Wonderful Tonight." It's the first song that we danced to, and God does Rachael ever look gorgeous this evening.

Her cream wedding dress skims her petite frame. The front is very modest, and it's long-sleeved with a simple beaded pattern. The back—well, the back is damn near orgasmic. A deep *V* exposes her toned back, ending just below her ribs.

There are no secrets on tour, which is when this entire wedding was planned. The designer flew to some remote part of the country that the tour was in for the week and did a fitting. Because the universe loves me and Rachael doesn't believe in superstitions, she asked for my opinion. Fortunately the designer gave us a few minutes alone so I could properly express it.

I stand up, offering her my hand. "Mrs. Jackson, care to dance?"

She grasps my fingers. "Thought you would never ask."

I lead her to the middle of the dance floor and the band begins to play the opening notes of our song. She molds perfectly to my body as I lead us around the parquet floor. "I'm so glad that you found the time to marry me," I whisper in her ear.

She giggles at my joke. We've been engaged for way more than a year, but with the tour schedule and our baby, planning a wedding was out of the question. Rachael stepped in to the role of CEO for the Sons or Liberty tour and had everyone whipped into shape in about a month. Slowly but surely, we began turning a profit, and when the tour ended a week ago we were financially successful enough that we were able to pay out bonuses to all the crew that had stood by us through the rocky road at the beginning.

Rachael made a lot of changes, but one of her boldest moves left us not speaking for two days. She fired our agent and convinced her ex-boyfriend to take us on as a client. Aiden. The man whose heart she broke, who is now married to her best friend's little sister. He's a nice enough guy, but I wasn't crazy about having to work so closely with someone who had seen my girl naked. So far, I'll give Rachael credit, it has been a good move. He was interested in branching out from just working with athletes, and he's a super smart guy. He's done well by us.

I drew the line at inviting him to the wedding. So, once again, we spent two days not talking, and now he and his lovely wife are sitting at a table with Caroline and Colin, laughing and enjoying the lobster that must be made of gold.

Aiden also found a loophole in the contract that we signed with Hank that let us fire him. We never recovered the stolen money, and we couldn't prove that he was the one who stole it, but I've learned to make peace with the situation. It was essentially a fifty thousand–dollar lesson on why Rachael was needed so desperately.

With tour management off my list of duties, I was able to focus on what I do best, and that's being the front man for the Sons of Liberty. The public responded, and the radio show is pulling in good numbers. I will say that I miss the tour and interacting with the crowds, but I'm looking forward to ditching The Cougar and sleeping in our bed again. What Rachael doesn't know is that The Cougar has one more trip in her.

"Did you see that Holden brought Aubrey as his date?" Rachael asks, as I spin her around. Holden is the first candidate that the Sons of Liberty have chosen to back. His girlfriend is presenting a bit of a problem. Tonight is his coming-out party, of sorts. Rachael and I, via the Sons of Liberty's support, are introducing him to the who's who of Washington politics.

"I thought you addressed that little issue. I mean, the guy is not stupid.

Sister fuckers don't get elected to Congress."

She pulls away to arm's length so she can properly chastise me without drawing attention. I can read her like a book. "Quit calling him a . . ." I spin her around so she has to shut up for a second. Of course, she can't be distracted. "She's the step-sister, and they didn't become family until just recently."

I tuck her back against me as the song comes to an end. Before we part, I remind her that this is the first candidate that the Sons of Liberty have plucked from obscurity and are backing with our support and dollars. It has to go well.

She smiles sweetly as she reaches up, straightening my tie. "There's a reason why this wedding and reception is a tax write-off."

And with that, Former President Jones asks her for a dance. She graciously accepts and leaves me standing in the middle of the dance floor.

I turn and walk over to the table where Max, Marissa, Jake and his date, Veronica, are sitting, along with Holden and Aubrey. When Rachael and Erin worked on the seating chart for the reception, this was a strategic move on Rachael's part. We have a current president and former president in attendance, along with numerous influential media personalities and huge players in Washington politics. This is Holden's endorsement party as much as it is our wedding reception.

Rachael's philosophy was that if she had to have a wedding—I insisted on it—that it might as well be one of the political events of the year. And that's one of the many reasons that I love her.

I'm greeted with a round of fist bumps and high fives by my brothers. Holden stands and shakes my hand, offering me his congratulations. I lean over and give Aubrey a kiss on the cheek. She's an absolutely stunning woman. I remember once seeing a story on the news about an artist who used Photoshop to create what the American female would look like, since we are a country with such diversity. The artist rendering looks very similar to her. She doesn't have one characteristic that defines her race. That's great for Holden's campaign. I just wish they weren't related by marriage and, well, that she didn't work as a bartender in a strip club. Both are issues that we're going to have to fix in the next six months.

"The wedding was beautiful," Aubrey gushes, and takes Holden's hand. He looks at her with big, puppy-dog eyes. I know the look. He's a man enamored.

Without looking in my direction, he replies, "It was."

"Jesus Christ, you two are making me sick," Max says, as his face twists in disgust. "You're a politician, man. Have some dignity."

"Oh wait! Politicians have no dignity." Jake follows up, and we laugh like crazy.

Holden's a good guy. I like him. He'll be a good choice for our new pet project, if Rachael can just get the Aubrey problem under control.

I sip on a bourbon that someone was kind enough to grab from the bar for me, while we discuss the important things in life, like who's going to win the Super Bowl, why my Orioles can't seem to pull their heads out their asses, and of course, the next UFC fight.

We're just getting into a fun debate over boxing versus MMA when Erin approaches me, as if I'm a caged lion and she's been hired to feed me raw steak from her palm. "Mr. Jackson," she says, as if I bite. In all fairness to her, I don't particularly like her and haven't been the nicest guy.

"Yes." I smile, hoping to redeem myself.

"It's really time to cut the cake."

I nod and scan the large space, looking for my wife. Finally, after searching for a bit, I spot her. She's on the dance floor, and her partner is Colin. He must have requested a country song from the band because I don't recognize the music. They're two-stepping like mad across the floor. Caroline is standing by the tables and laughing like crazy. What I've come to learn about Caroline and Colin is that they are Rachael's family, which now makes them mine.

I tell the guys goodbye, and tell Holden that I'll to introduce him to the other guests in a moment, but first I owe Caroline a dance.

She sees me approaching, and her smile grows as I draw closer. I reach my hand out. "Since your husband stole my wife, I thought it only fair that I dance with you."

"Oh. Yay!" She beams as I lead her out on to the dance floor.

Colin spies us and gives me a scowl, while Rachael laughs like a hyena. I take it that Colin isn't thrilled with me dancing with his wife. Well too damn bad I'm not particularly happy that he's dancing with mine.

The band begins a new country song. I think George Strait originally recorded it, but I'm not sure. I take Caroline in a strong hold and begin to two-step her across the floor. She's a fantastic dancer. Instead of having to strongly lead her like I have to with Rachael, we glide.

I compliment her. "You sure know how to dance."

"I do. It's one of the things that Colin and I enjoy doing together." She gets a twinkle in her eye that tells me that there is more to the story, but I don't ask.

We're silent for a couple of beats before she says, "Graham, be good to her. I know that she's got a strong personality and people think that she's tough, but she's not. She's got—"

"Shhh . . ." I silence her with a spin. When she comes back around, we resume two-stepping. "I love her. I'm crazy about her, and I'm determined to make her happy. Save your worries for someone else."

She nods, and we finish our dance without another word spoken. As soon as the song is over, Colin rushes to her side and steals my dance partner while I collect Rachael for cake-cutting time.

After we've shoved cake into each other's mouths, I ask Rachael if she's ready to make this wedding truly a business expense. "Am I ever not ready?" She smirks.

We grab Holden, who I've come to refer to in my head as Test Subject A, and introduce him first to former President Jones. It goes well. Rachael, Holden and the former President begin talking politics, so I slip away.

Rachael is much better at shaking hands and kissing babies than I am.

I make a beeline for the bar and order another bourbon, but before I'm able to take my first sip, Roan Perez stops me. He's another one I didn't want to invite, but Rachael reminded me that he is the Vice President and even though we both think he's an asshole, he's one that wields a lot of power.

"Never thought I would see the day that Rachael Early got married." Roan slaps me on my shoulder, as if we're old buddies.

I'm so tempted to brush my arm where he touched it, but I don't, because I've been told to play nicely tonight. "Guess she finally found the right guy." I hold my bourbon up in a toast.

Bourbon has never tasted so sweet slipping down my throat.

"Think she'd have any interest in working in my office?"

"Not on your life," I reply, slapping his shoulder in return and walking away.

Damn that felt good.

I shake a few more hands and thank more people for their congratulations before I decide that my wife has politicked enough, and it's time for us to leave.

Sliding up behind her while she visits with some guy who she used to work with who is now at CNN, I wrap my arms around her waist and whisper in her ear, "It's time for bed, Mrs. Jackson."

***

Rachael

Graham is in the baby's room, staring at his mini-me, while I sit in the middle of the floor, looking at the very expensive set of lingerie that I had purchased for tonight. I can't bring myself to slip it on. Instead, I stare at it trying to find the energy to put it on.

Tonight was amazing—a final destination to a very long journey that began at a diner in D.C. or maybe even the President's viewing room.

Malik and his wife were there. It was great seeing him again. I promised him long ago that I would invite him to the wedding. Rachael Early Jackson keeps her promises. Maggie came with a date. He seemed nice enough—Roger, I think is his name. She whispered that he loves cats. It was great seeing Lou and other friends from my former life, and a nice reminder that I'm so glad that I've ended up in this fantastic place.

Right now, I just crave silence. I feel like since I agreed to run Graham's tour that there hasn't been a moment of stillness. It's been great. I don't regret my decision for one second, but our life has been one crazy rollercoaster ride. Tomorrow, we get to be a family in a house that doesn't move and on a timeline that we now dictate. What a ride it has been.

"I'm just going to rip it off with my teeth and toss it on the floor," Graham says from behind me. I sigh.

He walks over the lingerie bag, pulls the delicate lace number from it and throws it over his left shoulder. "There. I saved me the hassle."

I'm bone tired, but strangely enough, when Graham's lips find my breasts, I have the energy to make love to him for the next hour.

After we're snuggled into bed, my head resting on his chest, I deliver my big news. "Did you see Candace at the reception?"

"You mean your book agent that sounds like she swallowed glass?" He runs his hand over my arm, causing goose pimples.

"Yes. That's the one." I swallow. "Well, she gave me the best wedding present ever."

"Really? A better present than me?" he asks, grabbing my wrist and running his finger over my diamond tennis bracelet.

"How about a different present?"

"I'll take that." He smirks.

"Well, you just made love to Rachael Early Jackson, *New York Times* bestselling author. *Anything, But Not Everything* will debut in tomorrow's paper at the top of the list," I proudly state.

"You did it, baby," he congratulates me, as his hand that was stroking my arm moves across my stomach and over my breast. "This calls for celebration sex. I need to be inside of a bestselling author."

So begins another round of Graham making sure that our marriage is properly consummated.

***

The next day, we pack our stuff and head to the lobby of the hotel to finally go home. It's only fitting that Graham pulls up in the pickup truck towing The Cougar behind it.

"Seriously?" I smirk.

"Yup," Graham says, smacking the side of the travel trailer. "It's only fitting, don't you think? It is what convinced you to give me a second chance."

"It was all The Cougar's doing," I reply, as I strap the baby into the car seat.

Graham loads our bags into the backseat. It feels empty without George, and I can't wait to get home to see my big wonderful boy.

As we pull out of the hotel parking lot, Graham slaps the steering wheel. "Got one more trip in you, old girl. Take us home."